One Bright Day
in the Middle of the Night

One Bright Day
in the Middle of the Night

Nigel Bowden

Prepared and printed by:

York Publishing Services Ltd
64 Hallfield Road
Layerthorpe
York YO31 7ZQ
Tel: 01904 431213

Website: www.yps-publishing.co.uk

Copies available from www.ypdbooks.com

"Where Fishes Fly," by the late Dr. Patrick Smith, has been most useful to me in reconstructing the background of one of the characters in these pages, while "Every Man for Himself," by Beryl Bainbridge, also plays a part in this tale. But Ray Herman's painstaking work and advice have been invaluable. He has been a true mentor.

N.B.

To Joana

The river is on fire. Among the boats that have been hit is a tanker, which is now listing to such a degree that its cargo of fuel oil is spilling out across the surface of the water. A further wave of bombers, failing to finish her off, has succeeded in igniting the slick, which in turn has engulfed a fire-fighting vessel. Rescue or escape from the ship is now impossible. The tanker's name, painted on the prow and blistering in the heat, is "Hope of Britain."

With the engine still running, Edith has the driver's window down, and with good reason. Since joining the Yeomanry she has seen as many horrific injuries from flying, fragmented glass as she has from bomb-blast itself. She turns to her co-driver and calls over the background roar of explosion and conflagration, "Get up to the front and see what's holding us up."

Her partner's eyes widen. She is frightened already and the thought of leaving the dubious but comparative safety of the truck's cab fills her with dread. She is about to argue, but there is an authority in Edith's clipped, aristocratic tone, and in any case she is out-ranked. Resentfully she climbs down on to the rubble-strewn road.

"Here, you better take my helmet," Edith says, passing it across to her. "Not the best of times to lose your own."

The nurse, who has been sitting squashed between them, eases herself over towards the passenger window.

"We're sitting ducks here," Edith murmurs, thinking of the large red cross on a white background painted like a target on the truck's roof.

As usual, the Luftwaffe commanders have chosen their time cleverly; low tide and full moon. The Thames will not supply the firefighters' hoses for long and, bathed as it was in moonlight, the first wave of bombers had no difficulty in locating the Capital, in spite of the strict blackout regulations. The second wave had no need even of the moon. It wasn't just the docks that were on fire but much of London's East End. All the planes had to do then, as they droned up "Bomb Alley," over Kent, was aim for a great orange glow on the western horizon.

Edith watches the steady stream of traffic coming away from the docks, their headlights blacked out pointlessly in this night as light as day. She smiles grimly and intones a line of doggerel she remembers from childhood.

"One bright day in the middle of the night."

The nurse eyes her furtively. She finds the image of the driver's face, its half-smile illuminated by the blazing destruction beyond, unnerving. Edith turns her gaze briefly on the nurse and thinks to herself, 'She's got the wind up.'

An ambulance identical to her own and travelling in the opposite direction halts briefly alongside her. The driver, whom she recognises, calls across to her.

"There's a heavy-rescue truck up ahead, gone into a bomb crater."

"Oh Lord!" Edith calls back, adding, as the other ambulance jerks forward, "Are you full?"

"Chocker!" she hears the driver shout. "It's absolute carnage down there."

Edith knows the driver well enough to know that she is not given to exaggeration. Indeed, their whole class tends towards ironic understatement. When she asked a then-friend and officer what it had been like to be involved in the Dunkirk evacuation he drawled, Noel Coward-like, "My dear! The noise, the people!"

'So,' thinks Edith, 'we're going to have to stick it out, or find another way in.'

Reaching around the steering wheel she plucks a packet of cigarettes from the dashboard. Woodbines. Not Edith's brand at all, but then there is a war on, as everyone keeps telling her. She offers one to the nurse who mutely declines with a shake of the head. Edith lights one and inhales deeply.

'I'd get a ticking off from my tutor if he could see me puffing away now,' she thinks, and she finds herself contemplating the strangeness of the times through which they are living. There she is, in uniform, at the wheel of an ambulance, attempting to get into an inferno while nearly everyone else is trying to get out of it, and only last night she was in a concert hall, on stage in a long frock, singing arias to a lot of other people in long frocks. (In fact half the audience was in uniform, as seems to be half the population of London).

What Edith had proposed to sing that night were not arias at all but her beloved "Four Last Songs" by Richard Strauss, but the management would not countenance it. While Germany was raining bombs on the Capital they did not think a German composer would be a popular choice.

"Art," she had told them, "is above that sort of thing," but they did not relent.

"Cretins!" she hears herself saying now, as she stares through the windscreen at the burning city. The nurse looks at her quizzically.

"I was thinking of the management of the Wigmore Hall. Not the German High Command."

The nurse gives a faltering smile and quickly looks away. She is used to eccentric behaviour from people like Edith, but in that moment she wonders if the ambulance driver is perhaps a little off her rocker.

A few seconds later a motorcycle can be heard approaching from behind. Peering around, Edith sees that it is ridden by a policeman wearing a tin hat. She steps from the truck and flags him down. As she watches him come to a halt she finds herself unable to take her eyes off the little toothbrush moustache he has sprouting beneath his stubby nose.

"Can you do something about this traffic?" she calls out to him over the phut-phut of the motorcycle engine.

"That's precisely what I'm on my way to do, Madam."

"Lieutenant."

"Lieutenant," he repeats with a sneer, making the word sound like an insult.

Edith sighs. In the course of her duties most men she comes across accept the role of women in uniform, but occasionally she comes across the kind of man she has before her now.

From his perspective he is not only looking at a woman in uniform but he can tell from the uniform that she is an officer in the First Aid Nursing Yeomanry, or F.A.N.Y.. "A Fanny," as he and his friends like leeringly to say. Knowing that many Fannys are drawn from the upper and aristocratic classes this marks them down as Toffs as far as he is concerned.

Without taking her eyes off his, Edith draws languidly on her cigarette and gives him a smile both patronising and dangerous.

"Don't let me detain you, Constable. The sooner you sort out the traffic, the sooner I can put my ambulance to some use." She nods her head in the direction of the blazing docks. "I gather there's quite a show down there."

Returning her ambiguous smile the policeman replies, "Not a very clever remark, Lieutenant. This isn't my idea of a show."

"No," she smartly comes back, "and not very clever wearing a Hitler moustache just now."

This isn't the first time he has suffered this jibe, and he had thought of shaving it off, but then a woman told him in a pub one night him that it gave him a certain authority. Being the kind of man upon whom irony is wasted, the twinkle in her eye as she said it he had interpreted as something else. Unable, now, to think of a riposte, he revs the engine, lets in the clutch and continues picking his way through the traffic. Edith watches him witheringly for a moment and then looks about her.

It is a truly miserable scene, frightening for many though not for her. Her autocratic father instilled in both herself and her sister a strong sense of self-reliance, and old-school as he is he taught them that they are every bit as capable of making their way in the world as any man. This partly explains why Edith is still unmarried. Most of the eligible men she has met are in awe, if not frightened of her. As a debutante she "came out" in 1926, the year of the General Strike, when she threw herself into the role of bus-driver in defiance of the striking workers. She was then presented at Buckingham Palace and paraded at all the obligatory balls, which provided her with both fun and tedium in equal measure. She was already determined upon a career as an opera singer and she viewed it with such single-mindedness that the business of finding a husband and having children were distractions to her. Over ten years on, and in her early thirties, she was beginning to reconsider her situation, but then the war intervened, and thoughts of marriage were once again postponed; until the night, that is, she met a naval officer at the Savoy, the one who in answer to her question about Dunkirk had drawled, "My dear, the noise, the people!" She warmed to him straight away and she allows herself to think of him now and to wonder where he is. She finds it frustrating that one is never allowed to know where friends and loved ones in the forces are being sent, and she feels relieved in that moment to have her own part to play in the war.

She looks beyond the line of slowly-moving vehicles on the other side of the road to another line, but this one of human traffic. It is a ragtag band, some shuffling resignedly, exhausted by yet another raid and evacuation, and others striding purposefully, as if by just swinging those arms and holding those heads high they will let the enemy know that they will not be cowed. She notices a young woman in a headscarf pushing a pram with one hand and holding with the other the hand of a little girl. The mother looks as if she might at any moment burst into tears and sink, a heap of rags, to the ground. Edith steps smartly between two cars and joins her on the pavement. She finds herself looking down at a face that has been worn well beyond its years. Edith smiles.

"You'll be at the shelter in a few minutes," she says, wondering if it will be full by the time they get there.

"I can't believe they're doin' this to us again."

The tone of her voice confirms the look of defeat in her face.

"They won't be doing it to us for much longer."

"But why are they doin' it to us at all? What 'ave we done to them?"

Edith is about to deliver a little rallying speech but she checks herself. Clearly the woman is exhausted by it all, while the baby in the pram, she notes, sleeps peacefully, oblivious to the Armageddon about him. She undoes the button of one of the pockets of her tunic, pulls out a lollipop and proffers it to the child.

"That's for being a brave girl and looking after your mummy."

The girl smiles shyly, revealing a gap in her front teeth. A piece of sticking plaster is wrapped around that part of her specs that bridges her nose, to prevent them chafing perhaps or to hold them together. She takes the sweet but otherwise remains quite still, staring up into a pair of piercing blue eyes in which she sees reflected the flames about them.

"Say thank you to the lady," the mother says, but the little girl remains mesmerised by this strange soldier in a skirt. Edith gives the girl a gentle push in the small of her back.

"Go on, young lady. Get mummy to the shelter. Double-quick time," and she watches them as they rejoin the sorry human flow, the girl tugging her mother on, until a bend in the street takes them out of sight. Edith looks across to her marooned ambulance and back to where mother, daughter and baby have just disappeared and feels in that moment utterly useless.

Taking a deep breath and pulling herself up to her full height she waves to the driver of another passing ambulance and steps nimbly across behind it. As she does so the vehicle stops momentarily then jerks forward and one of its rear doors swings open. Edith reaches up and grasps the handle to close it, and it is then that she catches sight of the scene inside.

Thinking back on it later in the cab of her own ambulance it probably wasn't anything worse than she had seen already, many times over, but it shocks her in that moment and stops her in her tracks.

To begin with, the interior is hopelessly overcrowded. There are two nurses and another woman from the

Yeomanry attempting to minister to the wounded but they hardly have room to move. The stretchers are full but there are several other injured men, some crouched and slumped against the bulkhead and others attempting to strap-hang as if they are on a bus; but the sight that confronts her the most is just a foot or two from her face, and on a level with it.

It appears to be a merchant seaman, but his tunic is so scorched it is hard to make out. His stretcher has been carried in so that his head is towards the door, but he must have shifted because the head is thrown back over the end of it, thus presenting his face upside down to Edith. She stares back at it.

It isn't a face any more. There is a mouth cavity, from which comes a low moan, but there are no discernible lips, and the nose looks like a rough daub in a child's painting. His hair is burnt away, as is much of the facial skin, leaving a pulpy mess. But it is the eyes that draw Edith's gaze, or rather the eye sockets. She can't make out if the eyeballs are still there; there is just a filmy redness.

Resisting the urge to take a step back, and knowing that other eyes are upon her, Edith looks up to her fellow yeoman, a corporal, and says, before she's had a chance to think, "Let's get him more comfortable on that stretcher."

As soon as she says it she knows what a preposterous remark it is. The only sort of comfort he can hope for now will be found in death. The Corporal silently shakes her head.

"I'd give you a hand," Edith goes on, lamely, "but I've got an ambulance over there myself. We're trying to get in."

"You won't be short of things to do," says the Corporal.

The ambulance moves forward again, Edith clicks the door shut, steps across the road and onto the foot-plate of her own truck. She swings the door open and climbs back in.

"We're going to have our work cut out," she says to the nurse, "if ever we get in there."

"I know."

Edith unbuttons another pocket of her tunic and pulls out a hip flask. She carries it mostly for the shocked and the injured but there are times when she feels as much in need of it herself.

"Care for a drop?"

The nurse nods.

"I wouldn't mind."

Edith can see that sitting in the cab doing nothing is getting to her. The job is always easier when you are active. While the nurse takes a swig of the brandy Edith lights two cigarettes and offers one to her. This time she doesn't refuse. Edith takes a swig herself and feels the spirit's warmth suffuse her. She takes a long draw on her cigarette and stares through the windscreen. After a moment she turns to the nurse.

"I've seen a lot of stuff doing this job. And it doesn't really shock me any more. But there's one thing I still have a kind of horror about."

The nurse looks across at her.

"Disfigurement," she goes on.

The nurse nods.

"It's not seeing it on some other poor blighter's face.

I can cope with that. It's just that when I see it ... it's as if I see it on my own face."

Both women stare through the windscreen and Edith silently recalls a night she had at the theatre a few weeks before. She was sitting just a few rows from the stage and the people around her were lit by spill from the stage lighting. A ripple of laughter ran through the audience and as she turned to smile at her companion she caught sight of a group of RAF airmen behind her, and as she looked at their laughing, upturned faces her smile froze. There was something featureless and mask-like about them, and she realised that she was looking at faces that had been horribly disfigured and then reconstructed. There were one or two uniformed nurses sitting with them and Edith guessed that this was probably an outing from one of the teaching hospitals specialising in plastic surgery. As she was thinking this, one of the young pilots looked back at her and she quickly turned away. The comedy they had been watching had distracted him until then, but he was reminded in that moment that no woman would ever look at him again as she might have done before.

The silence that has fallen upon both driver and nurse in the cab is suddenly broken by an explosion so close that it rocks the truck and causes some women on the opposite pavement to scream. The nurse gasps and Edith looks across at her.

"Wind your window down," she says. "You don't want that glass coming in on you."

Edith can be tough, but she is beginning to feel protective towards the nurse, as if she were a younger sister.

"D'you know what the official advice was in the last war," she goes on, "when we had the Zeppelins bombing London?"

"No?" says the nurse.

""TAKE YOUR WHISKY AND GO DOWN TO THE CELLAR.""

They smile.

"Headlines in the newspaper," she adds. "Pretty good advice I'd say."

"Yes," says the nurse.

They puff away at their cigarettes.

"We never thought it would be happening all over again. Just a generation on," Edith says.

"No … but it's a bit more serious this time, isn't it?" says the nurse, who was barely born during the First World War.

'Not to the people in the trenches,' thinks Edith, recalling members of her own family who laid down their lives in that so-called "war to end wars."

She looks up at the sky and wonders if there will be another raid that night. They are in a comparative lull – if crackling, burning buildings and exploding gas mains can be said to constitute a lull – but if the bombers return while they are still trying to sort things out, as they often do …

She tries not to think about it.

"What's your name?" she asks.

"Dorothy. But most people call me Dot. Or Dotty."

"How d'you come to be doing this sort of work?"

"I'm just finishing my training at Guy's. And I want to do military nursing. So I thought this might be useful experience. Until I get a posting."

"Where would you like to go?"

"Well, I won't get much choice, will I."

"No. But if you did."

"Well ... I'd quite like to go to the Middle East. Iraq, maybe. Or Palestine."

'With your looks,' thinks Edith, 'you'd blend in well.'

While Edith is striking in appearance, the nurse is beautiful, in a dark, Asiatic sort of way; which belies her origins, as does the accent she has cultivated since coming to London. She comes, in fact, from Porthcawl, and it was there, in that Welsh seaside resort, aged barely one, and during the terrible flu epidemic of 1918-19 that killed even more than the Great War just before it, that she managed to pitch head first into a grate full of burning coals. It has left her with an intriguing dark blemish to the side of one eye, which adds to her allure, and there is no shortage of junior doctors wanting to take her out. Indeed she has found herself, without quite meaning to, engaged to two of them at once.

"I wonder," Edith begins, thinking aloud, "if this is how the world will end? In one long traffic jam."

Leaving Dorothy to ponder this enigmatic remark, Edith springs from the cab and stands looking between the two lines of vehicles. Normally she would have just run the ambulance between them – her skill, even with a three-tonner, is well known within the Yeomanry – but the gap is so narrow here that this would force the out-flowing traffic onto the pavement where there is now a continuous stream of pedestrians. She climbs back in.

"There's got to be a break in the traffic soon," she says. "Or perhaps Constable Jobs-worth will sort it all out for us."

Dorothy grins. She hadn't liked the policeman either. Edith stares again at the back of the truck in front, as if by so doing she could make it move, then she takes another swig of brandy.

"Well, this certainly beats cocktails at the Savoy," she says.

As if to dispel this thought, or the even nicer one of sitting there with her naval officer, Edith reaches for the co-driver's map and studies it. For the nurse, Edith's reference to the Savoy puts her in mind of another place favoured by the better off, and of one night in particular.

"I attended the direct hit on the Café de Paris," she says.

Edith looks up from her map. The nurse looks for a moment as if she might burst into tears, but then a sort of dazed expression settles on her features.

The bombing of the Café de Paris, or what followed, was an incident so depraved and shocking that it was suppressed in the newspapers, but the rescue workers knew all about it. A fifty-kilogram bomb had passed through the Rialto cinema above and exploded by the bandstand killing thirty four people, including the bandleader, Snakehips Johnson. A hundred souls were trapped, but when the rescuers arrived they were confronted not so much by the devastation, to which they had become inured, but by another phenomenon altogether. When they started to claw away the rubble, they found the bodies of young women in blackened and bloody evening dresses with all the usual injuries save one; some of their fingers had been neatly, almost surgically, removed. For just a moment they were bemused, and then the awful truth hit them. Looters had got there first, and knowing that the rescue teams would arrive at any moment had decided upon the quickest means of removing those valuable diamond rings.

When Edith heard this story she felt an intense anger. She had come across looters before and they had received a summary admonishment from her and been quickly handed over to the police, but at the Café de Paris that night, human behaviour seemed to have plumbed a depth hitherto unimagined. It was one thing to believe the enemy capable of such atrocity, but quite another to come across it in one's fellow countrymen. The F.A.N.Y. was the only women's voluntary organisation authorised to bear arms, and Edith dearly wished *she* had arrived on the scene that night, promptly, service revolver at her side. She would have meted out some very rough justice.

The nurse pulls again on her cigarette.

"I just couldn't believe people could do things like that," she says.

Edith hands her the hip-flask again but remains silent. She wants to say something wise and irrefutable; something that will make sense of it all, but she can't think of a single thing. She studies the map again.

"There's a gap," she hears the nurse say.

Looking up, Edith sees that a break has opened up in the out-flowing traffic. Without hesitating she slips into first gear, lets in the clutch and swings the heavy wheel hard to the right. They jerk forward and move out from the line of stationary vehicles. Edith presses hard on the accelerator, unsure how much time she has before the oncoming traffic resumes. They press on over a series of hoses running across the road, which have gone flat through lack of water.

She slips into second gear and presses hard again on the accelerator. She feels exhilarated that at last she is doing something. The line of traffic to her left stretches out of sight. There is no way that she can get back in, and then suddenly a truck appears around the bend ahead coming straight towards them. The nurse gasps and grips the sides of her seat, while in the same moment a narrow street on the right comes into view. Edith races towards it, swings the wheel hard again and gives a sharp blast on the horn to clear the pedestrians. The ambulance clips the kerbstone but otherwise slides neatly into the side street, just ahead of the oncoming truck.

They find themselves now in a place eerily deserted. With high blank walls on either side, the street-lamps unlit for the blackout, and the truck's headlights cut down to thin strips of light, it suddenly seems very dark.

"We could be in a Dickens' novel," Edith calls out as they rush on between what she judges to be old factories or warehouses.

The nurse is not relishing the literary quality of their surroundings and wonders, as she watches Edith's eyes flashing even in the darkness, if they are about to become hopelessly lost. They then round a bend where the street, they find, ends abruptly in a junction with another road. Edith brings the truck to a halt and looks first left then right.

This larger road is also deserted. It has been cordoned off, with barriers either side of them that prevent them turning into it. Edith frowns. Each of the barriers bears the warning sign, "DANGER. UNEXPLODED BOMB." These barriers are normally manned, but, Edith supposes, with so much mayhem in the docks all available personnel have probably moved on there. Looking straight ahead she notices a collapsed wall. The rubble at its base looks flattened and it occurs to her that this might have been used by rescue vehicles as an alternative way in and out of the docks. She thinks quietly for a moment, considering their options. She doesn't want to drive through the barriers and risk coming too close to the unexploded bombs, wherever they might be, and there doesn't seem much point in turning around and going back only to get stuck in traffic again.

She eyes the gap in the wall. It seems to be their only option. But what lies beyond it, she wonders. From the cab, all Edith can see is a forbidding dark hole. If she drives into it might she get them irretrievably stuck? Sensing what is going through the driver's mind the nurse shifts uneasily in her seat.

Edith grabs a torch and springs down onto the road. The nurse watches as she clambers over the rubble and stares into the darkness beyond the wall. From this point, with the aid of the torch and the glow in the sky from the fires all around, there seems to be a way through. There is earth beyond the wall and she can clearly see tyre tracks from vehicles as large and larger than her own, but fifty yards on, where the torch cannot reach, there appears to be a dip in the ground that she ought to investigate before bringing the truck through. She is about to scramble across to it when she hears an explosion across to her right. She hesitates for a moment, then spins around and leaps gazelle-like over the rubble. Springing back into the cab she pushes into first gear and presses down on the accelerator. The nurse closes her eyes and over the revving of the engine she hears the driver cry, "Tally-ho!"

The truck lurches forward and the tyres spin up pieces of brick that crack sharply against the undercarriage. They are quickly on top of the mound and bouncing down the other side. The wheels then sink deep into the soft earth but there is enough momentum now to keep them turning. They plough on, and almost before she knows it they have traversed the fifty yards to the dip she saw in the ground, where she brings the truck to an abrupt halt. There before them, reflecting the orange glow from the sky, is what looks like a miniature lake.

Edith regards it quietly, wondering how deep it might be. The nurse opens her eyes and stares at the water. Surrounded as they are by destruction and chaos, there is something incongruous about its tranquillity. She hears the ratchet of the handbrake as the driver pulls on the lever, and then Edith jumps from the cab again and steps tentatively forward.

The water feels pleasantly cool as she paddles through it, but she winces as her ankle scrapes against something sharp and jagged. Soon she is midway across, where she has to hitch up her skirt as the water laps around her knees. That, she reckons, would be up to the floor of the cab. If she takes it very slowly she might just avoid getting water into the electrics, and so far the ground beneath her feet has felt firm. A few yards further and she realises that the water has become shallower. She turns around, wades back and climbs into the cab.

"I think we can just make it," she says, and gently eases the truck forward, water radiating out in circles as they inch on. There is a hiss of steam as the water comes into contact with the hot exhaust pipe, and then the nurse feels it lapping about her feet on the floor of the cab. She draws them up onto the dashboard. Edith keeps the truck moving steadily, but as slowly as she can so as not to cause any turbulence that might flood into the ignition system and stop them in their tracks. She isn't quite sure what concerns her more; the thought of putting her ambulance out of action when it is urgently needed, or the more ignominious thought of having to be rescued themselves.

They are midway across when Edith stops breathing. She has just seen the fins of an unexploded bomb breaking the surface. It is little more than three feet from the side of the truck. She stares, transfixed, and her brain begins to race. Should she stop or should she go on? If she stops, what then? Do they just sit there and sink into the mud? She asks herself these questions in just one second, and in the next she has answered them. Without altering course she presses on.

Unaware of the driver's furious mental process in that moment, the nurse gazes at the softly glowing water ahead of them. Looking down, she notices that it has started to drain from the floor. Edith notices it too and breathes a sigh of relief. Soon the rear wheels have cleared the far edge of the pool and she pushes down harder on the accelerator. With just a splutter or two the truck trundles on, bouncing here and there over piles of rubble.

They are moving over open ground still, towards a large square of light almost directly ahead. As they get closer, Edith sees that it is a hole in another wall and she feels convinced now that they are on some sort of improvised route into the docks. They bounce through the gap and find themselves in another deserted street. Using her in-built compass, Edith turns left, and as they accelerate away both women hear an explosion in the area through which they have just passed. Craning her neck around, Dorothy sees a column of water shoot a hundred feet into the air.

They press on. Edith smacks the steering wheel and starts singing something from Verdi. Knowing nothing of her operatic background, the nurse is becoming steadily more convinced that the driver is losing her marbles.

They are racing now towards an eerie glow in the night sky. A direct view of the docks is obscured once more by some buildings, but Edith reckons that they must be less than a mile away now. She is just beginning to believe that she has, against the odds, got them through, when the truck starts pulling to the right and she hears a sound from the offside front wheel that can only mean one thing. She presses on the brake pedal and quickly brings them to a halt.

"Dear Lord!" she calls out, slapping the wheel again and raising her eyes to the heavens. "It's just too much ODTAA!"

Her bright blue eyes are flashing dangerously and the nurse involuntarily presses herself against the passenger door.

"ODTAA?" she asks.

"One Damned Thing After Another," Edith growls, yanking on the handbrake and almost tearing it from its mounting. She springs down from the cab and walks to the front of the truck, her wet feet squelching as she goes. She kicks the punctured tyre and shouts up to the sky.

"Listen, Chum, I can take anything you care to dish out!" and with that she squelches around to the back. Unable to suppress a smile, Dorothy hears the rear doors wrenched open and Edith clattering around inside. A moment later she reappears at the front of the truck, a jack in one hand and a wheel-brace in the other.

"Nurse," she calls out, "kindly bring me the spare."

While Dorothy attempts to do as instructed, Edith applies the brace to the first wheel-nut and with a strength enhanced by anger gives it a powerful twist. By the time Dorothy has managed to work out where the spare is, Edith has already loosened all the nuts and has the jack in position under the front axle. As the nurse arrives, rolling the wheel along the road, the offside front of the truck is jerking up inch by inch as Edith cranks the handle of the jack. When the wheel is clear she whips it off and the two women manoeuvre the spare into place. Edith does up the nuts finger-tight, lets down the jack and then tightens them with the wheel-brace. They return the jack and wheel to the rear of the truck and are climbing back into the cab when they hear a sound that stops them in their tracks.

Motionless, they stare at one another across the interior of the cab; then, both women step down from the footplates and look up at the sky.

It isn't difficult to spot them, and for a moment Edith wonders why they hadn't been aware of them before.

'Just too wrapped up in what we were doing,' she thinks to herself.

As if quite indifferent to everything going on below, the bombers are flying in perfect formation, in spite of the anti-aircraft shells bursting around them.

It is what she had feared most: another raid, while they are still trying to sort out the chaos from the one before. She quickly loses count of the number of parachutes gliding down, which, she reckons, will be finding their targets just on the other side of the river, but even as she is thinking this, she notices that one of the parachutes is drifting away from the others and appears to be heading to their side of the river. Perhaps some freak gust of wind has caught it she thinks.

Dorothy has noticed it too, and is now staring mesmerised as it clears the north bank and falls lower and lower, seeming almost to be skimming the slate roofs, and in a moment of frozen stillness she thinks she hears the wind blowing eerily in the parachute lines.

Edith feels curiously detached from it all. The rush of adrenaline brought about by the approaching missile makes her feel that everything is happening unnaturally slowly; as if she is sitting in a picture house watching a film at the wrong speed. By now she can make out clearly the spikes protruding from the metal casing; the horns that will trigger the detonation on impact. Landmines – she knew that as soon as she saw the parachutes – or to be more exact, sea-mines, with enough power to blow up a battleship. Then she hears the nurse's voice coming from seemingly far away.

"Wrong time, wrong place," and in her surreal sense of detachment, Edith finds herself playing a curious word game.

"Wrong time, wrong place," she repeats. "Is that a double negative? That would make it a positive. Meaning this is the right time and the right place. Or perhaps we're in the wrong place at the right time, or the right place at the wrong time."

Dorothy turns and stares at her, and sees again the strange smile and the flashing blue eyes. She wants to slap her, but she doesn't dare; for she is convinced, now, that the driver *is* mad.

There is a crashing sound and the women turn to see that the mine has knocked off a chimney pot and sent it clattering onto the roof below. It hasn't detonated, but continues strangely and unerringly towards them. There is something uncanny about the way in which this one parachute with its bristling charge appears to have singled them out.

But then, as the saying goes, "If it's got your name on it."

*   *   *

Edith sits in her rambling garden in Hampstead, North West London. She is shaded by a large and ancient oak, but additionally she wears a broad-brimmed straw hat to keep the sun's rays off her reconstructed face. Her glass blue eyes stare sightlessly across the lawn. In 1970's Britain she finds herself in a very different world.

She has just been making a mental list. It is a human inventory of persons she plans to acquire. It comprises a nurse, a housekeeper and someone to read to her. In addition, there is to be a dog, and someone to walk the dog.

Her retinue planned, her little army, the Mistress, as she will soon become known, inclines her head, closes her unseeing eyes and sees, in her mind's eye, the red glow of the sun through her lids. She considers herself fortunate that she once had the experience of sight, so that now it is gone she can still conjure up an image of the world about her. And with that satisfying thought, sleep steals over her and she dreams of her future household.

As she drifts in and out of her doze, in the branches high above her, the buds are turning imperceptibly into tiny, bright green leaves. She can smell the Spring, in the earth and in the flora, and she senses the multitude of shoots and tendrils reaching towards her.

But there is something else creeping insidiously in her direction that she cannot sense: for she cannot know that in mustering her little army she will be drawing in to her life someone, or something, that will put her in as great a mortal danger as she was that night in the Blitz, more than thirty years before.

*

St. Dunstan's Rehabilitation Home for the
Blind, Brighton, Sussex.
1940, evening. My cell.

I can be myself here. Emotional, if I choose,
judgmental, biased, selfish, vain, scornful, passionate,
angry, intense, aggressive. All those aspects of myself
I am not supposed to present to the world. This is for
my eyes only (bad joke).

The Braille machine is well-suited to my mood.
I Punch the keys rather than tap them. It is a
remarkably simple system. The entire alphabet,
numerals and punctuation marks, from variations of
just six raised dots. Only a blind person could have
invented it. The tutor tells me the typewriter was
invented for Braille. I didn't know that. He tells me
also, "Keep it brief – you're not Proust."

I divide the tutors here into two groups – blind and
sighted. Group Alpha and Group Omega I call them, so
far are they apart. Alpha understands us. They know
what we are struggling with. Omega think we're just
a bunch of invalids and that an hour or so of basket
weaving will somehow fulfil us. I record an example
of the Omega mentality. Today, the Polish airman
asked if he could touch my face, so that he could get a
picture of it in his head. I was appalled! Not because I

didn't want to be touched – I yearn to be touched, as I was before – but because he wanted to touch my face. I can't imagine what it must look like (just as well) having been all but blown away. I thought he would be sure to feel just what a mess I now am, and I preferred him to know me simply by my voice, which is still strong.

But I like the Polish airman. We have a lot in common. Both the same age, more or less, both blinded by fire, and both angry at finding ourselves so helpless and dependent on others. Further, he has confided to me that he is also angry with the people who rescued him and forced him to go on living. When he is not being angry his voice is warm, like toast. He sounds assured, almost, but there's a trace of uncertainty in it. You hear it in all the inmates here. It is to do with having to make your way in a world you can no longer see. You hear it in the way the voice rises at the end of a sentence, as if they're forever asking a question.

So, I hesitated when he asked to touch my face, and the next thing I knew, he took my hands in his and put them on his own face. And we just stood there. I could feel the scars, like my own, but underneath, it was a face that fitted his voice. It was an open face. The features were diminished, as are mine, by the surgery, but there was nothing repulsive or frightening about it. So then I took his hands and put them on my own face. I was starting to enjoy myself. Not so Group Omega. I heard a woman say something about it being "inappropriate and unacceptable." It was said sotto voce, but deliberately loud enough for me to hear. My blood boiled. I wanted to scream, "Unacceptable!? I'll tell you what's unacceptable! Being blind is unacceptable! Why don't you try it and see?" I could have gouged out her eyes in that moment. It had been such an innocent thing but she was making it sound sordid. Of course, I said nothing at the time, but I got it out of system on the way back to my room. While tapping my way along the corridor I managed to send flying a large and apparently valuable porcelain vase. "Oh don't worry dear," they said, " it was just an accident." I intend to have several more such accidents while I am incarcerated here.

But if I am honest, which I promised myself to be in these pages, it hadn't been such an innocent moment, touching the airman's face. It was charged with sexual desire, and I think our warders are aware of this pervasive and underlying frustration we have. They feel they have to keep us under their thumbs or they will have bedlam here, and we'll be skipping in and out of one another's bedrooms as if we're in a Feydeau farce. Well ... I wouldn't mind the Polish airman skipping into my bedroom. I would rather like to hear his soft broken accent on my pillow.

Palla looks out over a spectacular seascape, but the sight only fills her with dread. She has trudged up the little, cane track that brings her to the top of Hackleton Cliff, and she stands staring out at the vast and tranquil ocean, but she feels none of its tranquillity. Occasionally she hears voices floating up from the three hundred or so feet below. They seem to be miles away, these murmured voices, and they emphasise the distance she feels from humanity.

This should have been a day of celebration for her, her thirtieth birthday, but she merely feels that her life is slipping away. Her youth has passed and she has nothing to show for it. In addition, the day coincides with her plummeting to the depths of a psychotic depression. Her mother had seen it coming and abandoned plans to celebrate her daughter's big day. Rolling her eyes she confided to her neighbour, "She back in the Mental by then."

The mother knows all about the mental hospital – or "Jenkins" as it is known in the island – for Palla's father lives there permanently now, and it is, as far as she is concerned, the best place for him. Her neighbour looked back at her fearfully, for the stigma of mental illness is strong in Barbados in the 1970s.

"She gone off the rails again?"

"She not just gone off the rails," the mother replied. "She gone down the embankment too."

Palla inches forward, but she feels no thrill as she peers over the edge; only a dull, moaning numbness. Inadvertently dislodging some stones she hears them clatter down the escarpment. She bites into her lip and tastes the blood on her tongue, and then she hears a voice much closer than those below; so close it seems to be right inside her head.

"You no going back to Jenkins," it whispers to her. "That be the end of you."

"No," she says, "I'm not going back there."

"So why you doan end it here?"

*

Dr. Patrick Smith looks far too young to be the Senior Consultant Psychiatrist; a look that is enhanced by his floppy, blonde hair and boyish demeanour. On Barbados he stands out as the archetypal Englishman, with his gentle civility and public school manners. He has brought with him from England an un-dogmatic and common sense approach to psychiatry. Looking up from the file, he smiles reassuringly at the woman sitting across the table from him.

"Palla," he says, "I think the best thing would be for you to stop with us again for a little while."

She keeps her eyes averted and Dr. Smith hears the low monotone of what sounds like an older woman.

"I no come back to Jenkins. That be the end of me."

"Hackleton Cliff might have been the end of you," he replies, wondering as he does whether or not she really would have jumped. A passer-by managed to intervene, but Patrick isn't sure that this wasn't simply the classic cry for help.

She remains staring into her lap.

"That's what the voice tell me to do."

Dr. Smith regards her for a moment and then looks back to the file.

The original diagnosis – not his – was schizophrenia. Patrick knows that he has to keep her in, for she is too great a danger to herself. Given the severity of her illness he has the power to detain her, but he wants her to feel that at least it is in her own best interest.

"Palla," he goes on gently, "you'll be safe here. We've kept your old bed for you. You won't need to stay any longer than is necessary. And Nurse Grace will take care of you. You trust her, don't you?"

Palla looks up to the well-rounded form of the motherly nurse standing next to her. Grace smiles, and Palla looks quickly back to her lap and her wringing hands.

"It's like I's in the wilderness. You gonna take me out of it?"

Dr. Smith hesitates just briefly. He is pretty sure that they can alleviate her depression but he fears for her in the longer term. There is already a well-established pattern here.

"Yes, Palla. We're going to take you out of the wilderness."

*

Nurse Grace sits at the side of the bath soaping Palla's shoulders and back. It is necessary not only hygienically, as her new patient has been living like a feral cat for some weeks, but it fulfils another function also; that of calming and reassuring her, and of making her feel cared for. In disrobing her, she has surreptitiously removed anything with which she could harm herself. This includes a sharp metal comb she found in the tangle of her long, unkempt hair. It will be a long business, Grace thinks, as she recalls Palla's history both in and out of hospital, and she has no delusions that they are in for an easy time with her. Only a few moments before, when she left her alone in the lavatory, she overheard Palla's voice, high and appealing.

"Doan talk so hard – nursie hear you." Then there was a pause, followed by a "No," and then a still more plaintive "No!" What Grace couldn't hear was the other voice, low and guttural, in Palla's head.

"I told you – you better off finishing it on Hackleton."

"Doan talk so hard – nursie hear you."

"You mean the jailer?"

" No ..."

"Now you in Jenkins, that doctor, he gonna rewire your brain the wrong way round."

"No!"

"Listen – I want you to hear me good. This what you do when the doctor, him come to see you…"

While Palla is being given this inward advice on how to deal with the doctor, the doctor himself is striding across the courtyard on his way to one of the male wards. He has decided that he will inform Palla's father, now long-term incumbent of that ward, that his daughter is back in. The man is so deluded that he doubts it will mean much to him, but the bush telegraph is so effective from patient to patient that he knows he will hear of it anyway and he, Dr. Smith, would rather be the one to tell him.

Just then Cosmic shoots past on his bicycle. Cosmic, another long-term in-patient is the self-appointed messenger within the hospital, or the "internal male," as dubbed by fellow-patients.

"Good Morning, Cosmic," Dr. Smith calls out.

Cosmic cranes his head round through almost one hundred and eighty degrees but continues on his way. As he turns the corner around Norman House, Patrick hears him calling out his standard valediction.

"The whores, the whores, the blasted whores!"

It is a tradition at the hospital, of which Patrick greatly approves, that any patient capable of performing tasks about the place should be given the opportunity to do so. It seems to him that it is often as good a therapy as any he has to offer.

The doctor stops and looks about him. The site is an old sugar plantation that the government acquired many years before as its mental hospital. The name of the plantation's owner stuck, and thus the unfortunate Jenkins bequeathed his name to the nation as a synonym for madness. Mothers threaten their children with "Jenkins," people abuse their fellows with "Jenkins!" and even Dr. Smith is known, on occasions, as Dr. Jenkins.

Patrick's thoughts return to Palla. Once stabilised, he wants to find some useful and therapeutic task for her about the place that might help restore some sense of self-worth – like Cosmic on his bicycle. As he is pondering this he feels the sun beating on the back of his neck, so he steps smartly into the shade of a tamarind tree and, following its outline towards the wall beyond, continues on his way to the ward.

*

"Doc, I do believe you's rewiring my brain the wrong way round."

"What makes you think that?"

"That's what you do in here, aint it?"

"No. We just try to make people feel better."

"Well, I aint feelin' no better."

"He'm an Indian doctor," says the voice. "He put some strong powders in you."

"Is you an Indian doctor, Doc?"

"Do I look like an Indian doctor?"

Palla hesitates.

"...No."

"That's where he'm clever," the voice says. "He change his shape. He'm a shape shifter."

"Is you a shape shifter, Doc?"

"What's that?" asks Patrick, knowing exactly what she means.

"Somebody who aint what he seem."

"I'm just plain old Dr.Smith."

"You aint old! You sure aint old enough to be the Skipper here."

Nurse Grace gently reprimands her.

"Now you show the doctor some respec', Palla," but Patrick smiles and says, "No, I think I agree with her."

"The one before you," Palla continues, "he old. And he have a liking for the rum."

The doctor recalls that his predecessor did indeed have a fondness for the stuff, as does much of the population. It is cheaper to drink in Barbados than it is to eat.

"And when he have in a few liquors, he have a way of looking at you."

Patrick isn't sure how far he should let this go. He doesn't want to encourage gossip about patients and staff, past or present, but at the same time she is managing at last to converse, and this external conversation is a good deal healthier than the internal ones she has been having.

"I'm sure a lot of men have a way of looking at you. You're an attractive woman."

Dr. Smith would not have said such a thing had Nurse Grace not been present. He knows how easy it is for vulnerable patients to become fixated on members of staff, but in any event it has the desired effect and he is treated to the first smile he has yet seen on Palla's tremulous face.

"He got sugar upon the tongue!" the voice hisses.

"Well, what if he do!?" Palla says out loud. Patrick quietly asks, "Palla, are those voices and things troubling you again?"

"Not rightly. ... Them's always at it."

"But the medication ... that's been helping?"

"Mm ... maybe."

Resistant to taking medication, Palla doesn't want to admit that it might be helping her. When Nurse Grace administers the Fluphenazine she refers to it as Vitamin F, but although this benign deception makes it more acceptable to many other patients, Palla is not so easily persuaded. Nevertheless, Dr. Smith has observed a marked stabilisation in her mental state and has already noted in her file, "Reduction in auditory hallucinations."

"You think I's funny-funny, Doc?"

"No, Palla. I don't think you're funny-funny."

"Then why's you keeping me here?"

'I walked straight into that one,' thinks Patrick.

"We're only keeping you here until you get better. And you are getting better. You can feel that, can't you?"

Palla shrugs but says nothing. There is silence for a moment. The doctor wants to keep the momentum of a good therapeutic conversation going but he decides to keep off the topic of her recovery as it clearly raises for her the question of whether or not she is ill at all.

"Has your mother been to see you lately?"

"She doan care 'bout me. She only birth me, but my grandmother raise me."

"But you live with your mother now."

"My grandmother – she gorn."

"She can't have been that old."

She shrugs, as if to make light of it, but her eyes become moist.

"No. She doan make old bones. And I doan make 'em neither."

"When did your grandmother die?"

"She'm gorn three years now."

The doctor nods, and makes a mental note to check when Palla had her first admission to the hospital. She was clearly fond of the grandmother, and her death may well be connected with the onset of her illness.

*

Patrick stands looking out of the window from his office to where patients wander, some going about their daily business, some working, and some simply standing around in small knots, gossiping and smoking in the morning sun. It could be a village street scene rather than that of the local asylum.

One of the patients, Soldo, an old soldier, has already drilled his little cohort of fellow-patients through the ceremony of running the flags up the poles on the pillars of the hospital gates. He must have been flustered, thinks Patrick, noting that the Union Jack is flying upside down.

Another patient, Fritzy, is parading his band of under-gardeners. He is a White Russian who jumped ship when it reached Barbados way back in 1918. He has a shock of hair that stands on end as if electrified and he wears the remains of his blue, matelot uniform. Someone in those early days spotted his potential as a gardener, and many of the magnificent shady trees have been planted by Fritzy himself. He has though learnt only the barest of communication skills. These consist of the numbers 1-10, specialised abuse and interesting misnomers for his beloved plants. Patrick listens to him now as he hands out the hoes and spades.

"You, number 1, to the plum tobagoes. You, number two, to the French pennies. Number 3 and 4 to the quottons."

Slow off the mark, number 3 is reprimanded.

"You big-belly-two-foot-rat!"

At that moment, a young woman appears around the side of one of the buildings and strides towards the doctor's office, if not confidently, with at least a bearing that Patrick has not noticed in her before. This is the first time Palla has been allowed to conduct herself unescorted to his consulting room and she is fully aware of the significance of the occasion. Patrick settles himself behind his desk and awaits the knock on the door. Nurse Grace comes in first.

"Palla is here to see you, Doctor."

"Good Morning, Palla. Sit yourself down."

"Mornin', Dr. Patterick."

"How have you been?"

"Fine. I's jus' fine."

She certainly looks fine. Her eyes and her skin shine and her copious hair is freshly braided. 'Clearly,' Patrick thinks, 'she's taking pride in her appearance once more.'

"When you'm gonna let me out?"

"Very soon," he says, and then decides to play a risky card.

"You could go now, if you wished, but I'd rather you stayed on, for ... a couple of weeks? Just so that we can make sure everything's absolutely alright."

He knows it is a gamble, for she might take him up on it, and he doesn't feel that she is ready to leave just yet. But at the same time he wants her to feel that she is taking the initiative, and thus taking some responsibility for herself.

She sits there looking at him. She wasn't expecting this.

"Well," she says slowly, "I s'pose the mental's no worse'n that old galvanised where I do have my being."

Patrick feels immensely relieved.

"So, you'll be going back to your mother?"

"Aint got no other place to go. But I aint going to let her play the arse with me. Not this time. She do that an' I deal with she."

"Palla, she's not a bad woman, your mother. She has your best interests at heart."

He has been to see the mother recently to assess how stable a life Palla might have there if she returns home. She lives in an old chattel house near Sweetbottom Saint George which, though basic, is clearly looked after with pride. The woman, he believes, cares for her daughter, but she is tired of all the emotional disturbance that her illness has brought her. She went through it all with the girl's father and now she is having to go through it again. Further, in talking to the mother about Palla's father, Patrick got the distinct impression that some abuse, possibly sexual, had been taking place.

"When he do have a few liquors in, I doan let him near my girl," the mother told him.

As the father is permanently incarcerated in the hospital this is no longer an immediate problem, but how much of a problem, Patrick wonders, is it still for Palla? Thus far he has not raised the question of sexual abuse with her in the hope that, given time, she will raise it herself.

"And we'll need to talk about your medication, Palla. How it's to be administered. We can send someone over but it would be a good thing for you to come and see us here from time to time."

"Doan need no medictation."

"You know that it's helped you, Palla. You don't hear the voices and things any more."

"Oh, I still hear 'em. Do this, Palla, do that. I jus' tell 'em I gonna please myself."

"Good. ... Now ... I believe Nurse Grace has something to say to you."

"Yes, Palla," the nurse says. "You know you've been very helpful with me about the ward, and helpful with the other patients. So over the next two weeks, we want you to think of yourself as a kind of nurse yourself. Just help out where you can."

"You gonna give me a uniform?"

"No," says Grace, "I don't think that will be necessary."

"So I an undress nurse?"

Patrick smiles. Plain-clothes police are known in the island as "the undress police."

"That's right," he says, "you'll be an undress nurse."

"What you gonna pay me?"

"You might earn something from the experience. If you have to think of a job one day."

Palla thinks for a moment.

"Doc ... they have nurses in England, right?"

"Of course. Why?"

"Cos one day my mind mentioned to me and say, Palla, you goin' to England some day."

"You'd find life very different there."

"Caint be no worse than here."

"I don't think you'd like the climate," says Patrick. "I didn't."

*

Two weeks later Patrick and Palla are sitting in the shade of one of Fritzy's specimen mahogany trees. This is the day of her discharge and all arrangements have been made. She is not to be sent home in the ambulance. The appearance of an ambulance, particularly in the more remote areas, is always an event, and the doctor wants to spare her the curiosity and gossip that would create. Instead, Patrick has asked Nurse Bennie to drive her in the doctor's ageing Renault.

"How are you feeling, Palla?"

She thinks for a moment.

"To tell you the truth, Doc ... I's feeling jumpy. I just don't know what I's goin' to do with myself."

"Just take things easy for the time being."

"Maybe that's what I's jumpy about. I doan wanna have too much time for the thoughts to come."

"Have you thought any more about nursing? Nurse Grace says you have an aptitude for it."

"What's an aptitude?"

"That you have a talent for it."

"Oh – right. Yeh, it's OK," and she thinks of her last two weeks in the role of nurse. "Man – you got some crazy people here!"

On cue, Cosmic shoots past on his bicycle.

"The whores! The whores! The blasted whores!"

Palla looks after him.

"Why's he keep sayin' that?"

"I wish I knew," says the doctor.

At that moment another patient comes into view on the other side of the courtyard.

'Damn!' thinks Patrick. 'He never leaves the ward. Why does he choose this moment?'

Throughout her stay, Patrick has tried to keep Palla and her father apart, as he isn't sure what effect he might have on her. Now, as she catches sight of him, she visibly stiffens. The father shuffles along, acknowledging none of the other patients milling about the grounds. Patrick and Palla watch him.

"First time I's seen him since I been here."

Palla's voice seems to have dropped an octave.

"No", says Patrick, "he normally stays in the ward."

Palla screws up her eyes.

"He'm a bad man."

"Palla," Patrick says, "he can't harm you, you know. Not now."

Palla regards her father quietly. Her initial apparent fear seems to be turning into something more like curiosity.

"No," she says slowly, "I can see that. ... He's just a little old man. I doan hardly recognise him."

At this point, the father stops and looks straight at her, but it is as if he is looking through her. He stands quite still for a few seconds, though it feels much longer, then he turns on his heel and walks away. It is a chilling moment and Patrick wonders at the effect on Palla.

"Man!" she says again. "I aint gonna get like that!"

She thinks for a second or two.

"You aint gonna let him out, are you?"

"I doubt very much he could cope on the outside."

They sit silently, and then Patrick says, "Palla. Is there anything you want to say? ... About him."

She looks at him steadily, as if trying to reach a decision. Then, "No, Doc. I aint got nuthin to say 'bout him."

"Well," he goes on, "if ever you do, you know where to find me."

Just then, Patrick's Renault appears around the side of Norman House with Nurse Benny at the wheel. A moment later, Grace steps out from one of the wards and walks towards them. The little car, which Benny has never driven before, comes to an unsteady halt and the rotund Benny clambers from it, as if tugging off an ill-fitting garment.

"Mornin', Doc. Mornin', Miss Palla."

Palla smiles shyly.

"Morning, Benny," says the doctor, noting that the nurse is wearing both his specs and his dentures: items he normally removes before dealing with the more truculent patients.

"Doc," Benny goes on, "that's the weirdest gear stick I ever saw."

It is. It sticks horizontally out of the dashboard just below shoulder height and hooks up at the end.

"It's good for hanging your shopping on," says the doctor.

"You take good care now, Palla," Nurse Grace chirps in. "I'll be out to see you next week."

"Don't need no medictation."

'Full marks for doggedness,' thinks Patrick.

Palla looks at the doctor and he can see that she is trying not to cry. Then she throws her arms around him, kisses him on the cheek and, mumbling an embarrassed, "Thank you, Dr. Patterick," she climbs into the car.

Emotional farewells are not unusual at such times, but as Grace watches this one she isn't sure that Palla hasn't become "a little sweet" on the English doctor.

When the car reaches the exit, hiccuping as Bennie struggles with the gearstick, Soldo, who has inadvertently got the Union Jack the right way up this morning, throws open the gates and salutes its occupants; for the discharge of a patient is a major event in the hospital calendar.

Patrick watches it all with a slight frown on his face. Palla's rehabilitation has been more straightforward than expected, but he senses that this is only a temporary respite.

'Please God,' he thinks, 'prove me wrong.'

*

God does not heed Patrick's prayer. Palla is re-admitted within the year and the whole process begins again. There is, however, an extra complication this time. During her brief period of freedom, and courtesy of one of the island's "romanderers," she has managed to get herself pregnant. The man is never identified and it is clear that the wilful Palla wants nothing more to do with him anyway. The baby is born in Jenkins and his presence appears to have a calming effect on the mother. When she isn't nursing him, she performs, as before, other, low-risk, nursing tasks about the ward. It isn't long then before another date is set for her discharge, back to her mother's home. Arrangements for post-natal care are made, alongside arrangements to continue her psychiatric treatment, but within weeks Nurse Benny is reporting to the doctor, "She plain disappeared, Doc. Jus' disappeared. An' left the baby with the mother."

"Dear God," says Patrick, "that poor woman."

Benny isn't sure if he is talking about Palla or her mother.

She had laid her plans carefully. The initial, positive effects of motherhood having quickly worn off, she then felt so overwhelmed by the burden of it all that her instinctive response was to flee. She waited for the nurse's weekly visit, compliantly proffered her arm to the syringe, and said the things necessary to reassure the nurse that all was well. After his departure she persuaded her mother that she needed to be away for a few days on the other side of the island to help a friend cope with some illness in the family. Her mother was far from convinced, as she wasn't sure that Palla had any friends any more, but she allowed herself to go along with it and agreed to look after the child. Palla promised that she would be back in time for the nurse's next call.

Thus it is that a full week goes by before the alarm is raised. The doctor informs the police immediately and some cursory searches are made. Patrick even drives himself up to Hackleton Cliff, and gazes down at the Caribbean, little knowing that he is looking out over the path of Palla's flight.

It hadn't occurred to anyone that Palla might have left the island, but as he stands there on the promontory, Palla is, in fact, several days steaming away, standing on the deck of a Geest banana boat bound for England. She had managed to convince the purser that she was a trained nurse, and was aided in this deception by the uniform she had stolen from Jenkins. As the medic due to sail with them had let them down at the last minute the purser wasn't inclined to check her qualifications, and it is pure luck for all concerned that no one becomes ill on the voyage. She had stood on the stern deck, as they sailed away, watching the salty splendour of wind and sea sparkling forever into the retreating wake, while the skittering schools of flying fish pursued their westward migration to someone's frying pan back in Barbados. Then she turned her back on it all, and walking resolutely round to the foredeck, she set her face towards England: for her, the land of opportunity and, even more important, a place where nobody would know anything about her and her unhappy past; somewhere she could reinvent herself.

*

After docking, Palla makes her way to the railway station and buys her ticket to London. In the weeks prior to her departure she had begged, borrowed and stolen to amass a little stash of money to keep her going until she found work. The luck she had in gaining free passage and a wage on the Geest boat meant that she had more than expected in reserve, but she is dismayed all the same to see just how much the purchase of the train ticket cuts into her resources. She gazes out of the window as the train rattles along, amazed by the sheer greenness of the country, and oblivious to the looks she is getting from some of her fellow passengers.

At the terminus, she is struck by the noise, size and grubbiness of it all, and she stares uncomprehendingly at a large map of the London Underground. Her eyes sweep back and forth across the strange and unfamiliar place names, all connected by different coloured lines, and then she lights upon the word, "Whitechapel," and to her it conjures up the image of a little white church on a hillside looking out over the azure-blue Caribbean, its reflection dazzling in the midday sun.

How she gets there she hardly knows. There is a labyrinth of subways to be negotiated, and tunnels from which the train bursts with a fearsome noise and looks as if it is coming straight at her. So it is with immense relief that she emerges from the subway, but she finds no church on a hill bathed in sunshine. There is no hill, no sunshine, and the churches she sees look drab: but one catches her attention, or rather the people outside it. They are all black, and the women are decked out in the sort of bright, silky colours that Palla is familiar with from back home. It is clearly a wedding, and they are all smiling and laughing and taking photos of one another. On a sign above the door are the words, "Unity Church," which Palla notes. She never had any time for religion in Barbados, partly because her mother had been such an ardent churchgoer. But not only is she older now and less rebellious, she is feeling lonely, vulnerable and lost, and in spite of her solitary ways she feels the need of some sort of community about her. On Sunday, she thinks, she might just pay this place a visit. But now she has more pressing tasks.

She walks along the high street. Apart from the bustle and the noise, her early impression of the city is one of greyness; grey pavements, grey buildings, grey sky. Among the many shops, the one that catches her attention bears the sign, "Employment Agency." She hadn't really known how to go about finding work, but she knows that it is the first thing she must do; her little stash, she now realises, is not going to last her long. She moves close to the glass and peers nervously in. There are two or three desks but only one is occupied, by a young woman who is looking at what appears to be a television on top of her desk. It is grey though, like everything else in London, and not like the black televisions they have in Barbados. At the same time she is typing, but the typewriter is unlike any Palla has seen before. It is flat and small and contains no paper.

'Is that what they do here?' Palla asks herself. 'They watches telly while they does their work?'

She forces herself to enter and stands uncertainly just inside the doorway. The woman ignores her and continues typing and watching the screen.

'That must be a good programme,' thinks Palla. After a while the woman looks up.

"Afternoon," she says without smiling.

"Afternoon."

"Can I help you?"

"I's looking for a job."

The woman gestures towards the seat on the other side of her desk.

"Sit down."

Palla does so. She is a pathetic sight, clutching on her knees the little bag that contains everything she now owns in the world.

"What kind of employment are you looking for?"

The woman has a twangy nasal accent that is strange to Palla. Her name is Dawn and she is a serial chewer of gum.

"You got any jobs for nurses?"

"Yes, we do."

She taps some more keys on the keyboard and looks again at the screen, which is turned away from Palla.

"What you watching?" Palla asks.

The girl looks back at her.

"Sorry?"

"What you watching? On the telly."

One of the girl's eyebrows goes up.

"On the telly?"

"Yeh. What you watching on the telly?"

Dawn wonders if the woman is taking the mick or not quite right in the head.

"I'm looking to see what jobs we have on offer."

"What – on the telly?"

The girl taps one or two more keys and, still looking at the screen, says, "What qualifications d'you have?"

"I got qualifictations."

"Yes but what? ... Are you an SRN or an SEN?"

"Beg pardon?"

"Are you a State Registered Nurse or a State Enrolled Nurse?"

"... I's just a nurse."

"What does it say on your certificate?"

"Dunno. Maybe you can just put me down as a mental nurse."

" ... D'you have your certificate with you?"

"No."

"Well, we'd have to see it, you know. Before we could send you for an interview."

"Right."

Although she wouldn't have expected a nurse to be wandering around with her certificate in her pocket, Dawn is becoming suspicious.

"Where did you do your training?"

Palla smiles, relieved to have a question she can answer.

"Jenkins," she says proudly.

"Jenkins?"

"That's right. Jenkins."

"What's Jenkins?"

"You not heard of Jenkins!?"

"No, I haven't."

Palla can't believe it.

"Jenkins. It's the big Mental."

"The big mental?"

"Yes."

"The big mental what?"

"The big mental hospital," Palla replies, unsure of herself again. "In Barbados."

The girl looks at her a moment longer, a frown still on her face, and then, Palla thinks, she almost smiles.

"So, you're from Barbados?"

"That's right," she says. "Jus' got here."

"Right. Well ... shall we get down some of your details? You want to register with us, do you?"

"Yes. Please."

"Alright," she says, and tapping some more keys she looks again at the screen. "Name?"

In that moment, the machine that is Palla's brain shifts up a gear. She thinks of why she has come here at all. It is to be a new person, and to put all that she once was behind her. Dawn looks back at her, suspicious once more, of someone who doesn't appear to know her own name. Still racing, Palla's mind conjures up the image of the wedding party she has just seen, at the Unity Church.

"Unity," she blurts out.

"Unity," the girl repeats, typing it onto her keyboard. "Second name?"

Palla's mind races still further back, to her epic voyage on the banana boat.

"Geest."

"Geest," repeats the girl. "Is that like in the bananas?"

"That's right," says Palla.

"G-E-E-S-T," spells Dawn, typing it on to the keyboard. "Unity Geest." 'Comic,' she thinks. "Address?"

"Er … like I said, I jus' got here."

"You mean you literally just got here?"

"Yes. Today."

"So where are you going to be staying?"

"I doan rightly know."

"We do accommodation here as well, you know."

"You do?"

Palla's eyes widen; she can't believe her luck, but then the girl starts quoting some prices, and when Palla's face falls, Dawn starts to feel sorry for her.

"Look," she says, "you could just get a B&B for a few nights. Just to tide you over. Until you start earning."

"A B&B?"

"Yes. Just for a few nights."

"Yes, but … what's a B&B?"

Dawn's heart tugs at her slightly. 'She really has just got here,' she thinks.

"A Bed & Breakfast. They give you a bed for the night – your own room – and then breakfast in the morning."

"Right!"

"I could tell you about some if you like."

She gives her some addresses and points them out to her on the street map, which Palla finds as confusing as the tube map.

"Maybe you ought to get yourself an A-Z," she adds. "You'll be needing one."

"An A-Z?"

"One of these," she says, holding up the book.

"Right!"

"So in the meantime, until you get a permanent address, *you'll* have to keep in touch with *us*. About a job, I mean."

"Right."

"But we will need to see those qualifications. Before we can send you for an interview."

"Right," says Palla, thinking about her non-existent qualifications. "They's back in Barbados."

"Well, you'll have to get them sent over."

"That could be taking some time."

"Perhaps you could get someone to fax them."

"Fax?"

"Yes, fax."

"You mean ... facts. Like in true things?"

"No – I mean fax, like in facsimile."

Palla's head is spinning again.

"You're going to need them," Dawn continues. "No one's going to take you on as a nurse. Not without qualifications."

"No one?"

"No," says the girl, and, getting a little haughty, adds, "*We* wouldn't and *they* wouldn't."

It is all too much for Palla and she feels her eyes prickling and starting to water. Dawn softens again.

"Listen," she says, and thinks for a moment. "You could maybe go somewhere privately. Approach someone direct."

"Who?"

"I don't know – some ... little old lady who can't quite manage any more."

"How do I do that?"

"Well, there's a magazine called *The Lady* for a start. They have ads for things like that. But they still might want qualifications. Or you could try the local papers. But not round here. You won't find anyone like that round here. You need to find someone with a bob or two."

"A bob or two?"

The girl smiles. There's something about this strange, exotic woman that makes her want to laugh and cry at the same time.

"I mean, someone with money," she says. "Someone who could afford to pay you. And you won't find that sort of person around here."

"Where'd I find them?"

"You need to look in some of the posher places. Like Kensington. Or Chelsea. Or Hampstead. Look in the local papers there."

To Palla this is all mind-boggling. Having just arrived in a city that is bigger than the entire country where she has lived her whole life, she is finding it hard to grasp that London should have within it so many different places, each with its own name, and apparently its own newspaper. Nevertheless, she rolls those names around in her head, like a mantra, committing them to memory. 'Kensin'ton. Chelseee. Ham'sted.'

Palla stands up to leave, her little bag clutched to her chest.

"Thank you, Miss. You's been very kind."

"You're welcome. Good Luck."

As she says this, the girl glances at the screen and taps a key to take her out of the file for nursing vacancies. Palla smiles.

"I think that's real neat. You'm bein' able to watch telly while you work."

For Dawn it is then that the penny drops, as she realises that this woman has never before seen a computer, and in that moment she almost does cry, thinking of all the trials that must lie ahead for her.

*

But it is Palla who cries, later that night, in the little room of her B&B. She curses herself for having walked into the employment agency that afternoon so ill-prepared.

"You'm a big fat-arse dunce," she tells herself.

Then she cries for the little boy she has left behind, to be looked after by her ageing mother, and she cries for her mother also. She sits on the floor cradling her knees to her chest, feeling isolated, lonely, and utterly helpless.

When she awakes, a pale, grey light is filtering through the thin curtains. She looks about her in bewilderment, not knowing for a moment where she is. She had cried herself to sleep and now her eyes are puffy and bloodshot. She goes to the basin and splashes water on her face, and then she goes over to the window where she pulls back the curtains and looks out over the waking city. She listens to the sounds starting up; the cars, faint voices, and even some birdsong, and the realisation comes to her that she no longer feels the devastation of the night before. It is as if she has expelled it all through her tears, and she stands now at the window looking out with a sense of determination and resolve.

The weeks that follow are difficult and full. She has a lot to learn, and she must find work quickly, for her money has almost run out. Nursing posts are unobtainable. It is the same response wherever she goes. "Where are your qualifications?" She fills in with cleaning work, which allows her to graduate to a modest bedsit. Also, her employers don't ask too many questions about her work status. She starts attending the Unity Church and doesn't feel so isolated any more. She even manages to register with a GP because one of her new friends at the church refers her to her own surgery as a visitor. This gives Palla some relief and reassurance, because she has enough insight to know that her mental state may not remain stable for much longer. It is some time since she has had administered the "Vitamin F," and there are fearful moments when she hears the voices whispering to her again. She had stolen some fluphenazine and syringes from the hospital, but although she has witnessed it being injected countless times, she isn't sure that she can bring herself to self-administer.

Throughout all this, she repeats the mantra, "Kensin'ton, Chelseee, Ham'sted." She has bought herself an A-Z and visited these areas at weekends. She still has a fear of going into the underground but she is less intimidated by the buses, where often she hears from the driver or conductor accents that she recognises from the Caribbean.

Kensington, Chelsea and Hampstead are indeed very different from Whitechapel. She can see it in the shops, she can hear it in the drawled accents, and she can see it on the pavement, which is freer of dog excrement.

At first she is unsuccessful. No rich old ladies appear to be seeking nursing assistance. But she keeps at it, weekend after weekend, until one Saturday, in the Hampstead & Highgate Express, she sees the words, "Elderly lady, blind but otherwise in reasonable health, requires a nurse."

"Yes!" but as she goes to underline it her eyes fall on the words, "Must have qualifications and references."

"Damn!" she says, and the person at the next table in the café looks sharply at her. Oblivious, Palla carries on her conversation, self to self.

"Now come on, Palla. You's talked yourself out of things, you can talk yourself into things," and she gets up and pays for her tea. The smart middle-aged woman at the next table thinks to herself, 'Why do they let people like that in here?' Palla is still blissfully unaware of the prejudice around her. When first she saw, daubed on a wall, "National Front – Wogs Go Home," she had no idea what it meant.

So, the following day, a fine, Sunday afternoon, she finds herself sitting in a dark, oak-panelled room, looking into the bluest eyes she has ever seen. So transparent are they, and so accurately do they fix her with their gaze, that she can't believe that they don't actually see her.

"Unity Geest," says the old lady. "What a memorable name. Would that be Geest as in the bananas?"

Palla has got used to this response, as used as she has got to introducing herself as such. It comes naturally to her now and she has even developed a fondness for her new name. Also, the old lady is right – people don't forget it.

"Yes'M," Palla says.

"What?" I'm a little deaf, you know."

"Yes'M," she repeats, raising her voice slightly.

"What?"

"Yes, Mam!" Palla calls back.

"There's no need to shout," she smiles, revealing a set of teeth as perfect as her false eyes.

'Them's caint be real,' thinks Palla.

"And there's no need to call me Mam. Just call me Edith. Now ... this business of your qualifications. You say you have the equivalent of an SRN 2 from the main hospital on Barbados."

"Yes 'M – Yes, Miss ... Edith.'"

In referring to her non-existent qualification, Palla has failed to mention that the hospital in question is a mental hospital and that she was, in fact, a patient there.

"I don't normally take someone on without seeing their qualifications. Or references."

"You got my ref'rence there, Miss. From the Doc."

Palla is rather proud of it. It took her three hours the night before, with the help of a friend from the church, on a borrowed typewriter.

"And the qualifictations," she continues, "they be here any time now."

The old lady thinks for a moment. Her previous nurse had left suddenly and under a cloud. As she came from an agency, Edith did not want to go back to them, and thus placed an ad in the local paper. So, she is without a nurse and in need of one, particularly as she can't ask the housekeeper to do the sort of things required of the nurse.

"I give you free trial for a week," chirps Palla hopefully.

Edith smiles. There is something she likes about this innocent, girlish woman.

"I couldn't possibly make use of your professional services without paying for them."

Thus it is that Edith takes her on, having no idea that she has just employed an unstable, diagnosed schizophrenic who is no longer taking her medication.

*

St. Dunstan's Gaol. New Year's Night, into 1941.

This is something I would have recorded before, back in hospital. But then, I couldn't write Braille. It is something that only two people know — myself and the feckless fiancé; which is how I have allowed people to perceive him.

When he came to me in hospital that time, the first thing I sensed was the sheer shock he felt at seeing what had happened to my face. But as I heard the clock ticking away, I sensed something else. Pity. And I couldn't bear it. The thought of a lifetime's dependence on him, and all that pity, was just too much for me.

"Peter," I said, choosing my words carefully, for I knew I had to hurt him badly, "I no longer feel anything for you."

"Edie!" he said.

"Don't call me that. You know I never allow anyone to call me that."

(True. Anyone who does gets a sharp, metaphorical slap and they don't do it again).

He thought for a moment.

"Edith," he said, "I know why you're doing this. You want to give me my freedom."

"I'm not that bloody noble!" though there was some truth in what he said.

"Yes, you are."

"Peter – when I drove the ambulance on, that night, instead of staying in the traffic and possibly avoiding it all, it wasn't anything to do with being noble. It's because I was buggered if I was going to let anything get in my way. Result? One young nurse blown up. Now, there's nothing noble about that."

"You don't know the nurse died."

"You didn't see what happened. I did.

"You survived it."

"I'm tougher than she was."

"Edith. I know why you're doing this. I know you too well."

"Peter, you're not a psychologist, you're a barrister. Or you will be. When we get this wretched war over and you get out of your little sailor suit."

I was giving the performance of my life. Cool, rational, even cynical, on the outside, while inside my heart was breaking, because I think I loved him even more in that moment than I had ever done before. Then, by way of a little theatrical flourish, I took off the ring and held it out to him. Needless to say he didn't take it, so I tossed it on the floor.

"I can't believe you're doing this," I heard him say.

"It's simple, Peter. If I became your wife, I'd be living a lie. I don't love you any more. That thing changed me. I see life differently. There's only one thing I want now. I want my career back, and I'm not going to let a little matter of blindness get in my way. So you see, I really don't want any distractions."

"I don't see why you can't be my wife and go on singing."

"No, Peter. I know you. I know how important it is for you to have children. And I would just resent them, because they'd be getting in my way."

I was almost starting to believe my own argument, but at the same time I wasn't quite sure how long I could keep it up, so I asked him to leave. Which he did. And I howled for hours.

So, I closed the door on him. It would have been nice if he'd pushed back against it a little more, but I could no more become the dutiful wife who always knew where his slippers were than I would wish him to become the dutiful husband who always knew where mine were.

The reason I have allowed people to think he walked out on me is because I knew that they would try to get me to change my mind if they knew what really happened. They might even have gone to him about it, and I simply couldn't face another meeting with him. I didn't know if my resolve would hold. Because I still loved him then, as I still do now.

There. That's that out of the way. I need to clear the decks. I am determined to get my life back. Just how drastic I shall have to be, how bloody-minded, how astute, how unwilling to compromise, how ruthless – in short, just how much of a bastard I shall have to become we will see.

"Will you look at that?" Bridie mutters.

She is in the Colonel's bedroom, which she is supposed to be cleaning. Instead, she is staring out to the grey North Sea, rolling away to a grey horizon. There are myriad lines of foam on the chopped-up waves; white horses galloping towards her. A strong on-shore wind is blowing the rain into a wash against the window. It has a depressing effect upon her, reminding her of her home town, Dundee, tucked away just inside the mouth of the Firth of Tay.

"God, that was dreek!" she says.

Bridie's memory is conveniently short-term, for it fits in neatly with her swings of mood not to recall that only two months before she was standing in this same spot looking in just the same direction and saying, "What a bonny view!" But the sea then was calm, and though it is never blue, the sky beyond it distinctly was. She listens now as the waves slap onto the beach and drag the shingle back into the sea, only to deposit it again further along the shore. The inexorable repetition of the process irks her, mimicking, as it seems to her, the repetitive quality of her own life.

It was Aldeburgh in summer that beguiled her; that hot dry summer of '76, when fields of wheat ignited spontaneously. The breezes on the Suffolk coast had made the relentless sun more bearable, and on just such a day Bridie had climbed aboard the train at Liverpool Street Station and watched the London suburbs dwindle away as she sped towards the flat but alluring landscape of East Anglia, counting along the way three crop-fires. In her bag she had her copy of *Country Life* in which she had ringed in biro one of the entries commencing "Housekeeper Required." When she arrived, the Colonel, a jovial old man with the complexion of a drinker, had taken to her immediately.

Once a simple fishing village, Aldeburgh's fishermen were gradually edged out of the centre, where their cramped, old higgledy-piggledy cottages on the seafront were now considered quaint and desirable by a more affluent class, the Colonel among them. By the time Bridie arrived that summer the gentrification of the town was complete, and she wandered contentedly around its little back lanes, where people in yachting caps sauntered in and out of pubs and teashops. Her duties would not be onerous. As long as she kept the house clean and tidy, the pantry well-stocked, and provided the Colonel with three square meals a day, that was all that was required of her. Indeed, there were days when, after breakfast, she had nothing more to do, the Colonel preferring to dine at the Yacht or the Golf Club, and if the day were fine she would pack a picnic lunch and a romantic novel into a basket and take herself along to one of her favoured spots on the steeply-shelving pebble beach. On less fine days, and there weren't many that summer, she would take sanctuary in the Crabbe Sisters' tea-shop, where the scones are fresh and home-baked. Later on, the Colonel would arrive home, a little pink in the face and with watery eyes and, in spite of the pot of freshly-brewed coffee she placed before him, would call for a large glass of single-malt, "and one for you, Miss Bridie."

She suddenly becomes aware of the Hoover, droning away at her side, immobile for the last few minutes. She turns it off and looks at the clock on the bedside table.

"Oh, that'll do," she sighs. "The Colonel will be wanting his dinner soon."

The rain is still washing against the window, and she doesn't know how she will get through the winter here. She wonders if the time has come already to hand in her notice.

*

The Colonel and Bridie sit either side of the fireplace in soft old leather armchairs that have been moulded over the years to the contours of the old soldier and his late wife. Both he and Bridie are widowed, the Colonel through sheer old age, and Bridie, quite prematurely, just after the birth of her second daughter. The shock of that bereavement is little more than a dull ache now. It had been a car crash, while she was driving, and she never got behind the wheel again.

The wood in the grate crackles and creaks and sighs, blending its wood-smoke aroma with that of the Colonel's cigar. Both are mellowed by the glow of the fire and the malt whisky beside them. In addition, the Colonel has dined well, for Bridie went down to the beach in the morning, as soon as the fishermen returned, and bought directly from them. This has become both a habit and a pleasure, for even the old ones flirt with her, and there is nothing quite like the taste and texture of fish so freshly caught. She pressed her coins into the fisherman's scaly palm and her eyes twinkled at him, just as the Colonel's are twinkling at her now. She smiles and looks quickly away, into the fire, where she sees the face of her elder daughter.

"Mum! Can't you see what you're doing? You're giving him the come-on."

She has said it to her scores of times before, and Bridie's response is generally the same – "It's just the way I smile, Emily." Which is true. She has that sort of smile.

The Colonel clears his throat.

"Bridie ..." he begins.

She looks at him, trying hard to give him some other sort of smile, but ending up looking slightly pained.

"Colonel?"

She finds herself wondering why, more than twenty years out of the services, he is still calling himself a colonel. He is even down in the phone book as one.

"Call me Jamie," he says.

This is a well-rehearsed conversation, but she is determined to keep things on a professional footing. She allowed herself to mix business with pleasure in her last post, and ended up without one. She decides on a compromise in her terminology.

"Mr. Jamie."

Now it sounds as if she is talking to the Laird. The Colonel smiles.

"Miss Bridie – why don't you make an honest man of me?"

"Colonel, you're an honest man, or not, without any help from me."

She hopes that she doesn't sound too uppity, and that she has extinguished any sexual tone from her voice.

The Colonel likes the lyrical quality of her speech. But there is something prim about it too. "A touch of the Miss Jean Brodie," he once teased her. He takes another slug from his glass and, giving her an impish look, replies, "You know damn well what I mean."

She knows exactly what he means and she makes a mental note not to sit with him again in the firelight, glass of whisky in her hand, but she knows that she probably will the very next evening.

"They're all starting to talk," the Colonel goes on, enjoying what he takes to be her discomfort. "Housekeeper indeed!"

Bridie is pretty sure that this is pure invention on his part.

"They can talk as much as they like," she says.

Though the rain has let off some hours ago, the wind is still strong and she can feel the old house almost bending to its force. But she feels cosy and warm. At ease, also, for she is used to being propositioned and is more experienced in such games than the Colonel.

"Come on, Bridie. Just say "yes." I'm too old to get down on one knee."

Bridie doesn't know if this is just another ploy to get her into bed, or if he really does want something more of her. She feels sorry for him. He probably doesn't have much time left, but she could no more get "chummy" with him than one of the old fishermen on the beach.

"I'd see you alright, you know," he adds hopefully, but to Bridie's relief not too earnestly. 'Too much dignity,' she thinks. 'Too much of the old regiment.'

She has often wondered about all that. He has told her many stories of derring-do, in World War Two, but she can't get out of her head the image of a very English chap, ex-public school, not bad-looking, just sitting behind a desk in a smart uniform shuffling pieces of paper around.

'Here was I,' she reflects, 'about to hand in my notice, and what does he do? He proposes to me. Again.'

She looks back into the fire, but her daughter's face has gone. There is no one to counsel her.

*

"Damn this gammy leg!" the Colonel exclaims one Spring morning. He is standing beside the old pine table in the kitchen, and as he says it he taps his walking stick against the offending limb, at the same time, behind his back, knocking his knuckles on the table top, thus giving the impression that he has a wooden leg. He grins at her. It is one of his little Music Hall turns. Bridie smiles.

"Well," he goes on, "I'll go and get the car out," and he hobbles out of the back door, for indeed he has a gammy leg, but it isn't made of wood.

Though Bridie has seen the routine before it still amuses her. She likes this boyish side to him. It contrasts nicely with his old Colonel image, which he positively cultivates, right down to the navy blue blazer with its yachting club crest, and the regimental tie, or, if he is feeling rakish, a cravat. The moustache, of course, is de rigueur and he keeps it impeccably trimmed.

She doesn't know if she is looking forward to today. "Spring is in the air," he had announced, "and I'm going to take you for a spin."

It was that last bit that alarmed her. She has never been driven by him but she has seen him driving around and she found the spectacle unnerving. As she hears him gunning the engine she looks briefly around the kitchen, as if for the last time, turns and steps out into the yard.

"Oh my God he's got the top down!"

Bridie steps back into the house to find a headscarf, while the Colonel sits contentedly behind the wheel, listening to the irregular tick-over of the old, six-cylinder engine. He takes a deep breath and inhales the unmistakable aroma of tanned leather and walnut. He loves his ancient car. They have a shared history – he and "The Duchess," as he calls her – for both are relics of the war.

A silk-scarfed Bridie appears and the Colonel leans over and pushes open the passenger door. She steps onto the running-board and lowers herself onto the seat, hoping that her trepidation isn't too apparent. She has only just clicked the door shut, a little too daintily for the Colonel who thinks car doors are for slamming, when the Duchess shoots forward as if she has been rammed from behind.

Their first destination is Thorpeness, less than three miles north. You can see its queer outline from the top of the house. As they tear along, Bridie's mouth twitches slightly at one corner, for underneath the relaxed façade she is a neurotic woman, but she can't deny that she is feeling more alive than she has all winter. The Colonel calls something to her that she doesn't catch, and when she looks enquiringly to him she sees that he too is looking remarkably alive. Beyond, the sea is tranquil, with not a single white horse, while above, the sky is azure-blue with just a few wisps of cirrus high in the ether.

Suddenly her head pitches forward as the Colonel brakes hard, causing the car to slew to the left. The Duchess comes to a halt in a cloud of dust and, still reeling, Bridie looks about her at the strange buildings of Thorpeness. 'They really are very queer,' she thinks to herself.

They roll on slowly through the village, which has a peculiar, unreal quality, as if it has not really been built for human habitation; a feeling reinforced by there being not a soul about.

"It's like toy-town," Bridie says.

"Used to be a holiday camp."

"A holiday camp?"

Bridie is incredulous, for the buildings look like proper houses.

"Yes," the Colonel goes on, "some cove built it in the twenties. Had a bit of a thing about Mock Tudor. Of course it's not a camp any more. People live here now."

"But where are they all? It's like a ghost town."

"No, wouldn't suit me. No pubs. Got its own golf course though," and he brings the car to a halt and waits for his passenger to react.

Bridie's attention has been on an old but well-preserved windmill, which looks curiously out of place, enhancing still further the atmosphere of unreality. Her instinct is more accurate than she realised.

"Didn't used to be here. He had it moved from somewhere else," the Colonel explains matter-of-factly, as if people move windmills about every day.

But this isn't why he has stopped the car there, and his glance flickers to a point just behind Bridie. She looks in the same direction and her jaw falls open.

"What's that!?"

She had been aware of another strange building as they approached but had become distracted by the windmill. She finds herself now attempting to take in the extraordinary sight of a house apparently built in the sky. There it is, a two-storey timber-clad house with a pitched roof, complete with chimneys, about fifty feet up in the air. Seeing it close to, it is clearly a house plonked on top of a tower; a tower of dark wood cladding, five storeys, with windows at every level, tapering towards the top, where the precariously perched house overhangs it on every side. But it still gives the impression of a house in the sky. Bridie turns back to her guide.

"What is it?"

"You're going to be a bit disappointed. It's a water tower."

Bridie looks at it again.

"A water tower?"

"Yes. The house at the top isn't really a house. It's just a big iron tank made to look like one. The actual house is the bit underneath."

"Oh my God!" cries Bridie, "I wouldn't want to live there. Imagine if it leaked."

The car rolls on.

"Bit of a joker, the old cove. He called it The House of Peter Pan. Says something about his state of mind. But the woman mad enough to live there, under thirty thousand gallons of water, called it The House in the Clouds. And that's the name that stuck."

Bridie tries it aloud. "The House in the Clouds." She smiles. 'I like that,' she thinks. And then she tries it again, more softly, "The House in the Clouds," and her brow furrows, for she wonders if that isn't where she is living herself – in the clouds.

Suddenly she becomes aware that the car is tearing through the village at breakneck speed.

"Have you got an appointment or something?" she calls out.

The Colonel beams at her, his look lingering a little too long, and she wishes he would just keep his eyes on the road.

"Just had an idea," he calls back. Which is a lie, because he has planned the whole day with military precision.

From out of nowhere, it seems, a lake looms up in front them, and even though she hasn't been behind the wheel of a car for years, Bridie instinctively jams her right foot hard on the floor, as if pressing down on the brake. The Colonel brings the automobile to a skidding halt just inches before the water. Bridie lets out a gasp and sits still as a statue, waiting for her heart to stop pounding.

The empty lake stretches out before her, lapping gently on to the shallow-sloping shore in front of the car. There are trees dotted aesthetically about its perimeter, and like everything else about the place it gives the impression that it has not evolved organically, but has been put there by a giant, unseen hand.

"Man-made," the Colonel confirms.

To either side of them, boats are pulled up on the sand; an assortment of punts, rowing boats and sailing dinghies. Beyond and on the left bank is an implausibly cute wooden cabin. Bridie is drinking it quietly in when she becomes aware that the Colonel is standing beside her, leaning on his stick and opening her door.

"Allow me," he says, and bends forward, offering his hand. Bridie takes it and is levitated from the car.

The next moment, that same hand is passing her across the gunnel of one of the punts and supporting her as she sits in the prow, her back towards the water. The Colonel nonchalantly tosses in his stick, pushes the vessel off the sand and springs in at the stern without so much as a drop of water on his highly-polished brogues. He stands for a moment, perfectly balanced, then picks up the pole and with five or six expert strokes projects the boat smoothly and rapidly towards the centre of the lake. Bridie is so transfixed by the spectacle of this seventy-odd-year-old man with a gammy leg displaying such agility and expertise that she can think of nothing to say but, "Er … aren't we supposed to pay someone?"

The Colonel scans the shore.

"I don't see anyone. Do you?"

Bridie doesn't, and hasn't. Not one sign of life since they arrived. It is as if the village has had a spell cast over it.

The punt glides on, smoothly skimming the surface, and Bridie sits back and acquiesces. She doesn't like being on water – it frightens her. 'But then,' she thinks, 'if you can punt on it, it can't be that deep,' and she trails her hand in its cool ripples. She watches the trees on the shore sliding past as if on a conveyor belt, but surreptitiously she is studying the boatman, and for a moment she has an image of a much younger man, wearing a boater, college tie around his waist, punting along the backs at Cambridge, squinting into the sun and showing off to a young woman in the prow with a parasol over her head.

"Learned to punt in Oxford," the Colonel says. "Didn't learn much else there though."

How uncanny, she thinks, that their minds were on the same track. But she doesn't believe him.

"Oxford," she says. "Would that have been a day trip?"

The Colonel looks at her quietly, his expression unreadable, and Bridie thinks for a moment that she has gone too far – got above her station – when suddenly the Colonel bursts out laughing and gives the pole another powerful stroke. Bridie looks away, and breathes a little sigh of relief.

In her line of vision now, on the other side of the lake, two swans glide serenely into view, giving Bridie a start. She is sure that they weren't there a moment ago, and she didn't see them land. Again she has that strange feeling that they are in a place outside reality, where an unseen hand, occasionally and on a whim, simply plonks things down.

How long this idyll lasts Bridie isn't sure. She has completely given herself over to it when the Colonel says, "Lunch. Want to get there in time for a snifter first," and he brings the boat about in a gentle arc and punts back to the shore. Moments later, The Duchess is transporting them away from the enchanted village, where still not one soul has appeared.

The lane that they are on, though not much wider than the car, is fairly straight. The Colonel presses his foot down and the hedgerows become a blur. He slows only slightly to take a bend, and as he accelerates out of it one of the wheels spins over the drainage ditch. Then a junction looms up and at first Bridie thinks that he hasn't seen it, but at the last moment the brakes are slammed on and The Duchess lurches to a halt. Bridie, whose fingers have been digging into the upholstery, lets out a little gasp and looks across at her lunatic chauffeur, her mouth twitching again at the corner.

"What would you have done if something was coming the other way? Or if a car just popped out of a side-turning or something?"

By way of reply, the Colonel recalls a joke. He enjoys telling jokes, though he doesn't always get things in the right order and sometimes tells the punch-line first.

"This chap gets himself a really fast car. A Jag. Could do a hundred and fifty. And he thinks where can I go to try it out? Not here. I'll get done. And a chum says Ireland. Long straight country roads. No one on them. So he takes it over to Ireland, finds a good stretch, nice and straight, and puts his foot down. Sure enough in no time at all he's up to one-fifty. But suddenly, just in front of him, this tractor pulls out of a field, two chaps on it, and just stops there in the middle of the road. Well it's too late to put on the anchors – he's nearly on top of them. So he just swings the wheel hard, goes crashing through the hedge, bounces along the field, which they've just been ploughing up, crashes back through the hedge the other side and goes tearing up the road out of sight. And one of the chaps on the tractor looks at the other and says, "Seamus, we only just got out of that field in time!"

Bridie laughs in spite of herself. She wanted to look disapproving, and to tell him that he isn't impressing her with his reckless driving, but when she looks at this pensioner-cum-schoolboy she can't help but smile.

They flash past a sign which Bridie thinks says "Snap." There are now houses around them, and one or two people walking about. They cross an old vaulted bridge and then the Colonel swings off left into a sandy, stony area, which gives him the opportunity to bring them to a halt in another cloud of dust.

"Come on," he says, pushing open the door, "I'll give you the tour first."

They are parked alongside a very traditional country pub, and although it is a weekday, there are a good number of people about, mostly young, thronging around the entrance and sitting at the outside tables, making the most of one of the first fine days of spring. The Colonel leads Bridie away from the pub, down towards a little stretch of river in the shadow of the bridge they have just crossed.

There are one or two boats moored there, the largest of which is called "The Jock." It is broad and has a tall mast, and its heavy brown canvas sails are neatly furled.

"Old Thames sailing barge," the Colonel informs her. "They used to ply the coast around here. Grain, coal, whatever. Flat bottom. Just run her up onto the bank when you want to stop, and float off at the next tide."

"You seem to know a lot about it."

"I've sailed 'em once or twice. I've even sailed this one," and to confirm it, he calls out, "Jimbo!"

A moment later, a man appears from below wearing a smock, corduroy trousers and canvas shoes. He beams back at his namesake.

"Jamie!"

"We're going to have some lunch in the local hostelry. Care to join us?"

"Don't mind if I do."

"Oh this is Bridie by the way. She's an old friend."

'Oh,' thinks Bridie, 'I'm an old friend now am I?'

"Pleased to meet you, Bridie," Jimbo calls back, but before she can reply the Colonel has taken her by the arm and is ushering her away.

"I'm just giving her the tour," he calls over his shoulder. "See you there in five minutes."

They walk on among tall red-brick buildings, which have a deserted feeling about them.

"These are the old Snape Maltings," the Colonel explains.

'Oh, Snape,' Bridie thinks, 'not Snap.'

"They're not malt houses any more, worse luck. Been done up. Concert hall, music festival, Benjamin Britten, all that stuff," and he sounds as if he doesn't have much time for all that stuff.

By now they have reached the edge of the outermost building and are standing staring out at a vast expanse of flat marshy land, covered to the sky-line with reeds that sway in pulses in the wind. The only real feature to break the monotonous but compelling vista is the river that lies across it, which is more a long, thin lake at this point.

Bridie's heart gives an unexpected lurch. She is more used to the dramatic splendour of the Scottish Highlands, but there is something about the desolate land before her now – under a sky made big by the sheer flatness of it all – that captivates her.

She could have stood there for an hour or more, gazing, spellbound. It is the first time since she came to this part of the country that she feels a real connection with it, but the Colonel, not being one for reflection, and thinking of his snifter, is getting restless, and so they amble back to the pub.

The Duchess is not the only convertible there with its roof down. There is a variety of sporty and more modern cars, parked haphazardly, as if their drivers jumped out before they came to a halt. There is a group of young people around the entrance, dressed casually but expensively in open-necked shirts and jeans or chords, and as they jostle their way in, Bridie hears the assured drawl of public-school accents, punctuated by neighing laughs.

By contrast to the bright, broad exterior, the interior seems dim and cluttered, but Bridie's eyes adjust as she is led to the bar, the Colonel calling out as they go, to a group of people sitting around a table in an alcove by one of the windows.

"The cider's good here," the Colonel advises. "Local brew. Aspall's. I'd go for the medium." Bridie says, "Alright, I'll give it a try," but notes when the bar-girl arrives that he orders a large Bell's for himself.

She looks about the place. It is busy, though the majority of indoor clients are of an older generation to those outside. She is just thinking how much of a type they all are when her eyes fall upon someone who is anything but stereotypical of the pub's clientele. He is just a few paces away, standing head and shoulders above his companions, listening to them with a slightly troubled and world-weary look, which seems at odds with his youthfulness. There is a dignity about him; he is lean, and his clear skin is blue-black, but what strikes Bridie most about him is not the colour of his skin, in this all-white bastion of the establishment, but his sheer beauty. For a moment she just stares, transfixed, but then she makes herself look away, worried that her stare will seem rude, and she becomes aware that the glances of others towards this tall young man are by no means as admiring as hers. She begins to feel discomforted, and she senses that the young man feels it too. As she looks at the people about her and briefly back at him, she feels an empathy for him, as if they are both of them in an alien world.

Suddenly, the Colonel is thrusting a large glass of cloudy amber liquid at her.

"Get yourself outside that," he says, motioning her towards the table where his friends sit. She looks at them and hesitates, and a feeling of trepidation rises up in her.

Taking her hesitation for shyness, the Colonel gently presses her forward, murmuring, "Come on. They won't bite you."

There are only two chairs left vacant, and she finds herself separated from her companion and sandwiched between Jimbo, the skipper of The Jock, and a woman in an Angora jumper. She is introduced once again as an "old friend" but she is less amused by it now. It is as if the Colonel doesn't want to be seen as associating with the hoi polloi.

Inevitably, the talk is all about sailing and golf, and she allows a sort of haze to settle over her, aided by the local cider, which is very drinkable and potent. The sun is glancing across the bay window at which they sit, pinpointing its way through the lace curtains and highlighting little motes of dust drifting up and down in its beams, and the conversation becomes as removed from her as the indistinct pattern of the worn carpet at her feet, when she catches the words, "... poor show when you can't go into your local." She hadn't heard the beginning of the sentence, but what she distinctly hears next is the word, "Wog."

Even though warm from the sun, a chill runs through her. She looks around the table to see who might have been speaking, but everyone has gone suddenly quiet. One or two are staring reflectively into their drinks, but one is looking across the bar to the tall black man. She looks in the same direction and finds herself looking straight into the troubled eyes of the man whose appearance had so transfixed her. Did he hear it, she wonders, quickly looking away. And if he did, is he now going to associate her with them?

She feels a sweat breaking out on her forehead and starts to feel trapped by the people around her. Her heart is palpitating and she feels faint and sick at the same time. She struggles to her feet and hears herself saying, "I think I need some air." As she squeezes around the table she catches the eye of the Colonel, who is looking confused, concerned and apologetic all at once. She hears a sharp intake of breath as she treads on the toes of the woman in the Angora, but at last she is away from them, standing at the threshold of the pub, looking down at her shaking hands, surprised to find that she is still holding her glass of cider.

In front of her, just down the step, the throng of people has increased and she can't get through. One tall young man in a striped shirt has his back directly to her. She says, "Excuse me," but he goes on talking and laughing with the people around him. She says, "Excuse me, could you let me through?" but still he doesn't hear her, so she says it again, this time raising her voice and adding, "I need to get some air." Someone in the group says something that she doesn't catch and everyone brays with laughter. She finds herself shouting.

"Are you deaf!?"

Bridie is aware that in times of high emotion her accent reasserts itself and she hears it as distinctly Scottish now.

On the other side of the group a young woman is watching her with a mocking smile on her face, and it is then that Bridie realises they are all deliberately ignoring her – that this is sport for them. She speaks directly to the woman.

"Would it be the accent that's a problem, Hen?" and so saying she raises her glass above the immovable, young man's head and tips a full three-quarter's of a pint of best, local cider onto his blond locks.

This time she gets his attention. He springs round and steps back, upsetting the glass of the young woman whose jaw is now hanging open. In the same moment he raises his hand to strike, but then he hesitates. Bridie can almost see the cogs of his brain whirring around, and she sees him, fleetingly, as a character in a comic strip with one of those thought-bubbles coming out of his head, and in the middle of the bubble are the words, "Bashing a woman in front of my chums? That's not going to look too good."

He starts blustering and remonstrating with her, but Bridie is already striding away, back towards that desolate and peaceful expanse of reeds and sky that she was gazing at just a quarter of an hour before. Her eyes are flashing and she bears a triumphant smile.

Not long after, she hears the unmistakable sound of the Colonel's car drawing up behind her. She takes a last look at the windblown reeds, treads out her cigarette, turns and climbs in. The Colonel is uncharacteristically quiet and thoughtful. Concerned for Bridie he had followed her to the doorway and had witnessed everything. Now he is feeling in awe of her.

They drive back onto the road.

"Thought we'd er ... cut lunch at the pub," the Colonel says.

"Good idea. I didn't care for that place.... Or the people," she adds.

The Colonel, she notes, is now driving with the caution of an elderly spinster who only takes the car out at weekends.

"D'you like oysters?" he asks.

"I can take them or leave them. But they do go down nicely with a little champagne."

"Well, I know this place down in Orford. Does a decent smoked salmon too. Little triangles of buttered brown bread. Slices of lemon."

"That sounds very pleasant," she says, 'providing,' she thinks, 'there aren't any more of your cronies there.'

She leans her head back and closes her eyes.

'This has been a most extraordinary day,' she thinks, 'and we're only halfway through it.'

The Duchess rolls serenely on, at a stately twenty miles per hour, collecting a procession of less venerable vehicles behind her.

*

Summer comes and Bridie forgets about handing in her notice. The arrival of the tourists lifts her, and distracts her from the more humdrum aspects of life there. The cream teas fill out her waistline a little more and she continues to flirt with the fishermen on the beach.

The Colonel doesn't share her feelings about the tourists. They clog up the pubs and force him to retreat to the yacht or the golf club, both of which Bridie refuses to frequent. Also, the tourists have an infuriating habit of parking their cars in front of the Colonel's garage, marooning The Duchess inside. On such occasions the errant tourist often returns to find he has a flat tyre.

Six more summers come and go, and Bridie becomes as much a fixture of the place as the Colonel himself. He continues to ask her to marry him and she continues to decline, reminding him that she is young enough to be his daughter.

In a sense they are married. They share the old house with the ease of two disparate people who have got to know one another well enough to mould themselves to the quirks and foibles each of the other. There is between them, if not a love, then certainly a fondness. No getting chummy, as Bridie would have put it, but decidedly something more than friendship.

The Colonel's leg becomes increasingly gammy, but it is still capable of getting him to and from the car and depressing the clutch pedal. They continue to go for their spins, and on one late summer day in 1983 they are returning from another trip to the village of Dunwich, just ten miles up the coast from Aldeburgh. There is not much to see there any more, but they like to go and sit in the car, looking out to the sea that swallowed the place up over the centuries. Hundreds of houses and nine churches have tumbled over those cliffs, as the waves nibbled and lashed from below, and it gives them both pause for thought. Then, Bridie will duck down behind the dashboard, light a cigarette and walk out to the headland, with her hair streaming out behind her if she hasn't thought to put on a scarf, while the Colonel watches her from behind the wheel, imprinting the picture, "Woman Looking out to Sea" on his inner eye. Though still a jovial man, he has found in recent years that he cannot look at something that moves him without wondering if he will ever do so again.

The car rolls out of Dunwich and is soon heading back towards Aldeburgh. The Colonel doesn't drive fast any more, for he knows that his speed of reaction is no longer up to it, but more particularly he has Bridie on board. Ever since that day in Snape, he has treated her with more deference. He is, in truth, a little frightened of her, and has referred to her in conversation as, "A not-so-dormant volcano." But one peculiar trait he has never shaken off is that of sitting at a T-junction and waiting, not until the road is clear, but until something is coming, and *then* he pulls out. Bridie has observed this over and over and can never work out if the Colonel is simply oblivious to the ton of metal bearing down on him, or if it is in fact a game to him. She once asked him if it might be a good idea for him to take his driving test again.

"Again?" he said. "I never took one in the first place. They didn't have daft things like driving tests in my day."

They sit now at a junction. In neither direction is there another car in sight. They wait, and they wait, and Bridie wonders if she might have time for another cigarette. They wait a little more and then a speck appears on the road away to the right and gets steadily larger. Bridie closes her eyes and prepares herself for the inevitable lurch forward, the rapid acceleration and angry hooting from behind. The car seems to take a long time coming, but then suddenly she hears it shooting past and, opening her eyes, she sees it rapidly becoming a speck again. Looking to the Colonel, she finds that he has slid down in his seat, so that his eyes are on a level with the dash; but they don't appear to be seeing anything. In what seems like total silence, but can't be because the engine is still running, she hears herself addressing him softly in a way that she has never done in the seven years that they have known one another.

"Jamie?"

*

In his several proposals of marriage, the Colonel never knew how close he had got on one occasion to extracting from her, "Oh alright, why not." But despite his failure to wed her, he had fulfilled his promise to see her "alright." In the aftermath of his death, his family is as ugly about it all as Bridie expected. They contest the will, without success, even though they have inherited the house and most of the old soldier's money. It is also clearly stipulated that she is to be given a decent period in which to make her plans, and yet she finds herself having to show potential buyers around the place the very day after the funeral.

She keeps the house pristine, more so perhaps than when the Colonel was alive, and when she is dusting in his bedroom one day, she looks out through one of the windows to where they had first driven together. There it is still – The House in the Clouds. Thinking more about that day, she picks up the phone by his bed and dials a number she has often dialled before, when the Colonel had had too much even by his own standards to get behind the wheel.

A quarter of an hour later she is sitting in the back of a cab. It isn't as exhilarating a ride as the Duchess provided, but it is a luxury all the same for Bridie to order a taxi, just for herself, and then, on arrival at her destination, to tell the driver to wait.

They pull up outside the pub, she steps out and strides, as she did some six years before, past the moored boats and the tall, red-bricked malt houses, on to the broad tranquil river, and the flat mysterious land of reeds and marsh, beneath the big East Anglian sky.

Little more than five minutes later she is back in the taxi, not because she is concerned about the meter ticking over, but because she has said her farewell.

Back in Aldeburgh she steps into the newsagent, buys a copy of *The Lady* and walks along to the Crabbe Sisters' tea room where, as she sips her tea, she rings in biro an ad. that runs:-

    Elderly lady living in Hampstead,
    blind but otherwise in good health,
    seeks experienced housekeeper/
    capable cook. References essential ...

The idea of working for a blind person intrigues her, though she can't quite say why, and she has decided too that it shall be a lady. She doesn't regret for one moment working for the Colonel, but she doesn't want the possible complications of working for a man again, not just yet.

A year or so later, and well established in her post in London's affluent Hampstead, she will revise her notion that it is any less complicated working for a woman, particularly one as strong-willed as Edith. Working for a man, she will discover, kept her emotions in check, but living under the same roof as another woman, she will find female rivalries coming to the fore, and there will be regular battles for supremacy.

Edith, too, will begin to wonder if there might be a "female problem," and she will determine to redress the imbalance in her next appointment. She will wonder also if her generally sound judgement of humankind is deserting her in old age. She has already taken on a nurse whose mental state she seriously questions on occasions, and now she has added to her entourage a woman decidedly neurotic and hot-tempered. Both, she knows, have redeeming features, and more or less get on with their jobs, but she will have to ensure that her next recruit is just a little more "normal."

*

Hampstead, 1947. Middle of the night. (Can't sleep).

London is still a mess. Though I can't see it, I know just how long it takes us to get around now. (In the Armstrong Siddley Hurricane. Beautiful car. Probably not for much longer, though. Not with Sis at the wheel). Anyway, there are diversions all over the place because of bomb damage. It'll take them years to clear it up.

Later in the day I decided to take advantage of Sis being out to tea. (She has really taken to life in Hampstead. All those piping women in twin-sets and pearls). So, I was singing to myself – my voice continues to strengthen – and I suddenly realised I was screaming the notes, and I could feel tears welling up.

"What's all this about?" I asked myself, and the answer was simple. Sheer frustration. I have lost patience with the conventional, blind-disabled person's life, and I refuse to settle for it. I know I must accommodate to it (I have had the carpets taken up, for instance, so I can hear people coming) but I will not settle for it. I will not let blindness define me. Describe me, perhaps, but not define me. It's just that … with blindness

you have to be sensible, all the time. All sense, and meanwhile my intelligence is withering. I only feel truly myself, and fully intelligent, when I am singing.

"Oh Lord!" I said, "Haven't we been through all this before?" ("I" seem to have become "We." It's true. We have regular conversations together. Sis caught me at it the other day and told me they'll be coming to take me away soon). "So," I replied to myself, "why don't you _do_ something about it!" to which I replied, "Alright. I will."

I went and picked up the phone and dialled my agent. I have been putting this off for some time. I told myself it was because I wanted to get my voice tip-top first, but the real reason was I had a pretty good idea how he would react. He didn't disappoint.

"Look," I said, "I want some engagements."

"Engagements?" he repeated, as if the word were strange to him. "What sort of engagements?"

"Concerts," I said. "I want you to get me some concerts. Or some recording work."

"Deary," he said (I think he's a pansy), "people don't want to be reminded of the war."

"What d'you mean?"

"How can I put this, deary? As soon as people see your face they'll be reminded of the war. And it's not going to help tucking you away in the recording studio because you won't sell records without personal appearances."

I was about to detonate, but I defused myself just in time.

"Thank you," I said, "you've just helped me make up my mind about something. But before we get on to that, let me tell you that I intend to go out, onto the concert platform, and with my broken face, I will remind people of the war. I am not going to be put away in a cupboard because I am seen by the feeble-minded as some sort of embarrassment. And by the way," I went on, "You're sacked."

After I had slammed the phone down I sat and thought. He really had got to me, with that talk about my face. Was I such a horror? I ran my fingers over it. My forehead, my temples, my lids, my useless eyes, my cheeks, my mouth, my chin ... It didn't _feel_ that bad.

Sis came back an hour or so later. I hadn't moved.

"What are you doing sitting here in the dark?"

"Is it?" I said and burst into tears.

She came and put her arms around me. Which made things worse, because I'm not used to her being caring.

"Hell's Bells!" I blubbed, "I don't even know if it's day or night!"

She was very patient and let me cry it all out.

"I'll make us a nice cup of tea," she said.

"I need something stronger," so she served up a couple of Scotches.

"Listen," she said, "I've been thinking ..." (I always get a bit alarmed when she thinks) "...Why don't you join a blind club? That'll be companionship for you. You might even meet a nice young man. And another thing. Why don't you get yourself a guide dog?"

If I could have located her quickly enough I'd have given her a black eye.

"Our sisterly moment didn't seem to last very long, did it," I said. "I do hope, Sis, that you haven't been discussing me with the Hampstead Intelligentsia."

She knows I've got no time for her snooty friends.

"I just want us to do what's best for you, dear."

I know I've got to watch out when she starts calling me "dear" so I got in first.

"I'm glad you used term "us," Sis, because I'm going to need your help. And by the way, I know exactly what's "best" for me. What's best for me is to get back up on that stage and start singing again."

There was a bit of a silence, and then I heard her voice, rather wary now.

"Why d'you need my help to do that?"

"Because I've just sacked my agent."

"Oh dear. What for?"

I paused. I was drained and I didn't want to get into it.

"... For being a pansy."

There was another silence, and I thought to myself I've got to try and make her understand.

"Sis ... the thing is ... I've got no choice. I _have_ to sing. If I don't, I'll just dry up and blow away. When I sing ... it's as if I'm walking this long, straight, graceful, unbroken line. It's magical for any singer, but it's even more so for a blind singer. Because when I'm singing,

I feel I'm more seeing than I ever was with eyes. I just …can't think of any other way of putting it."

There was just a pause, and then I heard her say, "I'll help you."

Ronnie Scott's is sweaty, dark and heaving. This Mecca for the jazz set, located in a Soho basement, never sees the light of day and seldom gets more than a cursory lick from the mop. London's Soho in the seventies is less seedy than it had been hitherto, but although its Ladies of the Night have been removed from the doorways, red lights glow in the windows above to indicate that it is business as usual, and it has yet to become the Capital's gay centre, thronged by young men with moustaches, cropped hair, tight vests and overdeveloped biceps.

Reg looks out from the tiny stage and through a pall of cigarette smoke that hovers above the punters' heads. Some sit at tables, some lean against walls, and some are propped up at the bar. Most look animated and keen, in an intoxicated sort of way, and their eyes sparkle in the dim light as the music reverberates around the room.

It has been a good set, Reg feels, as he wipes the mouthpiece of his saxophone. He reaches for his beer and takes a swig before rejoining his fellow musicians for the finale. He has just performed what he knows to be an accomplished, improvised solo, and he never feels more alive than in such moments. He unclips his sax, puts it in its case and picks his way to the bar, where Hedda is waiting for him.

"Not bad," she says from her perch on a stool. She lights a cigarette from her own and hands it to him. Reg smiles, unsure what is meant by, "not bad." They haven't been together long and don't yet know how to gauge the other's responses. They are still at that stage where they find one another interesting.

Reg was a child of the thirties, and he knows a bit about deprivation. Those were hard times for working class families and he learned to be wily. He had a natural but non-academic intelligence, so although he didn't do well in the classroom he could broker a good deal in the playground. During the Blitz he ran a lottery for two spare places in the family's Anderson shelter, but when his mother found out he got a clout that made his ears ring and was made to give the money back.

"If you thought that wasn't bad," he grins, "just wait ...," but whatever he says after that she is not to know, because the next set strikes up with a loud and brassy flourish. There isn't any point in trying to talk over it so he turns his attention to the band. He knows most of the musicians and has played with two of them. He listens to the sax and decides that he, Reg, has a better technique. He is unable to discern that the other player has more "soul," for there is a cool detachment about Reg which not only prevents him from putting such emotion into his own playing, but means also that he cannot recognise it in others.

He looks about the room and is immediately struck by two women sitting at a table by the edge of the stage. They are in such contrast to the bohemian clientele that he wonders why he hadn't noticed them before. They could be in their sixties, and with their permed, whitish-grey hair and smart, conservative clothes they look as if they would be more at home with afternoon tea and a palm tree orchestra at the Ritz. What is particularly striking about them is that the woman on the other side of the table, whom Reg can see better, has the most translucent, blue eyes. She is gazing towards the stage but there is something in her look that makes Reg wonder if she is actually taking it in. When the set concludes he hears Hedda asking him, "So, who plays a meaner sax?" He grins back at her and replies, without the hint of a question mark, "Who d'you think."

Over his shoulder Reg hears someone say, "Excuse me," so he moves over to let the woman get to the bar. When the "Excuse me" is repeated he turns and finds himself face to face with one of the old ladies from the table near the stage; not blue-eyes but the other one.

"My friend wanted me to tell you how much she enjoyed your playing," she says.

Reg smiles, not so much at the compliment but at the clipped, upper-class tone with which it is delivered. It is unusual to hear such an accent at Ronnie Scott's and it reminds Reg of the Queen's Christmas day broadcast. The woman orders two glasses of dry white wine, under the misapprehension that there is any other type of wine on offer, and then asks Reg if he would care for another drink, which is like asking a beggar if he would care for some money.

"Wouldn't say no," he replies. "This is Hedda, by the way," he adds quickly, neatly including her in the round.

"You'd be most welcome to join us," the woman goes on. "I know my friend would like to meet you. Unless, of course, you're playing again."

"No, that was my last set," Reg says, thinking this might be fun. As they make their way across to the table he catches Hedda's eye and they grin at one another.

As the introductions are made Reg notices that while the first woman's tone is squeaky and nasal, that of the second woman has a rich resonance, and at close quarters her eyes are mesmerising.

"I did enjoy your playing," she says. "The saxophone has such a mournful, yearning tone."

Again, Reg can't repress a smile. He just isn't used to hearing people talk like this and it puts him in mind of the announcers on Radio Three.

"Are you into music?" he asks.

"Oh, certainly," the blue-eyed woman replies, "though rather a different sort. It was my friend who brought me here."

"What's your sort of music then?" asks Reg, wondering at the same time what on earth brought her friend there in the first place.

"Opera," she says.

"Oh, you're an opera buff."

Reg is in unknown territory now and doesn't quite know how to carry on, but the squeaky woman helps him out.

"She's an opera singer."

"Concert singer," the blue-eyed lady corrects. "Had to give up the opera when I lost the peepers."

For a brief moment Reg doesn't know what she is talking about, and then it dawns on him that she is blind, and that those eyes that are looking at him so penetratingly can't actually see him. He feels awkward in that moment, and for some reason embarrassed, but fortunately the three women carry on chatting among themselves, allowing Reg time to reflect. He is intrigued by this old woman with the beautiful but useless eyes, but there is something else that is filtering into his senses. She positively smells of money.

"Can I get you ladies another drink?"

*

A year or so later, in the saloon of the Duck or Grouse, Reg stares into his glass of beer. He would have been enjoying it more but for the unexpected arrival of the man sitting opposite.

"Reg," says the man, "it's been a good six months now. The agreement was for two."

Reg smiles awkwardly, and inwardly resolves to avoid the Duck or Grouse for a while.

"It's been a difficult time," he replies.

The man smiles back at him, but there is something dangerous about the smile that makes Reg feel queasy. The man has the build of a bouncer.

"Reg … it's always a difficult time for you, isn't it."

"I haven't been getting that many gigs lately," he begins, but immediately trails off, sensing that he will have to try another tack. Before he can think of one the man says, "That's not what you told me when you asked for the loan. You said you were doing very well just now and could easily pay it off in a couple of months."

"Yeh ... well things have dried up a bit since then. And this business of the interest..."

"Those are my standard rates, Reg. And you knew all about that from the start."

The man isn't smiling any more. Reg looks at his beer again and then looks up hopefully.

"But things are picking up now. I've got some gigs coming up. And I've got this er ... day job."

"You've got a day job? What would that be?"

"I'm working for this old girl. She's blind — and I go and read for her."

There is a brief silence, then the man gives a humourless laugh.

"Straight up," Reg says. "I've been doing it for a while now."

Without taking his eyes off him, the man picks up his glass and drinks half a pint in just one draught. He wipes the foam from his upper lip and belches.

"Reg, do I look like I've just got off a banana boat?"

"Er ... no."

"Then why are treating me like some ignorant nig-nog?"

"I'm not," Reg mumbles, glancing nervously at two powerfully-built black men at the bar. The man follows his glance.

"They're getting bleedin' well everywhere now," says the man, seeming not to care whether they hear him or not. Reg has no prejudice about black people and works with them regularly in his gigs. He is about to say so but then thinks better of it. He is in enough trouble already.

"Listen," the man goes on, "are you seriously telling me this little old lady's paying you so well you're going to be able to clear a debt of two grand?"

"Two grand!?"

Reg's mouth hangs open, making him look decidedly imbecilic.

"But I only borrowed a thousand."

"Compound interest, my friend."

Reg gives him a bewildered look. This is not the type of man, he thinks, who should be using terms like "compound interest." The man gets up.

"I'm going for a slash. See if you can come up with something more... agreeable before I get back." He has a way of making the word "agreeable" sound threatening.

Reg watches the man's bulky frame roll towards the door marked "Gents." He then looks at the door marked "Exit" and wonders if he should do just that. But what would be the point, he thinks. He'd just be getting in deeper, and the man knows where to find him.

He considers his options and quickly realises he doesn't have any. Even if he could get a few more gigs, they pay so little that anything earned there would be cancelled out by the rapidly mounting interest on his loan. Session work is more lucrative but the recording side of the business is very competitive, and Reg neither has an agent nor the necessary contacts. And the man is right about the old lady. She pays him well, for what he does, but it barely keeps him in beer money.

He stares morosely into his empty glass. He is so desperate, he actually finds himself wondering how difficult it might be to rob a post office. A little sub post office, perhaps, in the country, miles from anywhere, with just a helpless old woman on the other side of the counter. And then he has another thought.

When the man returns, Reg looks up hopefully from the two fresh pints he has just bought.

"Look," he says, "I've had an idea."

*

Reg walks into Sotheby's with an air of confidence. Though he's never been to such a place before he knows how to blend in. He has donned his only suit and it is pinching him under the arms. A young man in a striped shirt looks up from some sort of ledger.

"Good afternoon, Sir."

"Good afternoon," Reg smiles back, mimicking instinctively the man's Oxford tones. "I'd like to have this valued."

"Certainly. If you would just like to put it on the table there."

Reg begins to unwrap the bulky item he had so much trouble with on the bus. The man watches him quietly, a superior smile on his face. He has already consigned Reg to the category marked "Common."

"Mm," he says when Reg has finished, "… interesting."

Revealed upon the table is a large engraving.

"It's the Duke of Wellington," Reg says, "with his Generals. At a banquet. After Waterloo."

"Yes," says the man in the striped shirt, studying it more closely, "It's a fine piece." He peers at the artist's signature. "Provenance?" he asks.

"I beg your pardon?"

"I can't quite make out this signature. Where does it come from?"

"Er – it belongs to my aunt. One of her ancestors is there. Not sure which one. He was one of Wellington's Generals."

"Mm," says the man, "I think this is one for Mr. Bletch," and he picks up the phone. "James. Got something here I think you might be interested in."

Mr. Bletch's valuation causes Reg to catch his breath, but he manages, just, to maintain his composure.

"Your aunt's going to miss it, isn't she?" queries Mr. Bletch. "Particularly with one of her ancestors in there."

"Oh, she says she can hardly move for family heirlooms," says Reg, and then, adopting a more confidential tone, "and between you and me, she's a bit strapped for cash just now."

It isn't too difficult for Reg, later that day, to manufacture a reasonably authoritative-looking letter confirming the ownership of the engraving, particularly as he has been practising Edith's signature for a while now, in the belief that it might come in handy one day. Thus the portrait goes into Sotheby's next sale of militaria, and fetches just a little more than Mr. Bletch suggested.

"Easy-peasy," Reg says. "Money for old rope."

The tell-tale gap on the wall of Edith's dining room, where once the Duke disported with his generals, indicates that the place needs a fresh coat of paint.

*

The ease with which Reg pays off his loan gives him a false confidence. He thinks that with all the valuable stuff there is in the old lady's home – the portraits, the furniture, the jewellery, the silverware – he could subsidise a nice lifestyle for some time to come. He knows that he has to be careful though, for although his employer can't see what is going on around her, there is the housekeeper who comes in every day, and she is bound to notice if one of Edith's portraits suddenly isn't there any more. Reg has shifted some of the other paintings around, to make less obvious the gap where once the engraving hung, but there is only so much he can take before suspicions might be aroused.

So, he concentrates on smaller items; her jewellery, for example, some miniature portraits, and even one or two pieces of furniture. He is careful to vary the places to which he goes to sell them, and he includes one or two antique dealers in his rounds, though on the whole he finds he makes more by selling through the auction houses, even after they have deducted their exorbitant commission, which is, to his mind, nothing short of criminal. Also, he enjoys the thrill of attending the auction, and of standing there, anonymous, as the bids go up and up on this or that item he has just purloined. He can't always work out who is bidding, and he even bids himself once, on one of his own pieces, just to push the price up. But he only does it once, as he ends up having to buy it.

Weeks, months, and eventually years pass in the service of his seemingly gullible employer, and little by little the valuable family stock, accumulated over generations, is diminished. (It is fortunate for Reg that all this takes place before Bridie takes the post of housekeeper, for he will get away with less once she is around).

He has, however, underestimated Edith's powers of perception. She is not so easily fooled, and she has noticed that certain things are missing. At first she thinks that the housekeeper has perhaps put them back in the wrong place after cleaning, but when she discovers that this is not the case, she begins to have her suspicions. By now, however, she has developed an almost maternal affection for Reg, whom she finds both roguish and amusing. He has worked his charm on her, and when he comes to read to her from the paper in the morning, they sit each in their own armchair, and he regales her with some anecdote from the jazz world, and then they finish the session with a Scotch and American Dry. He is not always punctual, and judging by his sometimes slurred speech, Edith suspects that he has put rather more whisky in his own glass than he has in hers, but she only half-heartedly admonishes him, and he always has a way of wriggling out of awkward situations.

Just as Edith is aware that something is going on, so too is Hedda. She notices the changes in Reg's lifestyle. He is spending more on clothes, socialising and the like, but he doesn't seem to be doing any more gigs than before, and he hardly ever gets session work, so where is the money coming from, she wonders. He is, however, spending more on her, so she decides to hold her tongue and keep her suspicions to herself.

In the course of his now livelier, social calendar, Reg takes to spending more also on alcohol, not only for himself but for his so-called friends, and there are plenty of those when Reg is buying the round. He loves to play the genial host, but as he begins to drink more heavily, his judgement becomes unsound, to the point where he finds that he is in fact spending more than he gets from exploiting the old lady. As time goes by, he finds that he is, bit by bit, getting into debt again. There is a little loan here and a little loan there, none of which he had any intention of repaying, but when his creditors start putting pressure on him he finds he has nowhere to turn. He has more or less exhausted the potential to pilfer from the Mistress, without, that is, taking something that would almost certainly be missed, and in his desperation he resorts to the worst remedy of all. He borrows from the same man who gave him such a scare in The Duck or Grouse those few years before.

It is hopeless. There is not the remotest possibility that he can repay the loan, and on this occasion the man does not let him off so lightly. On returning home late from a gig one night, which was followed by an exuberant drinking session, he finds himself in the alley outside his flat, unsteady on his legs, looking up into the meaty, round face of his chief creditor.

The next thing he knows he is being projected with considerable force into a group of large, cylindrical bins on wheels. They roll this way and that as he bounces off them, and somewhere not far off a dog starts barking. Slumped on the ground, and just trying to take in what is happening, he feels a finely-crafted Italian shoe kicking him in the kidneys. But he has hardly registered the pain when he feels himself hauled to his feet, only to be expertly head-butted on the nose. Just before he slips into unconsciousness he hears the man's low growl.

"You've got three days. Then I might have to hurt you."

Reg doesn't wait three days. The very next afternoon he can be seen loitering in a little country lane, just outside the town of Epping in Essex. He has remembered this place from childhood, when a real treat for a working class family from London's East End would be a charabanc trip to Epping Forest. Behind him, now, is an opulent, pink mansion, the property of a young newspaper proprietor by the name of Rupert Murdoch. Although, doubtless, this grand house is stuffed with valuable items, this is not the focus of Reg's attention. Instead, he is furtively eyeing the small, sub-post office on the other side of the lane. He waits until the old man he has just seen entering comes out, and then he crosses the lane and steps inside. Behind the counter is not the little old lady he had been hoping for but a burly, red-faced man. Reg has had enough of burly men. His kidneys are still aching from the kicking they had the night before, and he has an angry-looking bump on the bridge of his nose that makes him look, in profile, like Mr. Punch.

He approaches the screen. His heart is beating so fast it makes him giddy. The man looks up, raises a disinterested eyebrow and says, "Yes?"

To Reg, the voice seems to have come from a long way away. He opens his mouth to speak but nothing comes out, so, instead, he draws from his coat pocket the replica pistol he purchased that morning from a shop in Lower Regent Street. Or rather he attempts to, for the hammer of the gun gets snagged in the lining and he has to struggle with it, half in, half out. Thus, by the time he has extricated it the man isn't entirely surprised to find a revolver being waved at him, and he has already pressed the silent alarm button beneath the counter. They stare at one another for a moment, and then the man says, "Just what do you think you're doing, Mate?"

He looks as if he's about to leap over the counter. Reg's nerve, feeble from the start, breaks in that moment and he spins around and bolts from the shop. He is still running when the police car pulls up alongside him and two policemen spring out and propel him face first into a hedge. He hasn't even thought to throw away the gun.

It was a truly desperate and pathetic act, and the judge shows some leniency in sentencing him to only one year's detention at H.M.P. Wormwood Scrubs. A week or two into his sentence, Reg is startled by the news that his financial advisor has come to see him. He hadn't realised he had one, so more out of curiosity than anything else he allows himself to be led to the visitors' room where he finds, sitting on the other side of the screen, the big man who introduced his forehead to Reg's nose just a few weeks before. The man informs him that the interest on his loan will continue to accrue while he is "banged up," and that he will be waiting for him outside the gates on the day of his release, "to discuss the terms of repayment."

With this cheering news, Reg is led back to his cell.

The only other person to come and see him is the old woman he has been robbing for years. Edith has taken pity on Reg, and she becomes a stalwart and regular visitor, while the person he most hoped would stand by him, his ladyfriend, Hedda, stays away, so repelled is she by his sorry behaviour.

*

It is not an easy year for Reg. He is not hardened prisoner material and he suffers as a result. He is picked on, and somehow he just cannot get his innate wiles and charm to work on his fellow inmates. The truth is, he is traumatised, and he simply cannot understand why such a thing has happened to him. His one solace is his saxophone, which he is allowed to keep in his cell. As long as he rations his playing, so as not to irritate his hostile cellmates, he can play away to his heart's discontent, and he spends many hours improvising mournful, self-pitying laments. But the saxophone apart, he is left mostly alone to brood and feel sorry for himself.

Through all this introspection though, he never quite makes the connection between his actions and their consequences. To him, his current, abject situation has been somehow wished upon him. He can't quite identify by whom, or by what, but it is as if the world has conspired against him.

After a year's incarceration, Reg emerges blinking into an alien place that seems to have turned its back on him. He is an embittered man. This world, he now feels, owes him something. He does not once think that he has been paying his debt to society; society, he is convinced, owes a debt to him. Standing outside the gates is someone with another debt on his mind.

"Morning, Reg. Nice holiday?"

Reg winces, wishing, in that moment, that he was back behind the forbidding but protective prison walls. He manufactures an unconvincing smile.

"Oh certainly," he says, "four star accommodation that. I do hope you got my post card."

"That's it, Reg. Glad to see you've kept your pecker up. Now, let's not beat about the bush. When can we expect repayment?"

"Christ! I've only just come out."

"Yes, but we don't want you skipping off anywhere, do we."

"How d'you think I'm going to come up with a big bag of money? Just like that. After a year inside."

"Now then, Reg. Don't be putting obstacles."

"No, but seriously."

"Reg. Come on. I'm a reasonable man."

Reg thinks of the kicking he had from this reasonable man just over a year before.

"Listen," the man continues, "let's work out a little repayment plan."

At that point, Reg becomes aware of a black taxi parked just a few yards away. The windows are tinted, so he can't see who is inside, but just then, one of the windows is pushed down.

"Reg?" Edith calls out.

Reg is so surprised that he just stands there, his mouth slightly open. The man glances across at the old lady.

"Is that your mother or something?"

"Er ... no."

"Reg," Edith calls again, "Is that you? I've come to give you a lift."

Reg goes over to the taxi.

"That's er ... very kind of you. But I've got to do some business with this bloke first."

"What kind of business?"

Reg explains.

"Send him over," Edith commands.

The man is sent over.

"Come and sit beside me," Edith says, patting the seat to her right.

The man walks around and squeezes in through the other door.

"Now then," Edith goes on, "I gather Reg owes you some money. How much exactly?"

"Five grand," he replies, and then feels compelled to add, "Madam."

"But I only borrowed a thousand," Reg whines.

"Compound interest, Reg."

Reg starts to remonstrate but Edith cuts in.

"In view of the fact that Reg has hardly been in a position to earn any money in the last year, I think that's somewhat unreasonable. I would suggest repayment of the principal sum plus a half. Fifteen hundred pounds. I'll write you a cheque now."

So saying, Edith takes from her bag a Coutt's & Co. cheque book and a Mont Blanc fountain pen.

"Would you kindly place my left finger at the start of the first line."

The man does so. He is so astonished by the imperious command of the old lady that not only has he failed to notice until now that she is blind, but he has completely forgotten to play the hard man, which is his usual way of doing things. To Reg, peering in at the window, the sight of this bruiser squeezed up against the old girl, meekly guiding her hand, is both surreal and incredible.

When the business is done, Edith quickly bundles the man out and installs Reg in his place. The man stands and watches the taxi pull away, the cheque in his meaty hand, the purple ink still wet.

For a few moments neither Reg nor Edith say a word. Reg is still trying to adjust to his surroundings. He never expected to feel like this; a stranger in the city where he was born. He turns to Edith.

"Where are you taking me?"

"To Hedda's."

Reg is so shocked he is silent for a moment.

"Are you joking? She doesn't want to know me."

"Yes she does. I've had a word with her. She just couldn't believe you could do anything so stupid."

The taxi continues on its way east, towards Hedda's place, and to what Reg is sure will be another confrontation. His saxophone case clutched to his chest, he sits quietly reflecting on the last year. The old lady has been the only one to visit him inside, and now she has come to meet him. No one else did, apart from the moneylender, and she dealt with him in a way that Reg could not. She has paid off his debt and arranged for him to be reconciled with his old girlfriend, which, if he were honest with himself, he dearly wants, even though he resents her for deserting him when he needed her most. In addition, that reconciliation might mean that he has a roof over his head, which would be a bonus, for he had no idea where he was going to go when he came out. The old lady has done all this for him, and yet he can't bring himself to express any gratitude, let alone feel it.

"Why are you doing all this for me?"

"God knows. You certainly don't deserve it."

Reg continues to scowl at the road ahead of him. Far from feeling grateful, he feels humiliated by the old woman. 'And yet,' he thinks, 'if she hadn't turned up and done all that, where would I be now? Getting knocked about in some back street? Checking in to a doss house tonight?' And thinking that, he feels even more humiliated, and even more resentful.

*

After the inevitable recriminations, Hedda takes him back, though she makes him abundantly aware of the considerable favour she is doing him. Edith takes him back also, as her reader, "on the strict condition that you mend your ways," but at least it provides him with a modest income, while he tries to rebuild his life. Dependent, then, on these two women, Reg feels that his humiliation is complete, and as he sits before Edith, morning after morning, subserviently reading to her from that day's paper, he finds himself almost choked with a resentment that rises like bile from his stomach.

Not surprisingly, Reg's ways are not mended for long. As he comes to feel increasingly secure in his position with

Edith, so he begins to get sloppy and lazy again. He turns up later and later for his reading sessions, which irritates and frustrates Edith considerably, for, in her old age, time has become very precious to her. And he starts drinking heavily again. Rather than cure him of the habit, his year of enforced abstinence in Wormwood Scrubs has given him an even greater craving for the stuff, and when he mixes their drinks he mixes his strong. This not only has an effect on the quality of his reading, which was dreary to begin with, but it affects also his language, and he takes to passing comments on the day's news with words that Edith would not even have allowed herself to think, let alone utter. He does it partly because the more he drinks the less he cares, but he does it also deliberately, because he knows that such language greatly offends the old lady. He can almost see her wince as he curses and swears, and it brings an evil smile to his lips. Then, one day, Edith turns to him and says, "This simply isn't working, Reg."

She has considered it all carefully. It seems to her that she is falling a long way short of her ideal. In recruiting her little retinue, she has managed to employ an unreliable nurse of unsound mind, a neurotic housekeeper given to unpredictable bursts of rage, and now, she has added to her score a thieving, alcoholic ex-convict. How can she be getting it all so wrong, she asks herself.

Reg looks up from the paper.

"What d'you mean this isn't working?"

"It simply won't do," Edith replies. "This is supposed to be informative for me. To keep me in touch. And it's supposed to be a pleasure, but it's become a trial."

"I don't quite get you."

But Edith is not about to explain herself.

"I'm going to have to relieve you of your duties."

"Relieve me of my duties?"

"Precisely."

"... But I need the money."

"You should have thought of that before. What I intend to do is employ a reader who doesn't mumble, who doesn't turn up late, and drunk, and who doesn't swear."

The alcoholic flush has by now drained from Reg's face. Since returning from prison, the Mistress had increased his pay, partly because he suggested it, but partly because she really wanted to help re-establish him. He had found it difficult to get back into the professional jazz circuit, for many of his old contacts didn't want to know him any more, so he is very dependent on the money Edith gives him.

"But what'll I do?" he says lamely.

Edith smiles.

"I've thought of that too. From now on, you can walk the dog."

His expression goes from craven to perplexed.

"But you haven't got a dog."

"That's the next thing on my list."

It would seem then that Reg's humiliation had not quite been complete before, but it is now.

*

Hampstead. August, 1948.

When my sister agreed to help me get back into singing she didn't know just how much she was taking on. She certainly didn't envisage becoming my accompanist. Nor did I. I had more in mind the idea of her taking on the role of agent. Having sacked him, I couldn't see myself getting another one very easily. Who would want to represent a blind singer with a broken face? But I still needed an accompanist, and I thought, 'Well why not Big Sis?' She _is_ a good pianist (though I never tell her that). We have our father's musicality.

Anyway, after endless months working together, something happened between us today. Musically. I felt right. She sounded right.

We were working on the "Four Last Songs." (Not "last!" Definitely not "last!"). It all came together. I knew it would. Though I know she hates me for having bullied her so mercilessly into being my accompanist. I've thrown every kind of tantrum. Threatened to harm myself (cut my wrists). I said if she didn't do what I asked I would go mad. I would go out and get a tattoo – as vulgar as I could find – in a prominent place.

She says I've become more perverse and manipulative, taking advantage of my situation. Which is all true. My temper is short, for one thing through having to learn everything by ear, which makes me feel so childish and stupid.

We've rehearsed and rehearsed and rehearsed. Schumann, Schubert, spirituals, and of course Strauss.

"Why is it never right for you?" she asked.

We were going through "Im Abendrot." (They never get the translation right on that. "At Dusk" is the best they can do, whereas it translates more like "In the Sunset Glow." Which is rather different, and alters completely the way you go about it). Anyway, we were going through it for the umpteenth time and I suddenly shouted to her to stop, but she kept on bashing out the accompaniment as loud as she could right to the end.

We're growing alike.

And then, on the next take something happened between us. Everything went quiet. I waited for her to go on, but there was just silence. I began to wonder if she'd slipped out of the room – finally decided to throw in the towel. I could hardly have blamed her. And then I heard her voice. Low and curiously

reflective. Which is not her style at all. Reflection is
not something Sis goes in for.

"Your voice has got darker," she said.

George Orwell's novel, "Nineteen Eighty Four" – set in that year but first published in 1949 – is a nightmarish tale of a totalitarian state, and one man's hopeless struggle against it. In the Britain he envisaged, citizens could be called to account not only for what they did, but even for what they thought.

In 1984, Prime Minister Thatcher proudly announces that Orwell's vision has clearly not come about, but the book had not been intended as a prophecy; rather a warning. What *has* come about though, and helped along by the Prime Minister herself, is a culture of greed, and Henry is one of its disciples.

Dressed just like his fellows, he slicks back his hair and wears expensive, dark, two-piece suits over striped shirts and brightly-coloured braces. He drives a black BMW, though he has something more modest if he needs to reassure his clients that he isn't doing too well out of them, which invariably he is. What distinguishes him, however, from other estate agents is his public school background, unusual in that line of work, and it manifests itself in his accent and supercilious air. Having not been academic enough to get to university, his traditional, career choices had been limited to soldiering or the city, both of which seemed to him too much like hard work. But with the early eighties property boom, there was clearly money to be made in real estate, and it didn't seem to Henry that he would need to work too hard to make money there.

In addition to helping people buy and sell property, or in some cases positively hindering them, he goes in for a little property speculation. Thus it is that he acquires a handsome, three-storey, Victorian house in Clapham, South London. Clapham is not at that time a fashionable area, and property prices there are relatively low, but Henry guesses that it is an up-and-coming area, and so gets in at the right time. However, the purchase of his house at a favourable price is the result of considerable duplicity on his part. It is being offered for sale at his own agency, and he persuades the vendors that they have over-priced it. After they agree to drop the price, he then creates a fictional purchaser who comes in with a very low offer, which is justified on the grounds that the house needs a lot of renovation. It doesn't, but Henry convinces them that it does by sending round a carefully-vetted builder who points out various non-existent flaws in the building which will be costly to put right. So, the vendors are duped, and Henry becomes the new owner, but not content with the generous profit he has made, even if he sells the house the very next day, he decides that he will hang on to it for a year or two, while property prices rise in the area, and he might as well use it as his own home during that time.

Things start to go wrong almost as soon as he moves in. To begin with, his wife, who is a dealer in bonds, leaves him holding the baby; or rather their six-year-old daughter. Their relationship had been tenuous from the start. Henry has an ability to charm, but it is a superficial charm and its effects quickly wear off, so his wife soon tires of him, and being a subscriber herself to the greed culture, she feels no compunction about moving rapidly on and up.

His daughter is demanding, and there is one particular demand that recurs every birthday, in June, and at Christmas.

"Daddy – why can't we have a dog?"

"Because, Hen."

Hen is short for Henrietta.

"That's not a proper answer," she replies, chewing on her lip.

"It's perfectly proper. Because we've been through it all before."

"All my friends have got dogs."

"Not all your friends, Hen."

"Well, most of them."

"Yes. And most of them have got a daddy *and* a mummy."

"What's that got to do with it?"

"Everything. If you've got a mummy around you've got someone to look after the dog. I've got a business to run."

"I'll look after the dog."

"And who looks after it when you're at school?"

"It doesn't need looking after. It's got this big garden to play in."

Henry sips his gin and tonic and looks about the garden.

"That wouldn't be very fair on the dog, Hen. He'd get lonely."

Henry, of course, doesn't care whether the putative pet gets lonely or not.

End of conversation; but only for the time being, as far as Henrietta is concerned.

It is usually early December when Henry starts asking her what she wants for Christmas. She puts him off for a few days, and then one evening when he comes home from work he finds both Henrietta and the child-minder busy in the kitchen.

"What's all this?" he says, an eyebrow raised.

"I've made you dinner," his daughter announces proudly. In fact the child-minder has done most of the work, but she allows her charge to take the credit. After the carer has left, Henrietta comes through to her father in the living room, her serious face all concentration on not spilling the contents of the glass she is carrying.

"And now?" says Henry, the supercilious eyebrow raised again.

"Your aperitif," she replies.

He laughs and takes it from her.

"What are you after, little vixen?"

"Nothing," she says innocently. "I just thought you looked a bit tired."

He smiles and takes a sip.

"Cripes! This is strong!"

Dinner, by candlelight, is served with his favourite wine, a German Hock, and his glass is never allowed to be empty. By the end of it he seems about as mellow as he is likely to get.

"Dad?"

"Yes?"

"You asked me what I wanted for Christmas."

He smiles, a little bleary-eyed.

"I knew this was leading up to something."

Henrietta has decided to keep it simple.

"I want a dog, and I'm not going to take "no" for an answer this time."

There is a long silence as they quietly regard one another, then he bursts out laughing and says, "Oh, what the hell!"

'Got him!' she thinks, but then he says something that catches her completely off guard.

"OK. This weekend we'll go over to Battersea Dogs' Home."

Henrietta's face twists.

"I don't want a mutt!"

"What d'you mean, a mutt?"

"I don't want some ... scrawny mongrel."

"They don't just have mongrels at Battersea. They have pedigree dogs as well."

"You're just saying Battersea Dogs' Home because you don't want to have to pay for a dog."

"That's not true, Hen. I think they make a charge there. And doesn't it make more sense to give a home to a dog without one?"

He surprises himself with this ethical consideration. Henrietta chews on her lip and stares at the ground.

"I don't want a mutt."

But a mutt is what she gets. That very weekend, they drive over to the home and walk among the kennels looking at the eager dogs through the bars of the doors. Henry had been right, for there are pure breeds there; Red Setters, Dalmatians, Labradors, Spaniels, Border Collies, Poodles and even an Old English Sheep Dog.

"Look, Dad, a Dulux Dog!"

Henry moves her quickly on, visualising already the pristine upholstery of his BMW covered in long, grey and white hairs.

The next dog sits quietly in his kennel and takes little notice of them. Though still young, he is beyond puppy-hood, and what distinguishes him from the other dogs is that he makes no attempt whatsoever to ingratiate himself. He just sits in the far corner, looking resentful, and though barely one year old, there is a trace of world-weariness in his large, dark eyes. Henry is astonished when his daughter stops at this particular kennel and gazes in.

"I thought you didn't want a mutt, Hen."

Henry doesn't always engage his brain before opening his mouth, and Gaynor, the Re-homer, who is showing them around the sales block, looks at him sharply.

"It's not that we've got anything against mutts ... er ... mongrels," Henry blusters, "it's just I thought she wanted a pedigree dog."

"We've got plenty of those here," says Gaynor, coolly.

"What's his name?" asks Henrietta, deliberately and slowly.

"It's there on his chit," Gaynor replies, indicating the piece of paper to the side of the kennel door. "Tyson."

"Tyson," says Henrietta quietly, still looking at the dog, who is sitting motionless, looking back at her now. The word makes her think of typhoons, and of wildness. "That's a funny name."

"I think he's named after a boxer," Gaynor explains. The American boxer is not so well-known in 1984, though he was known to Tyson's first owner.

"He's not aggressive, is he?" asks Henry.

"He's not aggressive, so long as he's taken proper care of. Which he hasn't been, and that's why he's here. We don't re-home aggressive animals"

"What do you do with them?"

"They spend some time in the Behaviour Block. They can usually sort them out there." She doesn't add that Tyson has himself spent some time there.

"I want him," says Henrietta, who feels instinctively now that this is her dog. Perhaps she senses his rebelliousness, and empathises with it.

There are formalities to be gone through, but before they go into all that, Gaynor escorts them to the outside pens where the kennel-hands give the dogs some exercise, and where she can better observe them all together. Dominating this area are the great, towering chimneys of the old Battersea Power Station.

At the end of his lead, Tyson senses that something is about to happen. He allows himself to be led around by the little girl, while Henrietta tries to look composed and in control, but her heart is fluttering. Gaynor watches them carefully, and decides that they can move on to the next stage, which will be a visit to their home to ensure that it is suitable.

So, Tyson is installed in the Clapham house. The garden, even in winter, is a joy to him. Having spent the first few months of his life in a high-rise block of flats, rarely being taken for a walk, outdoors is a wonderful place, and he spends long periods there, sniffing out all the subtly different scents through his powerful nostrils. It is there that he gets his first whiff of fox, and on a crisp, frosty evening, comes face to face with one. Both stand stock still, each as startled as the other. Though it is a dark and shadowy part of the garden, they can see one another clearly, their large, dilated pupils well-adapted to seeing by night, but it is the fox that turns tail first, with Tyson fast on his heels, his instinctive sense of territory coming to the fore. However, the artful fox is able to scale the six-foot fence, which is a skill Tyson will never acquire.

Their favourite haunts are Clapham Common and Battersea Park. They can walk to the Common from the house, but the park requires a trip in the car, so they frequent that less. When he sees the lead being lifted down from the coat-rack in the hallway, Tyson is unable to contain his excitement. The withdrawn and subdued quality he displayed at the dogs' home melts away as he grows to trust more the two new humans in his life. What is curious about them, he finds, is that they don't beat him. In his previous home he could be thrashed for any number of reasons, most of which were a complete mystery to him, and sometimes he was thrashed so hard that blood was drawn. On those occasions his master was usually red in the face, and he stumbled, and there was a peculiar scent on his breath, which Tyson came to know well and fear.

He had just had such a beating one day when the bell rang, and Tyson let off a volley of barks and ran to the door. His master grabbed him, then cuffed and shouted at him, which Tyson could never understand, because surely, he reasoned, it was his duty to defend their territory. When the man opened the door, there were three other men outside, and one woman, and they seemed to Tyson to be dressed identically, but not so to his master. He knew immediately that two were police officers, and that the others were from the RSPCA, for he had had visits from them before.

They all came in. The RSPCA woman held Tyson, which he found curiously reassuring, because she seemed to know how to hold and talk to him, which his master had never done. As the dog watched, he saw his master at first aggressive, then defensive, and then he had a defeated look about him, which Tyson identified with immediately, and suddenly the man didn't seem so frightening any more.

He was taken away by the two policemen, the RSPCA officers following with Tyson on the lead. He could distinguish between their uniforms now, for while the police wore white shirts, the RSPCA wore blue. Tyson could see blue. He couldn't see the human's colour red, for this he saw as another colour altogether, so that when his master had made him bleed, it was a yellowish liquid he saw seeping through his fur. They put him in the back of a van. Normally he would have put up a fight, but they seemed to know how to reassure him and keep him calm.

Also, they let him relieve his bladder before putting him in, which he had been desperate to do for hours, but hadn't dared to, because he had noticed that his master was red in the face again, or yellow, and he had once more that familiar odour on his breath. Tyson's powerful sense of smell could detect that odour even in the man's perspiration. He didn't know it as he settled in his cage, but he would never see that man again.

In his first summer in Clapham, he and Henrietta go often to the Common. In early June it is still a verdant green, which he sees more as white, or sometimes a shade of grey. Today it is white, and he tears about on it, his exuberance seemingly inexhaustible. Though still something of a loner, he has become a little more sociable with other dogs, though Henrietta has to be careful in this regard for he can, without warning, become extremely aggressive, and will think nothing of taking on a dog twice his size.

Henrietta lies on the ground, tugging at the grass. Squinting in the sunlight she watches him now, playing with a few other dogs. She prays that it won't all turn nasty. As she watches him she thinks again what a good-looking dog he is. Not handsome exactly, like her friend's Red Setter, or another friend's Golden Retriever, but good-looking all the same. He is a medium-sized dog, with a broad back and neck, and sturdy shoulders. The dogs' home lady said that she thought he might have some Bull Terrier in him. His coat, which was long and curly when they got him, has been clipped, so that it is a smooth, shiny, mid-brown now, with streaks of grey. The shortness of hair accentuates his muscular torso, but for

Henrietta, his eyes are his most striking feature. Set in a dark mask, they are large and black, with correspondingly dark pupils, and when he looks at her he seems to be looking right into her.

"Tyson!" she calls out, but he ignores her.

"Still got that mutt, Hen?"

Henrietta swivels round and sees two friends coming towards her; the ones with the Red Setter and the Golden Retriever.

"He's not a mutt!" Henrietta insists. She is getting tired of having this word thrown back at her.

"Well, what is he then?"

"He's a ... Bull Terrier cum Mastiff."

The other girls laugh.

"He's a Mongrel cum Mutt," one of them says.

Henrietta screws up her face and looks back at the increasing pack of dogs.

"Are you having a party on your birthday, Hen?"

"Course I am."

"Are we invited?"

"Course you are."

"What d'you want for your birthday?"

"A new collar for Tyson."

"That's not much of a present."

'No, it's not,' thinks Henrietta. "Encrusted with diamonds," she adds, having discovered the word "encrusted" just the day before.

"Get you!"

"Anyway," the other girl persists, "it's not *his* birthday."

"When is his birthday?"

Henrietta pauses.

"Don't know," she has to admit.

"That's what happens when you get a mutt from the dogs' home."

"Stop calling him a mutt! At least he's not a girly dog."

"What's a girly dog?"

"Yours is. And yours!" Henrietta blurts, aware of an angry flush on her face.

"Who says?"

"My dad says."

"What does your dad know – he's an estate agent."

This is something else that rankles with Henrietta; the implication that estate agents are a lower form of life. She resents this very much, but she resents even more the fact that her father is an estate agent at all. She had dreams of being the daughter of an ambassador, or an astronaut.

"How can they be girly dogs anyway? They're bigger than Tyson."

"Tyson could take them both apart with one paw tied behind his back," Henrietta boasts.

Suddenly there is a furious snarling from Tyson as he goes for a German Shepherd.

"Oh shit!" Henrietta mutters, getting quickly to her feet. She doesn't know whether to try and grab him, which can be perilous, or to pretend that he isn't anything to do with her.

"I know what I'll get you for your birthday. A muzzle for your mutt."

The other girl giggles.

"That's it!" Henrietta shouts at them, "You're not coming to my party!"

"Didn't want to come anyway."

When Henry comes home that evening, he finds Henrietta lying on her front on the living room floor watching television, and Tyson outside in the garden, howling and irritating the neighbours. The dog is brought in, and after the child-minder has gone, Henry admonishes his daughter.

"You're really not looking after him properly, Henrietta."

"Stop calling me Henrietta!"

"Why not? It's your name."

"That's right. And it's just another rotten thing you've done to me. Like being an estate agent."

"What!?"

"Arabella says you don't know anything because you're an estate agent."

"That's because *she* doesn't know anything," Henry replies quickly, but it stings him all the same. "Anyway," he goes on, "it's this estate agent that keeps you in nice frocks and living in a nice house."

Henrietta turns back to the television.

"Turn that thing off, Hen. You're getting square eyes."

Tyson looks from one to the other of them, his dark muzzle resting on his paws. Glancing across at him, Henry goes on, "It's true, Hen. You're not looking after him properly."

"I am."

"Not like you used to. You don't take him out so much. And you ignore him when you're here."

Henry is right. In just six months, she has tired of the dog. Henry knows it, she knows it, and Tyson knows it. There is silence for a moment.

"What do you want for your birthday, Hen?" he asks unguardedly. (It's that time of year once more).

"A cat."

"Oh, Jesus!"

"All my friends have got cats."

'Here we go again,' thinks Henry.

"You are not having a cat. Tyson would have a cat for breakfast."

"Couldn't we go back to Battersea and sort of part exchange him? They do cats there as well."

"Christ, Hen! It's not a car dealer's."

Henrietta does not get a cat for her eighth birthday, nor does she for her ninth, but by then Tyson's days in the Clapham home are numbered. Henry has found that if *he* doesn't take the dog for a walk then nobody does, and as he doesn't feel much inclined to, Tyson is spending more and more time alone. But two events are about to occur that will determine the dog's fate.

Since buying his house, Henry has acquired two more properties, which are currently being renovated with a view to selling them on at highly-inflated prices. He has taken out two further mortgages to enable him to do this, and he is now stretched to the limit. But by now, the property boom has turned into a bubble, and when inevitably it bursts, Henry finds himself in negative equity. Having three mortgages and numerous outstanding bills to plumbers, electricians and builders, Henry is in despair. He is also acutely embarrassed, as someone who works in the property market and yet has somehow failed to see it all coming. He is still reeling when he receives another blow.

Someone else in the business, whom Henry has duped over a property deal, gets in touch with the original owner of Henry's Clapham house and lets him know that he has, in fact, sold his house to his own estate agent, and at a price far below its true value. So angry is the ex-owner that he goes straight round to Henry's agency, tells him he knows exactly what he has done, and that he is now on his way to his solicitor. As Henry watches him stalk out, he knows he is in serious trouble. There could be a charge of professional misconduct and he could well find himself in court. He might even have his business wound up.

On his way home he stops off at a bar, where he stares disconsolately into a large whisky and contemplates suicide. He has three properties, two of which are worth less than he paid for them, and which he probably can't sell even at their lower value. The third property, his home, might also be repossessed, and while he is in court over that... it doesn't bear thinking about. He could spend the next year of his life being sued by any number of people.

He buys himself another drink. He can't remember ever having been at such low ebb. The only thing that prevents him from driving straight to Battersea Bridge and throwing himself off is the thought of his daughter.

He buys himself another drink.

When he pulls up outside his house, he can hear Tyson howling in the garden even before he cuts the engine. He slams the car door and strides up the front path.

"Henrietta!" he shouts, crashing the front door shut behind him.

In front of the television in the living room, the girl freezes. She hadn't heard his key in the lock and was not expecting him home so early. The next thing she hears is the doorbell. Henry spins round and yanks open the door to find one of his neighbours standing there.

"Oh, sorry to trouble you, Henry …"

To Henry, the man has the pedantic tone of a train-spotter, and it grates on his already jangling nerves.

"… It's just that your dog has been howling in the garden for some time now."

He looks at his watch. "One hour and twenty three minutes, to be precise…"

Henry cuts in on him.

"I'm sorry old man – would you mind just kindly fucking off?"

He slams the door on his neighbour's startled face and strides into the living room. Henrietta still hasn't moved, and is transfixed now by the look of fury on her father's face. His bloodshot eyes stare down at her, and for a moment the only sounds are those of the television, and the howling dog outside. His anger is barely contained, but when he speaks, his voice is low and level.

"Turn that thing off. Bring the dog in. Take him for a walk. Bring him back. And feed him."

Henrietta cautiously gets up, turns off the television and leaves the room. This is not, she knows, a time to answer back.

When she returns with Tyson, about half an hour later, she finds her father sitting in an armchair in the living room, a glass of amber liquid in his hand, staring at the wall. He doesn't look up, and his daughter doesn't speak. Sensing the atmosphere, Tyson slinks away to the kitchen. Still not looking up, Henry says, "Now make yourself some supper and take it up to your room."

Henry sits on, waiting for the dark. He gets up only twice, to pour another drink, and he doesn't turn any lights on. A little while later, Tyson is surprised to see him standing unsteadily in the doorway to the kitchen, and holding his lead.

"Come on, old boy," he says.

He gets up and goes with him to the front door. Normally he would have been elated to be given this second walk, but he senses that something is very wrong.

Outside, the stars are bright and the street is quiet. The neighbour, watching from the darkened window of his bedroom, sees Henry open a rear door of his car, and the dog jump in. Then they drive off up the road.

Had Henry been stopped and breathalysed that night he would have been arrested. Nevertheless, he manages to drive without incident for ten minutes or so until he reaches Prince of Wales Drive, where he stops the BMW but keeps the engine running.

The oppressive atmosphere inside the car is made more so for Tyson by the unmistakable odour of alcohol on his master's breath. It reminds him of the beatings he had in his last home, and he is fearful of what is to come. Henry then reaches over from the driver's seat and, instead of attaching his lead, removes his collar. Tyson is baffled, but in the same moment, the door to his side is pushed open and he instinctively jumps out. Just before the door is slammed shut, he hears his master's voice for the last time.

"Goodbye, old boy. Good luck," and he watches the yellow tail-lights getting smaller and smaller as the car speeds away.

Tyson sits at the roadside for a full fifteen minutes. He doesn't understand the significance of the removal of his collar, for he doesn't realise that the collar is a means of identifying him. To Tyson, it is simply the thing to which his lead is attached. He sits waiting for a few more minutes, and then he decides that it is pointless to stay there any longer.

He looks across the road at the great, dark trees of Battersea Park. It seems a fearful place in this light, but he is familiar with it and he thinks that he will feel safer there than on the street. He trots across to the small, wooden gate that they normally use. It is closed and padlocked, so he pads alongside the low fence of pales, sniffing as he goes. A human walking in the opposite direction, with a dog on a lead, stops and looks curiously at him.

He trots quickly on until he reaches a part of the paling where the fence is broken. He squeezes through, but before going further he stops and urinates so as to leave his marker, then he presses on into the undergrowth.

He immediately feels safer, away from curious humans and the street lamps. His pupils dilate as he focuses on the dark outlines of trees and bushes. He reaches an area of open grass and stops, still within the dark of the perimeter. The grass is a pale grey to him in the starlight. He instinctively avoids it, for he knows that he will be too exposed there. He snuffles on through the undergrowth for another five minutes or so, and then he stops dead, his hackles rising. He sniffs again and recognises the acrid whiff of a male fox. He remains stock still, for it is vital that he doesn't make a sound. He knows, too, that he could give himself away by moving, for it is the movement of an object rather than its outline that attracts attention. A worker in the dogs' home had a name for this – "prey-drive."

He moves his head minutely, trying to locate the fox's scent on the still, night air. Then he catches it again, just off to his right. Turning silently, he slowly crouches, ready to spring. He doesn't see the fox at first, but as he looks in its direction, it crouches also, and gives itself away. It is only ten yards off, and he knows he can make that in just a few bounds. It is close enough for him to see that its hackles, too, are up. There is no need for silence any more, so Tyson issues a warning growl and the fox spins round and makes a dash for it. As he goes, he gives the submissive signal of the tail between the legs, hoping that this will discourage the dog from giving chase, but it doesn't. Tyson has learnt in his short life that attack is the best form of defence. So he leaps after the fox and is soon within range. He gives it two or three sharp nips on the heels, just to let it know whose territory this now is, pulls himself up and watches the fox streak off into the night. He stands still for a moment, checking the air for any other threatening scents, and then he puts down another marker and retraces his steps.

*

On its far side, the park is bounded by the Thames. Tyson watches the sun rise over the water. He has become chilled overnight and is enjoying the sun's warming rays. The park is still locked, and there is no one about, so he feels fairly safe in the open. Most of the nocturnal creatures with whom he has shared the night have sought their shelter, to be replaced by the birds, the squirrels, the rabbits and the waterfowl. The city around is still sleeping and quiet, which makes the dawn chorus sound all the more intense. The night has seemed long to him, and he hasn't slept much, which has given him time to think.

Fundamentally, he has had his innate trust in humans badly shaken. As in most domesticated dogs, his sense of loyalty to humans is supremely powerful, but already in his short life it has been twice abused. Although Henry never beat him, as his first master did, he has nevertheless betrayed him, and he will not forget it.

He hears his stomach rumble and wonders, momentarily, how he's going to survive without humans. Then he trots back towards the centre of the park, in the hope of finding some sort of breakfast.

Over the days that follow, the park wardens become aware of an increase in attacks on the waterfowl. It is not unusual for them to be attacked, as there is more wildlife in the park than people realise, but it is the sudden increase in attacks that gives them pause for thought. One of the wardens, Stefan, a dog-owner himself, has an idea about the possible cause, but he keeps it to himself, and sets himself the one-man task of tracking down the culprit.

Apart from the rubbish bins and the discarded litter, where Tyson often finds a tasty morsel, there seems to be plenty of prey in the park. The squirrels he gives up on almost immediately, for they are much too quick off the mark and can be up a tree in seconds. He has little more success with the rabbits, which are also fleet of foot, and often shoot into thickets where his stocky body cannot follow.

He does most of his hunting at night, when there are no humans about to trouble him, save the occasional tramp or drunk who might have scaled the fence.

The prey he finds the easiest are the waterfowl. If he catches them off guard, he can usually grab one before it has a chance to get airborne. Then there will be a great cacophony, as the alarm goes up along the lake, but by then, Tyson will be back in his lair, tucking into a still-warm supper.

One day, he hears an unusually high-pitched sound. He cocks his ears towards it and feels impelled to investigate. Keeping as much as he can to the undergrowth, he trots off in the direction of the noise, and finds himself eventually in one of the more out of the way parts of the park. There is a bench there but no one is on it, indeed there are no humans about at all, but there are several other dogs, all similarly attracted by the sound, and they are fighting for some scraps of meat that have been left on the ground. Tyson quietly watches them.

Quietly watching him, from the shade of some nearby trees, stands a man in jeans, working boots and a green T-shirt, and as he watches him, Stefan notes that he is the one dog present that is not wearing a collar.

At the same time, next day, the same thing happens, but Tyson does not just trot to the spot this time; he goes as fast as his legs will carry him, and by the most direct route, only to find that several other dogs have still got there before him and are already squabbling over the meat. Again, he just watches, and as he watches he begins to form a plan.

At the same time the following day, Tyson is already there. He has become, without knowing it, Pavlov's dog, responding automatically to a sound stimulus indicating that a meal awaits him. There is, however, no sound today, for Stefan has judged that the dog-whistle might no longer be necessary, but the meat is there all the same, scattered about, and it is all just for Tyson now, for there is not another dog in sight.

This pattern repeats itself several more times, until the day when Tyson arrives to find not only the meat there, but a man sitting on the bench. He wears boots, jeans and a green T-shirt, which Tyson sees as white. He is eating sandwiches, and reading a newspaper. Tyson hesitates. He has seen this man before; indeed he has seen him often in the park. He always seems to be busy with something, unlike most of the other humans who just wander about, or play games with their dogs, which makes Tyson wistful.

He looks at the meat and back at the man. Then he warily approaches the tantalising, raw flesh, throwing glances all the time in the direction of the man, whose attention appears still to be on the large piece of paper that he is holding; but out of the corner of his eyes, Stefan is watching him keenly.

This routine becomes established over the several days that follow, the only change being that each time the meat is placed just a little closer to the bench. At first, Tyson doesn't notice this, but by the time he does, he has become so used to the man's presence that he no longer sees him as a threat. After a little hesitation, he goes and picks up the meat, while the man, as usual, appears not to notice him.

And so it all goes on, until one day the meat is almost at the foot of the bench itself. Tyson circles for a moment or two, then he dashes in, seizes the meat and makes off with it, all the time keeping his eyes on the man.

Stefan appears to be supremely patient, but the truth is, he is enjoying himself. He has to go somewhere for his lunch, after all, but he feels an empathy for this apparent stray. As a Pole trying to make his way in a foreign land he is something of a stray himself.

When Tyson arrives the next day, he is disappointed to find no meat on the ground, but before he has time to turn away, the man casually opens up his sandwich and throws the contents to him. Tyson starts but does not run off. He cautiously goes and picks up the cooked meat, and finds it even more appetising than the usual fare, for Stefan has prepared his sandwiches carefully that day.

As this new arrangement becomes established, Stefan starts talking to the dog, sometimes in English, sometimes in Polish, and sometimes a mixture of the two. In spite of his strange accent, Tyson finds the tone of his voice reassuring, and it isn't long before he even allows him to stroke him. It feels curious at first, after the feral life he has been leading, but he soon gets used to it again, and in spite of the distrust he has developed for humans, he allows himself to relax, as he feels the strong, outdoor hands stroking him firmly along his spine.

It is in just such a moment of relaxation that he suddenly feels the rope around his neck. He springs back, but Stefan is too quick for him, and has prepared himself well. Hidden beneath his newspaper is a noose he has made from some rope they keep in one of the sheds. Tyson struggles and snarls and tries to bite him, but the man avoids his nips, talking to him softly all the while.

"Come on, yong lad," he says. "Yo're going to thenk me for this one day."

The dog keeps struggling, furiously at first, but gradually he becomes more subdued. Also, the man's voice is having a calming effect on him.

Stefan leaves his newspaper and lunchbox on the bench. He will collect them later, for just at the moment he needs both hands. As they walk through the park, Tyson looks about him at the place that has become his home, and he has mixed feelings about leaving it. On the way, Stefan stops off at one of the larger sheds, where he finds the Head Warden.

"I think I have found the colprit."

The warden smiles and looks astonished at the same time.

"So that's the little bugger!"

"I think so. I'm just going to take him over the road."

Tyson hadn't realised that he was almost back at the very spot where his journey began – Battersea Dogs' Home. He had had his suspicions, as he looked out from the park, to the four great chimneys of the old disused power station. He knew that he had seen them somewhere before. So, all Stefan has to do now is lead his captive over Battersea Bridge Road. He knows a number of the people who work in the home, as they often exercise dogs in the park.

"Blimey!" says one of them. "Hello, Tyson."

Tyson is as startled as Stefan.

"You know him?"

"Oh yes. Wouldn't forget Tyson in a hurry. Bit of a character."

This would have been news to Tyson, for his self-esteem is low, and in that moment he manages just a faint wag of the tail.

Back in his kennel, the dog resumes his solitary ruminations. Because of his mistrust of humans, he occasionally feels inclined to growl at them, or even snap if they get too close, and this earns him another spell in the Behaviour Block

The weeks go by, and Tyson watches the customary human procession through the bars of his door, remaining, as before, withdrawn from it all. He has just woken from a doze one afternoon when he hears a sing-song, lyrical voice.

"Oh, this one looks a bit sad," Bridie says.

He looks up to see a kindly face looking down at him. Next to the face, and slightly above it, is another, much older, with piercing, blue eyes. Tyson returns her gaze.

"What's sad about him?" the old lady asks.

"Oh, I don't know … he looks like he's seen it all before."

She is right. Tyson has a distinct feeling of déjà-vu.

"Describe him to me," Edith commands.

"Well, he's youngish," Bridie begins.

"We reckon about four," chips in Brenda, the Rehomer who is accompanying them.

"Right," Bridie goes on. "He's got a brown coat, streaked with grey."

"Brindled," says Brenda, who likes to show off her canine knowledge. "It's nothing to do with his age. We think he might have a bit of Bull Terrier in him."

"He's a mongrel?" Edith queries.

"Yes."

This seems to please the old lady. Being herself of impeccable pedigree, she likes the idea of having a little bit of "rough" about the place, even though she already has Reg.

"Go on, Bridie."

"Well, he looks strong. He's sort of ... medium-sized. And he's got big, dark, sad eyes," she continues, with emphasis on the "sad."

Those big, dark eyes are still fixed on the old lady. He is intrigued by the way she is looking at him. There is something penetrating about the look, and yet it doesn't seem quite to be taking him in. As an experiment, he walks slowly to the other side of the pen, without taking his eyes off hers, and notes, curiously, that the eyes do not follow him.

"Well, he's certainly taking an interest in you," Bridie says to Edith. "He hasn't taken his eyes off you."

Edith smiles, for she is beginning to take an interest in the dog.

"What's his name?" she asks.

"Tyson," Brenda replies, and is about to add, "It's there on the chit to the side of the door," but checks herself just in time. Again, it is that something in the way Edith conducts herself that makes people forget she is blind.

By now, Mike Tyson has gained his World Heavyweight Championship, and there aren't many who haven't heard of him. Bridie's mouth twitches at one corner.

"He's not aggressive, is he?"

"Not if he's properly looked after," Brenda assures her.

"There won't be any doubt about that," Edith comes back sharply, as if her own integrity is being questioned.

While all this is going on, Tyson decides to modify his experiment, and he gives a soft, non-aggressive bark. Immediately Edith's eyes fix on him, and she smiles.

"Hello, Tyson," she says, as if greeting an old friend.

"That's funny," says the Brenda, "He doesn't normally do that."

"Do what?" Bridie asks.

"Bark. Unless he's warning you. Or he wants something."

"I think he wanted to say hello," Edith says confidently, though Bridie isn't so sure it wasn't a warning. Edith starts to take her Coutt's & Co. cheque book from her handbag.

"We'll take him."

'This old woman,' Brenda thinks, 'doesn't seem to understand that I will decide whether or not you take him.'

"I don't think we've got to the cheque book stage yet," she says.

"That's alright," Edith replies. "I just want to make a donation. Shall we say five hundred?"

"That's ... very kind of you," Brenda falters. "But there are some formalities to be gone through first."

"Bridie can deal with all that," Edith says. Formalities bore her.

'Oh, can she?' thinks Bridie, suddenly cast in the role of lackey. But she has her ways of retaliating, and the Mistress might not get such a nice supper tonight. In the meantime, though, there is something Bridie wants to settle first.

"Er ... why would they have called him Tyson in the first place?"

But she is too late. Edith has bent down and stuck her fingers through the bars of the door. Tyson has come forward and is licking the ancient digits. Normally, Brenda would have told someone off for that, because it could be hazardous, and there are plenty of signs about warning people against it – which are, she suddenly realises, useless if you're showing a blind person around – but there is something about Edith that makes people think twice about confronting her, so all Brenda says is, "That's funny. He doesn't normally do that either."

On their way home in the taxi, Bridie is still questioning the wisdom of the Mistress, in acquiring a dog named after an aggressive and volatile heavyweight boxer. Her mouth twitching again at one corner, she says to Edith, "And he's positively neurotic, you know."

"Is he?" she says, thinking at the same time what a wonderful example that is of the pot calling the kettle black.

"Oh yes. And he can be fierce too. That woman told me – they've had to keep him in what they call the Behaviour Block," she says ominously.

Edith remains silent for a moment, and then replies, "I'm sure they wouldn't be sending him out if there were any question about his behaviour," but even as she says it, there is a question running through her own mind.

'I haven't just done it again, have I?'

*

15th April, 1977. Night time. The Den.
Hampstead.

We had been touring as "The X Sisters." I'd only meant it as a joke, but Sis took it seriously and the name stuck.

Anyway, we were in the middle of "Woman's Life and Love" (beautiful music – awful words!) when I heard her gasp. In the interval I said, "What was that funny noise you made?"

"I've a pain … here," she said at last, and she put my hand on her chest.

"When are you supposed to be seeing that doctor?"

"Two week's time."

"We're getting the earlier train," I said. "The 9.27."

"There'll be encores."

"We'll cut the encores," I said. "I hate the encores."

"But people love the encores – seeing you unbuttoned." (They wish!) "Makes them feel closer to you."

"I don't do this for them," I said. "I don't do this to make them feel anything. I don't really want them there at all."

"If we're not doing it for them, why _are_ we doing it?" she said.

"For me! For sodding me! So don't sodding argue! We're getting the 9.27 and you're seeing that doctor tomorrow."

"Edith! ... I don't think your time in uniform has done you any favours."

"Well! That must be the understatement of the century."

She suddenly realised what she'd said and started to bluster. I left her to it.

The thing is – she didn't know how much she'd frightened me. But I didn't know whom I was most frightened for. Herself or myself?

God! What a horrifically selfish woman I've become.

Eighteen months and three operations later: the morning they told me at the Royal Free that my sister has about four weeks to live. The doctor – the third doctor: I got rid of the first two – has just told me, and told me that she knows.

"She won't be coming home," he said.

I pushed aside the nurse's arm and tapped my way in to see her.

We sat, saying nothing. I could feel her eyes on me. I couldn't speak.

"Your hair's starting to go grey," she said finally.

I heard the clink of glass as she drank some water. I could have done with something stronger.

"I've never said," she went on, "but mine went white years ago. You're spared all that – seeing yourself getting old."

In the evening I went back to the hospital.

"I've been thinking," she said. "You're going to have to get some people in."

"Get some people in?"

"Now that I'm not going to be around to look after you."

I felt my heart turn over.

"I don't want other people."

"True," she said, and fell silent. Then she seemed to brighten.

"A dog's not "other people,"" she said. "I've been your dog, Edie. Do something to please me for once. Get a real dog."

Not once in our adult lives had she called me "Edie." Which surprised me when I came to think about it. Because she knew how much I hated it, and she didn't normally miss an opportunity to get a rise out of me. I just smiled at her, and I could sense she was smiling back at me.

"I've got an image," I said, "of this perfect dog. Sleek, dark, graceful, long legs."

"Sounds not unlike a person of many years ago in naval uniform."

I said nothing. I couldn't work out if she was just having a fling at me again. That's another thing about being blind. You don't always get the nuance. Sometimes you need to see the face.

"What did you mean when you said "true" just now?"

She didn't answer.

"You must have meant something," I pursued.

I waited.

"You only trust ... you only feel ..." (I could sense her groping for the word) "safe ... you're only bearable, with people ... like you."

"You mean blind."

"Heaven forbid! Not the blind. You can't abide the poor blind. No – like yourself. With a bit of you in them. Well ... survivors, for a start."

"Like you," I said.

For the first time in my life I found myself biting my tongue.

"No, Edie," she said. "Not any more."

Again, my heart flipped over, and there would have been another unbearable silence, but she seemed to want to carry on.

"If I think of all the people you're prepared to have something to do with. The friends you choose. Even the lackeys. The gardener. The chauffeur."

I came back sharply on that.

"She's not a chauffeur."

I'm often not comfortable being rich.

"What is she then?"

"She's just someone who drives for me occasionally."

She laughed.

"However you want to put it. But the thing is – in all of them, there's a bit of you. A bit of the good you, and a bit of the bad you."

I sat quietly and thought about it. Had she got something there? Did I go for people in whom I saw something of myself? Including the "lackeys," as she put it.

"What are you smiling at?" she said.

"I was just thinking, Sis. You haven't changed a bit. You're still an incorrigible snob. And yet … to me – _for_ me – over the last twenty or so years … you have transformed yourself."

The rain is sheeting down as Eric drives the hired van into Cheltenham. It is dark and he has the headlights on. He has all the usual trepidation an actor feels on arriving in a strange place to take up a new job, but something else is nagging at him. When looking through the digs list the theatre had sent him he selected a place simply because it offered a bedroom with its own shower. He booked it over the phone, and then the man at the other end had said, "I think you ought to know, we're gay." Eric hadn't known how to reply to this. "I just thought you ought to know," the landlord went on. "It isn't alright for everyone."

Eric finds himself thinking about this again now, as the wipers sweep across the windscreen double-quick time, and it gives him a vague sense of unease. He can't understand why it had been an issue at all.

The house is in a typical Victorian terrace, and inside all is immaculate and everything in its place. The landlord and owner is well-built, and turns out to be a builder, though his physique looks as if it owes more to the gym than the building site. As he shows Eric around, he proudly tells him that he has done all the refurbishment himself. They finish in the galley kitchen, which opens off the living room, and, where Eric notes, a row of a dozen identical mugs hang from identical hooks, all pointing in the same direction. Its orderliness seems to typify the place.

"Of course you can have full use of the kitchen," the landlord says, "we've cleared some space for you," and he shows Eric a little nook in an out-of-reach cupboard which might accommodate two or three cans of soup.

While the landlord is voluble, his partner seems to have nothing to say whatsoever, beyond a nasal, "Hi", when Eric first came in. He must be fifteen years younger than the landlord, and standing next to that robust builder he looks as delicate as a piece of porcelain.

As a part of his welcoming routine, the landlord informs Eric that he is expected to vacate his room at weekends.

"Really?" says Eric, recalling that the rent was shown as "per week" in the digs list.

"Well, you actors usually go away at weekends, don't you," says the landlord.

"I hadn't really intended to," replies Eric, who enjoys being away from home and exploring places.

"Well, I suppose we could let you stay some weekends. But we'd have to charge you extra."

An hour or so later, feeling distinctly unwelcome, and keenly aware that he has a long, hard day ahead of him, Eric retires to his room.

When he comes down in the morning he is relieved to find no sign of the builder or his mate, indeed no sign of human habitation whatsoever. Everything is exactly in its place, giving the feeling that one is in a show-house rather than a home in which people live, breathe and have their being. Eric drinks a quick coffee, rinses and dries the mug and hangs it back on its hook alongside its uniform brothers, all facing in the same direction. Then, as an afterthought, he turns it around to face the other way.

That day at the theatre is every bit as long and hard as he expected it to be. He is in Cheltenham to perform a one-man play about the First World War poet and soldier, Wilfred Owen. In the morning, he and the stage manager, whom Eric has never met before, go through the performance purely technically, plotting the many sound and lighting cues. In the afternoon they have their dress rehearsal, which should have been more or less up to performance standard, but isn't. There have been too many technical problems and Eric isn't feeling as confident with the stage manager as he would have liked. But the first performance, which is sold out, is due to begin in little more than an hour, and all Eric can do now is retire to his lonely dressing room and prepare himself.

*

"I am the enemy you killed, my friend.
I knew you in this dark: for so you frowned
Yesterday through me as you jabbed and killed.
I parried; but my hands were loath and cold.
Let us sleep now ..."

Those are the last lines of Owen's grim and nightmarish poem, "Strange Meeting," in which he, the soldier, finds himself plucked from the hell of battle only to be plunged into Hell itself. They are also the last lines of Eric's play. He delivers them and stands motionless, centre stage, tin helmet on his head, service revolver in hand, as the lights slowly fade. It has been a wretched performance, and everything that could go wrong, in terms of lighting and sound, *has* gone wrong.

As the sweet darkness of the final blackout envelopes him, he makes his way uncertainly across the unfamiliar stage of the studio theatre to the door at the back that is his exit. In the silence that immediately follows the play's conclusion, his free hand finds the door handle, turns it and pushes. Nothing happens.

There are several versions of the actor's nightmare. In one, you find yourself waiting in the wings to make your entrance. You hear your cue, but the door through which you must enter refuses to open. So now, Eric finds himself living out a variation of that one: it isn't that he can't get on stage – he can't get off.

He tries the door again, but still nothing. Just a few yards away the audience sits quietly in the darkness. There is an expectant hush about the place. Eric's nerves are already jangling from the unfortunate performance that has preceded this moment, but now he can feel his heart pounding as his panic rises.

That night, the stage manager has managed to bring up lighting on just about any part of the stage where Eric was not, and the hapless actor found himself delivering many of his lines in semi-darkness, or scurrying over to the light only to find it disappear as soon as he got there. Also, sound effects occurred where he had never heard them before, and where there should have been sound there was silence.

Eric tries the door again but still it will not budge. Just as he is starting to wonder how long it will take the stage manager to realise that something is wrong and bring the lights up anyway, the audience, feeling perhaps that they have been sitting in the dark long enough doing nothing, breaks into applause. Taking advantage of the noise, Eric shoulders the door hard three times, the lights coming up sharp and bright on the third assault. He spins around, straightens, smiles and walks towards the audience, but as he takes his bows, he can think of nothing but the door behind him that will not let him get off stage. As the lights go again to blackout, he turns and walks towards it once more.

Two or three seconds later, the auditorium lights come up, revealing a stage empty but for the few pieces of furniture integral to the action of the play. The spectators murmur to one another, rise, stretch, gather their things together and slowly leave the theatre.

And how slowly it seems to Eric, crouching uncomfortably under a table, behind a long, black drape at the back of the stage. Just before reaching the exit door, he had remembered a curtained-off storage area immediately to its right, and in that brief moment of darkness shot into it with the dexterity of a cat. On hands and knees now, his heart still thumping, he listens to the audience dwindling away. He waits a full five minutes, even from hearing the ushers leave, before stealing a look through the curtains. It is all clear. He steps smartly out, crosses to the door, turns the handle, and it opens – just like that.

Ten minutes later, Eric is still sitting at his dressing table, looking at his miserable face in the mirror. He can't face going to the bar, so he pours himself a hefty slug of port, knocks it back and feels its warmth against the back of his throat. Among the audience that night had been a soon-to-be famous author of a novel set in the First World War, which has just been published. He is, at that moment, giving the audience an after-show talk about it.

'What a night for him to be in,' thinks Eric, and he changes out of his costume, finishes his port and slinks off into the night.

Just before he gets to his digs it occurs to him that he hasn't eaten anything that day, so he stops off at a late-night store and buys a prepared meal from the chill display, and a very necessary bottle of wine.

When he enters the living room to make his way to the kitchen, both builder and builder's mate are arranged as per the previous evening, on the sofa, watching the television.

"I thought you actors went to the bar after the show," the landlord says.

"That's where I've just been," Eric lies, and as he goes into the kitchen he notices that his mug had been turned around. He puts his supper into the microwave.

"I thought you actors ate out," the landlord calls to him.

'He seems to know an awful lot about us actors,' thinks Eric, before calling back, "Just thought I'd make use of the kitchen."

The landlord makes a mental note to have the words, "Full use of kitchen" removed from his entry in the digs list. A few minutes later, Eric passes back through the living room. Indicating the tray in his hand, he says, "I thought I'd have this in my room. If that's alright with you."

"Of course. Not at all," says the landlord, who had been about to suggest it himself.

Eric steps out into the hall and begins to climb the stairs.

"Oh by the way," he hears over his shoulder, "we do expect our guests to supply their own toilet paper. If that's alright with you."

"Of course," Eric calls back. "Not at all."

'This has been the most perfect day!' he thinks, as he pushes his bedroom door shut behind him. He places the tray on the bed, himself beside it, and pours a glass of wine. It bubbles for a moment on the surface and its claret colour reflects warmly in the restricted glow of the bedside lamp. He looks about the cheerless room, quaffs some wine and feels his spirits restored just slightly.

At the end of the meal, Eric goes to the window, throws it open wide and stands there blowing cigarette smoke out into the cool, night air, looking beyond to where the moon, newly risen, is reflected on the wet, slate roofs. Then he recalls the show that evening, and the sheer heart-in-the-mouth, bowel-loosening, white-knuckle-ride of it all.

"There must be an easier way to earn a living," he says to the moon.

The next morning follows the pattern of the previous one. Eric comes down to find no one about, with everything clean, tidy and in its place. He has his essential shot of caffeine, washes and dries the mug, then hangs it back on its hook, facing the wrong way. He knows that it is childish, but it amuses him to think that on the one hand it irritates his inhospitable hosts, and on the other that it is such a trivial transgression they won't be able to raise it without sounding trivial themselves. He just can't work out why they seem almost to be going out of their way to make him feel unwelcome.

He arrives at the theatre round about eleven am. It is absurdly early, as the show doesn't start until half past seven in the evening, but he has things to do. He climbs the stairs to the offices and knocks on the door of the artistic director's secretary. She looks up brightly when she sees Eric. They already know one another from an earlier stint he has done at the theatre.

"Hello. How did it go last night?"

"Don't ask. Dreadful."

"Oh."

Not knowing what to say she looks troubled for a moment, but then brightens again.

"Well, you got a good review."

"Really?" says Eric, genuinely astonished.

"Yes, I've got it here. I'll do a copy for you," and she goes over to the photocopier. She hands him the copy which Eric looks at uncertainly.

"Are you sure it's safe for me to look at this?" he asks.

She smiles at him again. She is used to actors and their fragile egos.

"Perfectly safe."

To Eric, it isn't a matter of ego, it is a purely practical consideration. A critic can be utterly damning about an actor, but the actor still has to go on and do the show. The policy Eric has adopted is not to read reviews until the run has finished.

He says his thanks and hurries off, because it isn't to see the secretary that he has come to the theatre so early. A few moments later he is sitting across the desk from Clare, the Company Manager.

"I think we need some more rehearsal. Technical rehearsal," he tells her.

"Oh?"

"We had a few problems last night," he goes on, and smiles inwardly at the understatement. He gives only a few examples of the technical hitches of the night before, but enough to make it clear that the stage manager is not on top of the job. Clare has picked up the phone even before he finishes.

"Hi. We're doing another tech. on "Dark Star" this afternoon," she says into the mouthpiece. She listens only briefly to the voice at the other end, cutting in with, "Yes, I know you were. Cancel it. We're going at ..."

She looks at Eric.

"Is two-thirty OK?"

He nods.

"We're going at two thirty," she concludes, and puts down the phone.

"I'll be there too," she adds.

While awaiting the rehearsal, Eric gets himself a sandwich and coffee in the staff canteen. He looks wistfully at the dancers around him, for a modern ballet company is performing in the main house that week. His first real love had been a ballet dancer, and it has left him with the notion that theirs is the ideal female form.

He sighs, gets up and goes to his dressing room, where he puts on just those pieces of costume necessary for any stage-business: the army tunic and the Sam Browne belt with its holster and service revolver. When he arrives in the studio Clare is already there, with the stage manager, who looks sulky and resentful at having been called in to rehearse again.

"Unless you want to do it all," Clare says to Eric, "I thought we'd cut from cue to cue."

"That's fine by me," Eric replies. "There are just one or two sequences we'll have to go right through."

"OK. Just let us know when we get to them."

The stage manager makes his way up to the sound-proof control box above. Eric watches him go, wishing it were the efficient Clare who was going up there to run the show and not him.

Two hours later, they reach the final lighting cue. All the mistakes of the night before have been talked through and resolved. There had been just one moment when tempers almost flared. Eric had placed himself in the customary position for one of the scenes in the dugout. It was in this place the previous evening that he delivered an entire speech in almost total darkness, the lighting having come up on the wrong side of the stage.

"This is where the light should be at this point," Eric said.

The stage manager's petulant voice was transmitted via the speaker on-stage.

"Well you weren't in that position last night."

There was a charged silence, then Eric called back, through clenched teeth, "That's because you brought up the light on the wrong side of the stage. I just went to where the light was."

"Well that's where it was plotted," came the disembodied voice.

Seeing the set of his jaw, Clare said quickly, "Just ignore him." She then called up to the control box, "That's where the light should be. Have you got it plotted?"

"I have now."

"Good. Let's get on with it."

The show goes well that night. Another full house, and no technical hitches, which allows Eric to focus his mind solely on performing the part. He feels so much better about it all that he allows himself a drink in the bar afterwards. When, later, he walks back to his digs, he feels none of the weight upon him that he had the previous night, and when he gets there he is relieved to find all the lights out save that in the hall. He makes his way through to the kitchen, where a note has been left on the work-surface.

"Dear Eric, Just to say, we've got some friends coming to stay this weekend, so we'll be needing your room. Hope you had a fab show. Nighty-night."

"Nighty-night," says Eric to the empty room.

The week continues well. Another two favourable reviews come out, which have a good effect at the box office, so Eric is in good humour when he returns to his digs on Thursday night, but dismayed to find the downstairs lights still on. He leaves his shoes in the porch, intending to take them up with him when he goes to his room. This has become his habit, for the place is so immaculately kept, and he doesn't want to give his landlord any excuse to give him another ticking off; which is precisely what is about to happen.

He taps on the living room door and lets himself in. They say their hellos and he makes his way into the kitchen. As he is taking some leftovers from the fridge for a makeshift supper, he becomes aware of the landlord standing at the galley entrance. Eric looks up. The landlord is smiling but there is a distinct hint of, "I've got a bone to pick with you" about the smile.

"Good show?" he asks.

"Yes thanks."

"Smashing. Look – I need to have a word with you."

"Oh yes?"

"Yes. When I came down this morning, I found some doggy-do in the hallway."

As he says, "doggy-do" his lip curls, as if someone is holding the stuff beneath his nostrils.

"Oh dear," Eric replies, making an effort to look concerned.

"And I'm sure it wasn't there when we went up to bed."

Eric just looks at him.

"I've really got to ask you to be more careful."

"I'm being pretty careful as it is," says Eric, and points to his shoe-less feet. "I've been doing that every time I come back in. You'll find my shoes in the porch. And I don't think you'll find any doggy-do on them."

First the landlord looks suspicious, then he looks at a loss, then he looks suspicious again, but now he is looking at his partner on the sofa.

'Time to go up to my room,' thinks Eric. He says goodnight, closes the door behind him, and as he climbs the stairs he hears petulant voices raised.

Saturday morning arrives, and Eric doesn't have the luxury of the house to himself, but he doesn't care any more. He goes to the kitchen and brews some coffee, then takes it into the garden and lights a cigarette. There has been an unexpected frost overnight and the air is fresh and enlivening. He smiles as he watches the comic acrobatics of two squirrels in a tree next door.

"Lovely morning."

Eric turns. The landlord is beaming at him from the doorway.

"Yes, isn't it," he replies, waiting to be told off about the cigarette.

"You haven't forgotten about our friends coming this weekend," the landlord continues. He seems also to be in a good mood.

"No, I haven't."

Eric stubs out his cigarette on the paving and, taking care to wipe his shoes, first on the outdoor then the indoor mats, he steps back in to the kitchen, drops the stub into the waste-bin, then washes and dries his mug. Before he has a chance to hang it back on its hook the landlord snatches it from him and does it himself.

When next they meet, Eric is in front of the house, packing his things into the van.

"You're taking a lot of things just for the weekend," the landlord says.

"I thought you wanted the room cleared."

"Well ... yes. ... When will you be back?"

"I won't."

It comes out before he even has a chance to think, and Eric is as surprised by his answer as the landlord.

"Won't you?"

"No. Well," Eric goes on, thinking it through now, "it's obviously not very convenient for you, having me here, when you've got friends coming to stay. And it's not very convenient for me, having to move out every weekend."

The landlord considers asking for a week's rent in lieu of notice, but then he thinks better of it. He will be relieved to get rid of this troublesome tenant, who will insist on making use of the place.

"No. Well ... Got somewhere else to go, have you?"

"Yes," Eric lies.

"Right. Er ... Don't forget to leave your keys."

"They're on the hall table."

As he drives away he feels immensely relieved. Even if he has to spend the night in the back of the van, he knows that he will feel more welcome there than he has with the builder and his mate.

The following week sees the arrival of Monsieur Hulot. Eric's father, George, has a curious ability to be oblivious to things around him. Indeed, he is able, on occasions, to create chaotic situations of which he is quite unaware. Thus he has become known, within the family, as Monsieur Hulot, that genial and bumbling character created by the French actor, Jacques Tati, in his film, "Mon Oncle." The resemblance has become even more remarkable as George has grown older, and more vague, and he has even started to look like Hulot, with his characteristic raincoat, furled umbrella and hat.

By now, Eric is installed in a small hotel just outside the centre, which is modest but clean and comfortable. He has decided not to risk digs again, and he feels justified in the expense when he arrives at the theatre on the Monday to find the show still booking well.

His father comes to the play on the Thursday, as does Eric's agent, Bernard, with his "husband," Ray. After the performance, Eric makes his way through to the theatre bar, where he finds George, Bernard and Ray drinking and chatting together. Eric joins them, and for a little while they all talk about the production, Bernard doing most of the talking. His studied pose upon the chair is markedly feminine, as are his theatrical gestures. Late middle-aged and bespectacled, his thin, grey hair is combed back from his temples. He wears a double-breasted blazer and white polo-neck top, with grey, flannel trousers, over elegantly crossed knees, so that one trouser leg ends halfway up his calf, revealing an expanse of bare white skin and even whiter sock. He has a heavy, gold chain on one wrist and an equally flamboyant watch on the other.

When conversation about the play has been exhausted, George encourages Eric to tell the story about the digs he had been staying in the previous week. Eric tells it, and at the end, everyone agrees that *they* would have got out too just as soon as they could, and it seems that the conversation is about to move on when George chips in.

"And they were a couple of Nancy-boys."

This is followed by a deathly silence. The smile that had formed on Bernard's face at the conclusion of the story now freezes, his wine glass held motionless on its way to his lips. The silence seems endless, and Eric hears himself mumbling awkwardly, "What a quaint expression, George."

Three jaws are hanging open, and only the fourth, belonging to Monsieur Hulot, is still functioning.

"Yes," Hulot adds, in case they missed it the first time, "a couple of Nancy-boys."

Eric prays for the floor to open up and swallow him. He knows his father to be a fair-minded man, and that this expression is simply a crass articulation of the received opinion of his generation, but what an occasion, he thinks, to use it. Bernard could have been sitting there in a cocktail dress and high-heels, and it would still have passed his father by.

Eric downs his drink in one, even though he still has half a glass. Rising from the table he says, "It's been a long week. And it's not over yet. Come on George, I'll run you to your hotel."

His father looks perplexed at the abruptness of their departure, but for Bernard and Ray no explanation is necessary. Within seconds, however, of getting him out of the bar, Eric is back at the table, apologising profusely for any offence given. Ray is forgiving and understanding, saying that his own father might have used such an expression, but Bernard still looks thunderous.

On the way back to the hotel, Eric is seething, and doesn't know quite if he will be able to say anything articulate to his father.

"Didn't you happen to notice," he finally manages, "that you were actually talking to "a couple of Nancy-boys?""

He quotes the phrase with a heavy irony, which is quite lost on his father.

George looks at him uncomprehendingly, a half-smile on his face. The look is pure Hulot, and Eric realises that there is little point in saying any more. He swings the van off the road into the hotel car park.

"Don't worry about it, George," he goes on, as the engine ticks over. "I'll probably have to start looking for a new agent tomorrow. But don't worry about it."

In the event, it isn't a new agent that Eric finds himself looking for the next day but the artistic director of the theatre. It had been agreed, when they scheduled the performances of "Dark Star," that a week should be left open at the end of the run to allow them time to extend, should the bookings be good enough. Now, all the tickets have been sold, but Eric has heard nothing from the director, so after dropping his father off at the station, to catch his train home, Eric drives to the theatre, only to find that the director is away for the weekend. Unaccountably, they have no contact number for him, and when Eric catches up with the person who is deputising for him, she tells him that she doesn't have the authority to make such a decision.

It is one of those administrative cock-ups, Eric tells himself as he sets off back to London on the Sunday, that one just has to put down to experience, but it leaves him with a feeling of anti-climax. In spite of the trials of the last fortnight – the disastrous opening night, his inhospitable host, his father's oblivious insult to his agent – the show had been well-received, and could have gone on for another week.

The van climbs east out of Cheltenham and is soon up on the ridgeway, heading in the direction of Oxford. There is an uninterrupted vista to the north and south, across the Cotswold fields divided by their dry-stone walls, where the trees blaze out their autumn livery. Not a bad day, Eric thinks, to be moving on, and he has one of those brief, inexplicable moments of optimism.

It is late afternoon by the time he pulls up outside his flat in Alexandra Palace, North London, and another hour or so before he has unpacked the van and started to put away the various props, bits of furniture and articles of costume from the play. Having toured it around the country for ten years or so, on and off, he has decided that this will be its last outing. He is getting too old to be playing Wilfred Owen, who had been killed when he was only twenty five. Nevertheless, he feels that over the decade he has got to know something of the soldier-poet, whose words still resonate down the years, and he feels, as he hangs the tunic in the wardrobe, that he is taking leave of an old friend.

He sleeps fairly well that night and has little recourse, as he often has, to the BBC World Service, to help him through the long, dark hours; a habit inherited from his father. He is already half-awake when the phone by the bed rings early the following morning.

"Hello?"

"Eric – it's Ron here."

Now he is fully awake. Ron is the warden who looks after the old folks in the sheltered housing where Eric's father has a flat.

"Sorry to wake you so early," he goes on, "but Dad's had an accident."

Ron talks like this. He so identifies with his job that your dad becomes his dad, and your mum his mum. Eric and his cousins, George's nieces, refer to him as "Da-Do-Ron-Ron."

"Truth is, he's had a stroke. It's quite …"

Ron hesitates, but Eric already knows what the next word will be.

"… serious."

*

The trees along the roadside flash past in a golden-brown blur, but Eric is not admiring their autumnal splendour, as he had the day before. He is hardly registering the journey at all, or his speed, and the sign, "Harold Wood Hospital" seems to rear up before him almost as soon as he has set out, even though it must have taken him over half an hour to get there.

He finds his father on a metal trolley in A&E, covered by what looks like kitchen foil. His face is grimacing, his eyes tight shut, and he seems to be in neither this world nor the next. A doctor in a white coat comes up and says to him, "If it comes to it, I don't think we should try to resuscitate him."

For Eric, everything is happening too fast. Looking down at the doctor, he is still taking her in and thinking, 'She's so young.'

Some time later – he couldn't have said how long – he finds himself sitting at his father's bedside, in a ward he doesn't know the name of. Outside the window, he can see the upper branches of a line of trees, so he assumes that they are no longer on the ground floor, but he can't remember how they got there.

The day continues in a timeless haze, but as night comes on, the atmosphere, for Eric, becomes hellish. George seems to stir from the remote world he had been occupying. He becomes agitated and voluble, and succeeds in waking up those around him. He clearly has no real understanding of where he is or what has happened to him, and as Eric tries to settle and calm him, he hears a voice from a nearby bed call, "Fucking shut up!"

It is a very long night, for everyone in the ward, and in the morning a side-room containing just one bed is quickly found for them. While nurses wash the inert form of his father, who in the space of just twenty four hours has regressed from able-bodied octogenarian to helpless baby, Eric goes and makes some phone calls; one to his father's sister in Wales. He then buys himself a strong, take-away coffee and goes out into the car park and rolls a cigarette – thin as a crochet needle.

For most of the day he sits in an armchair by the bed, attempting a rudimentary communication in those moments when his father seems less comatose. George's breathing is erratic and alarming, in that for extended and regular periods he doesn't appear to be breathing at all. In those moments, Eric feels his own breathing to be suspended, and he doesn't feel much assured when another young doctor comes and puts a name to it.

"It's called Cheyne-Stoking," he says. "It can happen to coma patients, after severe brain injury. It may not seem like he's breathing, but he is. It's just very shallow."

For Eric, the diagnosis might have been more reassuring if the doctor had not used the words, "severe brain injury."

One of Eric's tasks is to dip a small piece of pink sponge on the end of a short, white stick, into a cup of water, squeeze it out and then use it to moisten his father's lips, gums and tongue. One of the effects of the stroke has been to knock out his ability to swallow, and without that reflex, any liquid taken orally could go straight down to his lungs. Thus his only form of sustenance and hydration is the saline solution in the bag slung above the bed, which feeds down through a tube and a cruel-looking needle inserted into his frail and mottled hand.

His father appears to sleep through the night. Now that they have the privacy of a side-ward, where they won't disturb anyone, he is quiet and tranquil. Eric tucks his legs up beneath him on the seat of the armchair and pulls the hospital blanket tighter around him.

The next day George's sister arrives, driven from Wales by their niece, Eric's cousin, Liz. Dorothy strides into the little room with a camel coat draped over her shoulders, a Liberty's, silk scarf knotted loosely at her neck, and her long, dark hair, grey at the temples, swept dramatically back from her handsome face. She reminds Eric of the actress, Ann Bancroft.

She had trained as a nurse in London during the Blitz, served with the Queen Alexandra's later in the war in the Middle East, and spent her post-war years working as a health visitor. With such a history behind her, she knows exactly what she is looking at when she enters the room. She is on familiar territory, and as she stands there, with a distinct air of authority, she knows that neither she nor anyone else in that place can do anything for her brother.

She looks at the notice above his bed.

"Nil by Mouth," she reads.

"He can't swallow," Eric explains. "We're waiting for a speech therapist to come and pronounce on that. She's taking her time."

The three of them spend the afternoon sitting around the bed, feeling vaguely useless. Dorothy takes a comb from her bag and runs it slowly and gently through George's fine, grey hair, sweeping it back from his high forehead. It seems to soothe him, and connect them, and becoming more aware of her presence, he starts trying to communicate, but in a child-like way, as if the stroke has wiped away the seventy or so years that have elapsed since his boyhood.

The windows of the room darken, and Dorothy and Liz take themselves off to spend the night in George's apartment. Eric prepares himself for another night in the unlit room.

By the time the two women arrive the next day, the speech therapist has finally put in an appearance. Eric relays her verdict to them.

"No swallow-reflex," he repeats.

"Well we knew that, darling," Dorothy replies.

"I think she meant not now or ever," Eric says.

'We knew that too,' thinks Dorothy.

The two women depart for Wales early in the afternoon, and when George's sister says goodbye to her brother, it is clear both to Eric and Liz that she is taking her leave of him for the last time.

The following evening, Eric is sitting in the hospital canteen, having just pushed aside a plate of something he can't identify, and certainly can't eat. Part of his mind is wondering what he is doing in the canteen at all, and part of it is reflecting on the night before. He must finally have fallen asleep in the armchair, to which he has moulded himself over the week, because he suddenly found himself woken by a movement in the room. Looking across to the bed, he was astonished to see his father sitting bolt upright, eyes wide open, staring straight ahead at a point high up on the wall opposite.

"What are you looking at, George?"

"Heaven," was the simple reply; the word enunciated perfectly, as if the stroke had never happened.

As a young man, his father had been destined for the priesthood, but he had been forced to pursue another career altogether, due to the straitened circumstances of his family. Watching him in that moment, suddenly alert and his eyes bright, Eric, long-time agnostic, believed him utterly.

He looks again at the inedible stuff on his plate and rises from the table. Pausing only to get a take-away coffee, he retraces his steps along the labyrinth of corridors and stairways that lead back to the ward. Something impels him to increase his pace, and he takes the stairs two at a time. When he comes through the doors of the ward he is at a run, driven on by an inexplicable urge to get back to his father as quickly as possible, but as he passes the nurses' station, the Staff Sister stands up quickly, and something about her look arrests him.

"He's just er... we sent someone to look for you."

Eric runs on, but she is almost on his heels as he bursts through the door to his father's room.

Before him, catching the moonlight, is a grey face on a glowing, white pillow. The hands are folded one on top of the other, and the needle of the intravenous drip has been removed. As he looks at the face, Eric sees that it is drained not only of life, but of pain also. There is a peacefulness about it, and a serenity. He is just taking this in when, from behind him, he hears the Sister's voice.

"It often happens like that, you know. When you're out of the room. It gives them a chance to let go."

*

The car speeds up the Great North Road. On the passenger seat next to Eric is a rectangular, cardboard box, inside which is a plastic flask, the size of a Thermos, containing the ashes of his father. It weighs seven pounds – which was roughly George's weight when he entered this world. Beside the box is a grainy, black and white photograph of a young man and woman, leaning back against the parapet of a low, stone bridge. The woman is stylish, with shoulder-length dark hair, swept back, and a white blouse open at the neck, under a two-piece suit with a knee-length skirt. She is posing more than the man, who stands with his hands in his pockets, his jacket pushed back to reveal a patterned, V-neck jumper. They are a handsome couple. Behind them, a narrow lane snakes up between two mountains. On the back of the photo is the inscription, "Honister Pass. Aug. 1947."

This is Eric's mother and father, in a picture taken four years before he was born, and Honister Pass, in the Lake District, is his destination now. The journey is an exact re-enactment of one he undertook some ten years before, only then his father was sitting next to him in the flesh. On the back seat, on that earlier journey, was an identical plastic flask, containing the ashes of his wife, Eric's mother, whom George called, "Potts," that having been her maiden name. At intervals along the way, George would call over his shoulder to the flask, "Nearly there now, Potts. Nearly home."

Potts had been born and brought up in the then steel town of Workington, Cumbria, and Eric and George had agreed that her final resting-place should be her beloved Lake District. Eric recalls that journey now, almost reliving it as the car heads north.

They hadn't got off to a good start. Not far up the A1, they became ensnared in a traffic jam, which crawled ahead of them out of sight.

"This isn't a road it's a car park," Eric grumbled, while George went on chatting to Potts in her Thermos.

Thus they arrived at their destination later than planned. The light had started to go, but they found the spot relatively easily, considering how indistinct it was in the photograph. They climbed out of the car and were buffeted by a gale-force wind, on which they could feel the first spots of rain, and then scrambled down a bank to the edge of a beck. Eric opened the plastic container and held it across to George, who scooped out a handful of the dust and threw it towards the water, but the wind whipped it sharply up and deposited it further down stream.

"That's it, Potts," he called out. "Wild to the last!"

They carried on this process until all the ash had been dispersed and was swirling away in the lively stream, and then they stood quietly for some moments, each with his own thoughts, while the wind dropped off, as if to allow them some quiet reflection. Eric recalled a snatch of something he had learnt as a boy at school.

"Long stood Sir Bedivere, revolving many memories, 'til on the mere the wailing died away."

"What's that, young man?" George asked.

"Mort d'Arthur. Tennyson."

They climbed the bank, Eric started the engine and they drove on up the pass, the old car straining on the one-in-four gradient.

They had a long journey back ahead of them. It is more than three hundred miles from the south to that part of the Lake District, and George was relieved that he no longer did any driving. On their way towards the motorway, Eric remarked that they were getting low on fuel. They seemed to be on long, desolate stretches of road with few buildings, let alone a petrol station. They passed one almost before they had seen it, and George suggested that they turn around and go back.

"It's alright. We'll stop at the next one," said Eric, unconcerned.

There wasn't a next one. Suddenly they were on the motorway, streaking past a sign that said, "Petrol 25 Miles." George looked uneasily at Eric, but in the lights from the approaching headlamps he still seemed unconcerned. It was just as they were passing a sign that said "Shap Summit" when the car, which had been labouring up the long climb, started to slow down.

"Why are you slowing down, Young Man?"

"I'm not slowing down. The car is slowing down. We've run out of petrol."

"Ah ..."

Eric turned on the left-hand indicator and manoeuvred the car on to the hard shoulder. They heard gravel hitting the undercarriage.

Mobile phones were in their infancy then. Neither George nor Eric had one, and even when, years later, they became ubiquitous, Eric still eschewed them.

"I like being out of touch," he said.

George turned to him now.

"You'd better let the car run on until we see an emergency phone."

"What for?" said Eric, bringing the car to a halt with not a telephone in sight. "Oh well," he went on, "looks like I'm going to have to get a bit wet."

"Which direction are you going to head in?"

Eric looked at George quizzically and said, "In the direction of the boot, of course."

"Why?" asked George.

"Because that's where the spare can is."

Suddenly George realised why Eric had not been bothered about running out of petrol. He hesitated before replying.

"Er... No, it's not."

Another headlamp passed across Eric's mystified face.

"No it's not what?" he asked.

"It's not in the boot," George replied, again after a little hesitation.

"Where is it?"

"It's at home. In the garage."

"No, it's not. It's in the boot."

"No. I took it out of the boot. Before we set out."

There followed one of those pauses that George was later to observe when Eric was in a play by Harold Pinter.

"... You did fucking what!?"

George didn't like swearing, particularly that word.

"Young Man," he began.

"Don't "Young Man" me, I'm over forty. Just tell me you didn't do what you just said you did."

"Well ... I did."

"Why?"

"To make more room."

"For what?"

"So that we could put in any bags we wanted to bring."

"What bags? We haven't brought any bags. We weren't stopping over, remember?"

George decided to say no more, as everything he did say seemed to be raising the temperature, so to speak; though in fact the temperature in the car was now rapidly falling.

There was another of those pauses, and then Eric said, "No, this is a wind-up, you're pulling my leg," and with that he opened the door, which was immediately caught by the gale and bent back against its hinges. Somehow, he managed to close it and went to the rear of the car, where he opened the tailgate. George felt an icy, wet blast on the back of his neck and over the howling wind he could just make out the words, "I don't fucking believe it! You've done another Hulot on me!"

He heard the tailgate slam shut, and watched Eric walking away. He was bent over almost at right angles against the wind, and he was pulling the Hulot raincoat over his already-drenched back. George watched his dwindling form, picked out by the headlights of the rapidly-passing vehicles, and sat listening to the buffeting wind, which rocked the flimsy car from side to side. He couldn't understand why people kept calling him Hulot. He had never seen a Jacques Tati film, but even if he had he would still not have made the connection, so completely was he Monsieur Hulot.

A little while later, peering through the windscreen, the rain coursing down it, George could just discern the figure of Eric coming back into view, bent double still against the wind and the rain, which appeared to be travelling horizontally. Eventually he was at the driver's door and climbing back in. Once behind the wheel, he sat looking pensively through the windscreen, the rain still running down his face. Casting furtive glances in his direction, George decided that the only word to describe his son in that moment was "saturated." After a moment, Eric spoke.

"Well, I wouldn't want to get caught out in that, would you?" he said, and started to roll a cigarette. George minutely relaxed.

"I wouldn't normally smoke in the car," he went on, "but given the circumstances." Then, as if from nowhere, he magically produced a hip flask and offered it to George.

"Drop of brandy?"

Given the temperature on Shap Fell that night, it seemed to George the most welcome and warming drop of brandy he had ever had. As they quaffed, and Eric puffed away, he told his father that the AA said that they should be able to get to them in about an hour.

Two hours later, George was still sitting there, watching Eric disappear in to the night once more, as he made his way back to the telephone. When eventually he returned, he seemed to his father even wetter than before. Being very correct in his use of English, George found himself wondering if it is possible to be wetter than saturated. Meanwhile, Eric told his father that the AA had, apparently, been looking for them on the other carriageway, and that they had, in fact, passed them several times already. Eric suggested to his father that he join the RAC.

As they sat on, awaiting rescue, watching the dark Cumberland fells about them lashed with rain, and feeling the car sway with every gust of wind, they were both having a very similar thought. That even after death, the turbulent and troubled Potts was still exerting her influence.

When, after this second journey to transport his parent's remains to their last resting-place, Eric finally reaches the location of the photograph, the weather is less wild than it had been those ten years before. It accords with his father's more tranquil nature. He scrambles down the bank and confers George's ashes to the clear, mountain stream.

He looks at the dark fells about him. There is an atmosphere of expectation about the place, as if the immutable mountains are waiting for something. It seems to him that as graveyards go this is pretty good. It would be a hard one to desecrate, and now, he reflects, only he knows where it is. Looking again into the stream, he notices that his father's ashes have formed little silver filigrees.

*

Back in London, Eric determines upon one thing; to keep busy. He picks up the phone and calls his agent. This is something he rarely does, as it is generally pointless. Bernard has been frosty with him since the Nancy-boy incident, but thawed a little on hearing of the death of his father. However, it has not made him any more useful, and he comes out now with the well-worn phrases that Eric has heard so many times before; such as, "Oh, it's very quiet at the moment."

Eric tries one or two of his own contacts, but they have all been casting recently and will not be looking for any more actors for some time. So he walks down to the newsagent and picks up one of the local papers, The Ham & High. In it, he finds the ad that Edith placed the week before when, exasperated by the wayward Reg, she determined to employ another reader. Eric dials the number and hears the lilting, Scottish tones of her housekeeper.

"Well," Bridie says, "we have seen quite a few people now, and we had more or less decided on someone," but when she asks him a little more about himself and discovers that he is an actor, her tone seems to change, for the people they have seen so far have been local, middle-aged, Hampstead women, and their piping tones have grated on the old lady's ears.

It turns out to be one of Eric's more unusual auditions. Sitting regally in her chair, Edith asks him to read to her from that Sunday's *Telegraph*, and Eric finds himself having to adjust projection, delivery and intonation to make himself heard. It seems that many of the vocal skills he acquired at RADA twenty or more years before will be required for this job. Eventually Edith turns her clear, blue eyes upon him and asks, "When could you start?"

In the ensuing weeks, Edith breathes a sigh of relief. It seems to her that after employing first a nurse of unsound mind, then a housekeeper of uncertain temperament, then a reader – now dog-walker – of uncertain principles, and then acquiring a dog as unpredictable as the weather, she has finally taken into her household someone who just seems "normal."

He has been there less than a month when one of the articles he reads to her concerns a man who has just been convicted of a series of horrific murders. Without exception, his appalled and shocked neighbours describe him as "quiet ... kept himself to himself ... always polite ... just seemed *normal*."

Edith looked up at him curiously.

*

1ˢᵗ May, 1977. Night time. Back in my den.

I'd been camping out at the Royal Free, and this morning, I was sitting by Sis's bed and talking to her. She'd been in a coma for two or three days now, but I've always wondered about that; whether something still gets through. They say the hearing's the last thing to go.

"Sis," I was saying, "you have driven me to distraction. And I you. And now you're going to leave me, you thoughtless woman …"

I stopped. My flippancy was out of place now, but my emotions were boiling up inside me.

And then, in the silence I suddenly felt her leave me. It was as distinct as that. I simply knew that she wasn't there any more.

I got up and sat on the bed and rested a finger lightly on her jugular vein, which is where the pulse is most prominent. (Did I learn that in the Fannys?) There was nothing there of course. I already knew that. And then I lightly ran my fingers over her face. The eyes were shut, the skin surprisingly soft, and I could tell that the expression was one of repose. (It's true that when you lose one sense you sharpen up on the others).

I pushed back some wisps of hair from her forehead (White, eh, Sis? You could have kept quiet about that. I need never have known), and then I ran a finger along her lips, and I could tell that there was the ghost of a smile there.

I got up, and stood as still as statue. I hadn't felt as devastated as this since I was blinded.

"Sweet Jesus!" I cried out. "What am I going to do now!?"

A moment later I heard the door open, and a young female voice said, "Is everything alright?"

"Yes, nurse. Everything's alright. Now."

There was a silence. She must have been looking at my sister and thinking, 'She's looking a bit grey around the gills.'

"Nurse — would you just leave us alone for a moment?"

"Of course," and I heard the door close.

I sat down and tried to collect my thoughts.

"Sis … It's all over. All the stupid bickering. We can put all that behind us now. I dearly wish we'd been more alike, but it doesn't matter any more. We're reconciled at last."

I heard voices outside the door.

"Look, Sis … I just want to say this. Thank you. From the bottom of my heart. Because of you, I got my career back. I couldn't have done it without you. You sacrificed yourself for me, which I would never have expected. Had things been the other way around, I'm not sure I could have done the same for you. I'd like to think I could, but I'm not sure I'd have had the strength. So … Thank you."

I kissed her on the forehead, and then heard the door open.

"Miss Parr?"

"Hello, Matron. …I'm going now. I just had to say goodbye."

She came over and put her hands on my shoulders.

'Oh God please don't do that!' I thought. 'I'm going to blub.'

"Matron," I said, "You've all looked after my sister so well. Thank you for that. From both of us."

I got up and headed towards the door but I didn't make it. My body – no, my being – was crumpling. As I tumbled I felt two pairs of hands take hold of me.

"It's alright, Miss Parr. We've got you. We'll just put you back on your chair."

"No," I said, "I want you to put me on the bed."

Without a moment's hesitation I heard the Matron say, "Of course," as if it were the most natural request.

They put me on the bed and I lay down. I heard the door close.

I put my arm around Sis and snuggled up to her. Her body was cold but still she was giving me warmth. I didn't say anything – I just lay there. And then, I think, I must have fallen asleep, because the next thing I knew, I heard the door opening, and the Matron was saying, "How are you, Miss Parr?"

"I'm alright now," I said. "We've just had a little nap."

And then I got up, left the room and tapped my way down the stairs

I walked out of the building, and into the rest of my life.

Eric ties a piece of tape around the bottom of his right trouser leg, to stop it snagging in the chain, and hops on his bike. He cycles up through Alexandra Park, past the animal compound, where two lamas and a donkey live. The locals are woken early by the donkey, braying mournfully for the mate he once had. Eric then skirts around the back of Alexandra Palace, which he had watched ablaze soon after moving to that part of London, and cycles along the old railway track where steam trains once brought day-trippers to the so-called "People's Palace." A group of young women step to one side to let him pass and as he does so he hears one of them say, "Nice looking bike," and not, he notes, "Nice looking bloke." He knows he is not prepossessing.

He cycles on through Highgate Woods. To his left, and on the other side of the road, are Queen's Woods, which had been a burial ground during the Black Death in the fourteenth century. He is always on the lookout at this point for wardens from the Corporation of London, which owns the woods and forbids cycling there. If they challenge him he generally pretends to be a foreigner, although the last time that happened, and he pretended to be French, he found himself being reprimanded by a warden who was himself French. Eventually he crosses the Great North Road and begins the climb up Bishop's Avenue, or Millionaire's Row, as it is also known. Looking at the gaudy mansions set back from the road he thinks, not for the first time, that money and taste don't necessarily go together. He then re-enters one of those parts of Hampstead Heath where single men wander around alone looking for other single men wandering around alone. As they do always seem to be alone, Eric wrongly assumes that they aren't having much luck. It is exactly quarter to eleven by his watch as he pushes his bike along Edith's gravel drive.

The house has seen better days. It was never attractive, except perhaps to the well-to-do actor who had it built in the 1920's, and even he had been disappointed with the result, but in recent years it has clearly suffered neglect. The paint-work is chipped and stained, the floorboards are worn and creak underfoot, the rugs are threadbare, and on the grimy walls there are tell-tale patches where once hung gloomy portraits of the Mistress's long-dead ancestors, until Eric's predecessor, Reg, carried them off. Some still remain though, looking sternly out upon a world that they would no longer recognise. In almost every room, ancient clocks tick away the hours in a mellow, measured way, and none of them agree on the time.

As has become his routine, Eric lets himself in with the key entrusted to him, removes the tape from his trouser leg and calls out but receives no reply. He then goes in to the smaller of the two reception rooms to make a fuss of Tyson, who, if he has yet been returned by Reg, will be attached by his leash to a radiator. Eric has discovered that making a fuss of Tyson pays dividends. Not many pay the dog much attention, save to give him a wide berth, but when Eric arrives in the morning, he greets the irascible and unpredictable creature like an old friend, so that Tyson, in his thankfulness, hardly ever attempts to bite him. On that particular morning Tyson is not there.

Eric then goes off to the kitchen and collects two glasses, most of which are chipped and not quite clean. He returns to the sitting room with them in one hand and a bottle of whisky and a bottle of American Dry clutched in the other. He pours a thumb of whisky into one glass and tops it up with the ginger ale. He then pours a thumb of whisky into the other glass, stops, and looks around furtively. He goes back out into the hallway where he stands and listens for a moment, but can hear no sounds closer than the two female voices he is accustomed to hearing from upstairs at that time of day. He slips back into the living room and, after a quick glance through the window to assure himself that there is no one in the garden, he undoes his fly buttons and urinates into the second glass. As he does so, his eyes meet those of one of the ancestors on the wall, and Eric isn't sure that a quizzical eyebrow isn't raised. He quickly does up his buttons and tops up the glass with American Dry. Picking up the first glass, he goes over to the window and holds both glasses side by side, checking for any inconsistencies in colour. He seems satisfied with the result.

A product of the English public school system, Eric tends towards self-effacement and self-deprecation. He is a mild, almost timid-looking man and he wears round specs, sleeveless patterned jumpers and baggy trousers, which give him the appearance of an escapee from the 1940's. He certainly does not look like the kind of person to do the kind of thing he has just done.

Careful not to mix up the glasses, he places the first on a small table beside a large, ugly armchair from which trails an electrical cable, and the second on the table by his own chair. He picks up the *Daily Telegraph*, sits down and settles in to wait. In another part of the house a clock begins chiming eleven and Eric hears feet on the stairs. A moment later Bridie appears in the doorway.

"Oh, Good Morning, Eric. I didn't hear you arrive."

"Morning, Bridie. No, I just got here. I did call out."

"Oh, I didn't hear you."

Bridie's tone is still lyrical, though her Scottish accent has softened over the many years she has been away from that country. A little overweight now in her late middle age, she remains an attractive woman, and when her eyes twinkle she can seem quite flirtatious. She has a relaxed voluptuousness about her, which does not, however, disguise the fact that she is highly-strung. Her mouth still twitches at one corner, particularly when in the vicinity of Tyson.

"You've got the drinks, I see," she says. "That's good."

"Yes. I thought I might just get them in while I was waiting."

"Well ... I'll just get off to the kitchen then."

As she does so, another clock begins chiming eleven, the front door opens and closes again, and then a very different figure appears in the doorway.

Reg's face has taken on an aspect of meanness over the years. It looks both puffy and emaciated at the same time, and in the centre of it is a long, broken-veined nose made more prominent by its bluish redness. His cap is pulled down over his thinning, unkempt, grey hair, and he stands unsteadily in the doorway, his look seeming both to see and not see Eric. In one hand he holds an open beer can, while from the other a dog's lead trails on the floor. Deciding to make no observation about the absence of dog at the end of the lead, Eric simply says, "Morning, Reg. Nice walk?" and gets an inarticulate grunt by way of reply.

When Eric took up his post with Edith he little knew what malevolent feelings he had engendered in someone who didn't even know him. Reduced to the lowly status of dog-walker, Reg is determined that he will one day get back at this younger man who has usurped his position.

He is about to lurch away when his beady eyes light on the drink at Eric's side. He hesitates, involuntarily half-stepping into the room. Feigning not to be keenly watching him, Eric looks down at the newspaper, but as he awaits the next move, Bridie's lilting voice sing-songs down the hallway.

"Is that you, Reg? I need a word with you."

Lilting as the voice is, there is an authority about it, and after a moment's further hesitation Reg toddles off towards it. Eric awaits the inevitable, and sure enough, seconds later, Bridie's raised voice can be heard.

"Oh no! You haven't lost him again."

Reg's voice is less distinct but just discernible.

"What?"

"Where's the dog for heaven's sake?"

"He ran off."

"How much have you had?"

"How much what?"

"It's eleven A.M. Antemeridian. Before noon."

Bridie's Scottish accent has reasserted itself, indicating that her emotional temperature is raised. Eric smiles. This morning is going to be even more fun than he had anticipated. Reg begins offering his routine excuses but a door is slammed shut, cutting off the sound, and Eric hears Bridie's cross steps approaching.

"Would you believe – that man has lost the dog again?"

"Oh dear," says Eric.

"If he doesn't turn up before Edith comes down … well, she won't be very pleased."

"No."

"She's very late this morning. But then Unity was late. Problem with the buses."

The last phrase has a decidedly ironic tone.

"She seems to have a lot of problems with the buses," Eric says.

"She does. She does."

To work off her agitation, Bridie begins dusting randomly, which is more a process of simply transferring dust from one surface to another.

"I don't know how much he's had," she goes on. "I told him – it's eleven a.m. Antemeridian. He's just blathering away out there. I shut the door on him. I believe he got my drift."

"I'm sure he did."

Tired already of her pointless dusting, Bridie stops and takes a sip from the glass of wine she had left on top of the sideboard.

"I wonder how long we're going to have you with us, Eric?"

Eric smiles. It sounds to him as if she has just heard that he has a fatal disease but the prognosis is uncertain.

"Er ... what d'you mean?"

"Well ...in your line of work. In and out of jobs. Or "resting" as you actors say."

Eric represses a sigh. In his twenty or so years in the theatre he can't recall hearing any actor using that particular euphemism, because they would have known with what derision it would be received by their peers, and yet he is constantly being told, by people who don't know anything about the business, that this is what actors say.

"Actually, Bridie, we don't."

"You don't what?"

"We don't say "resting.""

Bridie raises an eyebrow.

"What *do* you say?"

"We say "out of work.""

Bridie looks disappointed, and not entirely convinced. She seems about to argue the point but is interrupted by a raised voice from the landing.

"Don't you blame me! You gettin' slower an' slower!"

Unity descends the stairs. Nobody quite knows how she acquired her limp – an accident, they have extrapolated, while running for one of her buses – but it makes her downward progress now look somewhat alarming. She is carrying a tray that seems about to shed its load of discarded breakfast things. Dangling over the edge of it is a pair of stained surgical gloves. Step by uncertain step, she continues her solitary conversation.

"She gettin' slower an' slower. An' don't blame Unity! Blame the buses. Not my fault the buses doan come. Then three come together. What's the use in that? No, you gettin' slower an' slower, my girl! Soon the Lord's big red bus come to take you away, and you can bet, three come along together."

Having somehow made it intact to the bottom of the stairs, and tired of talking to herself, Unity addresses herself to Bridie and Eric.

"Nothin' to do with the buses. She gettin' slower an' slower. An' why I come anyway? Look, she no eat her breakfast. She got no sustenance. No wonder she slow."

While Bridie's accent has mellowed over the years, Unity's seems no less Bajan than when she left the island, all those years before.

"Well, she is in her nineties," Bridie suggests.

"I know that."

There is a pause, for neither of them can quite remember just how old Edith is. Bridie eyes the tray in Unity's tenuous grasp.

"Er ... is that entirely hygienic?"

"What," Unity shoots back, immediately defensive.

"We-ell ... the gloves and the food together. I don't even like to think what's on those gloves. "

"You doan teach me hygiene. I done my nurse's trainin'."

"Oh, I wasn't suggesting you hadn't, my dear. I just wondered ..."

"What's the difference? She no eat it anyway."

"No-o. I think she's a little off her food."

"Off her trolley more like. And I tell her – I no frightened of she. Doan blame me. Blame the buses. I can't get a bus which aint there."

Bridie decides to slip into placatory mode.

"No-o. They really are the limit those buses. Is she coming down soon?"

"Doan ask me. First she do this, then she do that. I go put the tray in the kitchen."

"I believe you'll find *that man* is still there. Would you credit it? He's managed to lose the dog again."

Unity's truculent face suddenly creases into a smile, as she undergoes one of her regular and instantaneous mood changes.

"Oh, just wait till the Mistress hear that!" she chuckles.

"That's what I told him," Bridie says, "but he doesn't listen. It's eleven a.m. and he's as tight as a cat's posterior."

Unity hobbles away and Bridie starts to follow, but she stops in the doorway and, turning a soft smile upon Eric, she murmurs, "If she's a trained nurse, I'm Mary Queen of Scots," and with that she is gone, leaving Eric once more to his musings.

He picks up the glass next to him, sniffs it and puts it down. For a moment all is quiet, save the ticking of the innumerable clocks, then Eric hears a brief barking from outside. He smiles, and is about to go to the front door when a low, mechanical hum vibrates through the stillness. It becomes steadily louder, and then, turning first one corner and then another, the chair of the Stannah stair lift comes into view, and sitting regally upon it, her unseeing eyes staring straight ahead, is … The Mistress.

Just before the chair reaches the bottom, Unity limps back into the hallway, pulling a Zimmer frame after her, which she places at the foot of the stairs, just as the chair comes to a halt. The Mistress raises one arm of the chair, struggles out of it, then calls out in a stentorian tone, surprising from one so seemingly frail, "Unity! Unity!"

"I here! I here! You wanna make me deaf too?"

Unity is all truculence again.

"How can I know that you're there," Edith asks, "if you don't tell me?"

"I always here. I here every day for …," and she pauses, unable to remember how many years she has been in the old lady's employ, "… God knows how long when you come down. The Zimmer here."

As Edith grasps hold of it, Unity begins dragging both frame and occupant across the floor.

"Don't yank me like that!" Edith chides.

"I no yank. You do the yankin'," and they continue this well-trodden conversation as Unity pulls her back and forth across the hallway, for this is Edith's morning exercise.

"Is Reg back? Is Tyson here?" the old lady enquires.

"Reg back but Tyson no with he."

"Oh no! He hasn't lost him again!"

"What you expect? The man's brain affected."

"Has he been drinking again?"

"He still drunk from last night," and then Unity chuckles to herself, "That man!"

By now, they have reached one end of the hallway, where Unity jerks the frame around to bring Edith back in the other direction. By way of reminding her just who is mistress of the house, Edith jerks the frame back towards herself.

"I told you not to yank it like that!"

"You do all the yankin'!" Unity shoots back, and then continues to herself, "She do all the yankin' then she tell me I yank," at which point Bridie appears once more from the kitchen, a tray in her hands, upon which are two whiskies and ginger.

"Good morning, Edith," she sings out.

"Oh, good morning Bridie. And how are you today?"

"O-oh, mustn't grumble. We're not getting any younger, are we. How are you?"

"Oh, just the same. I had a terrible night."

This is Edith's standard reply, for truly her nights are terrible to her, as she lies awake staring blindly at the cracked ceiling, listening to the sighs and groans of the house, and sensing the ghosts of her ancestors about her.

"Did you? Oh dear."

And this is Bridie's standard reply, for what else can one say to someone who has simply lived too long?

"Oh, Eric," she continues, as she steps into the living room and catches sight of the glass by his side, "I forgot you'd already done the drinks."

Eric doubts this, as he watches her take a glass from the tray and raise it to her lips.

"Pity to waste it," she goes on, and then, calling back towards the hallway, "Oh, Edith, has Unity told you about Tyson?"

"Yes, she has. Reg really is the limit. Unity! Will you stop yanking!"

"I fed up with this job. I go back to Barbados."

Unity threatens regularly to go back to Barbados.

"I think I've had enough exercise for the time being," Edith says. "Just take me to my chair. Before you pull my arms from their sockets."

Unity gives the Zimmer one final jerk and then guides it and her mistress through the doorway and over to the armchair, whose seat awaits the ancient bottom.

"What time is it?" asks Edith.

"It's past eleven," Bridie replies.

"Oh, we're so late again."

Unity is on the defence once more.

"Now doan you ..." but Bridie cuts in with, "I'm surprised you need to ask, Edith. Time's quite a feature here."

"They all go off at different times," Edith says. "One doesn't know where one is."

"Or *when* one is," Bridie corrects.

"Nothing works in this house. That chair lift. The number of times it stops before the bottom. And how am I to know? I'll break my neck one day."

"Hang on a minute, Edith," says Eric, springing from his chair, "the seat's not up."

He presses a button on the remote control, the electric motor whines and the seat slowly rises.

"Oh, good morning Eric. How are you today?"

"Fine thanks, Edith. How are you?"

"Oh, I had another bad night."

"I'm sorry. … There – it's all ready for you."

In spite of Unity's unhelpful assistance, Edith is now more or less in position, so pressing her meagre rump against the seat she manipulates the control and is gently lowered into place. While Unity fusses about with the foot-stool, and Eric collects a clutch of shawls and blankets, Bridie takes another sip of her whisky.

"Oh, be careful!" Edith moans, as Unity wrenches her feet up on to the stool. "That doesn't feel very comfortable."

"I think you've got it the wrong way round," Eric suggests.

"Eric, would you adjust the head cushion?" Edith asks.

"Sure."

"Do this. Do that," Unity mutters.

"Unity," Edith cuts in, "don't let us make you late for your next appointment."

"I goin' – I goin'."

"Is that alright?" Eric asks.

"Just up a little more."

"I don't know why you don't get a new chair," Bridie says between sips, "the trouble that one gives you."

"It's not the chair," Edith says, "it's the body. I need a new body."

"Well, get me one while you're at it," Bridie replies, gazing out of the window with a faraway look in her eyes, "… though I can still attract."

"What did you say?" Edith asks.

"I may be well-upholstered ..." Bridie continues.

"What did she say?" Edith asks again.

"Something about upholstery," Eric says.

"Oh, is she still going on about the chair?"

"... But I can still attract," Bridie goes on.

A sudden burst of birdsong brings her out of her reverie, and turning to Edith she says, "Well, I had better attend to your lunch."

"What are we having today?" Edith asks.

"Filet d'Agneau de Lait Roti en Croute de Sel," Bridie announces, her Scottish accent imparting to the French language a sexual allure.

"Ah ... lovely," Edith hesitates, "... well, don't give me too much. My stomach's still unsettled."

Bridie, not yet entirely back in the real world, passes through the doorway without comment, Unity close behind.

"I must have spent the entire night on the lavatory," Edith says, to no one in particular.

After the little bustle of activity, the silence of the next few moments seems peculiarly peaceful. Indeed whenever Unity leaves the room there is a sense of peace. The bird calls again in the garden.

"Have they gone?" Edith asks.

"Yes."

"I think Bridie's got a new recipe book. I do wish she'd stop experimenting on me. ... Well, we'd better get on, Eric. It's very late."

"Right."

Eric picks up the paper and sits in the chair next to Edith.

"Unity comes later and later," she goes on. "I think she's off her rocker, you know."

Eric is of the same opinion, though none of them know anything of Unity's history of mental illness. He gives a non-committal, "Mm," quickly scans the front page, and begins with the main headline.

""TORIES DISCLOSE FOREIGN,"" but that is as far as he gets before a high-pitched and piercing sound emanates from Edith's double hearing aid.

"Oh no!" she moans, and begins frantically trying to adjust it. "I think it must be the other one."

It is, and the sound abates.

"That's better. What were you saying?"

""TORIES DISCLOSE FOREIGN FUNDING.""

"I don't think so. What's the main picture?"

"William Hague and Ffion Jenkins."

"Go on."

""Guess who came to the wedding party. William Hague and bride to be Ffion Jenkins appear unruffled after being ambushed by strippers at last night's reception.""

"Where?"

"Er ... The Carlton Club."

"What do they look like?"

"She's pretty. Blonde. He looks like a little boy. A little bald boy."

"Mm ... What else?"

""PARISHES DEFY BISHOP ON GAYS.""

This last phrase is almost drowned out as a gale of laughter blows in from the kitchen.

"I can't hear a word you're saying," Edith complains. "Are they having a party out there?"

"Sounds like it."

"Who's there?"

"Just Bridie and Unity, I think."

Eric guesses that Reg will have been booted out of the kitchen by now.

"Has Bridie brought the drinks in?"

"I already did them myself. Yours is by your right hand."

Edith picks up her glass with a practised hand and raises it towards Eric.

"Cheers."

"Cheers."

Eric raises his own glass and clinks it against Edith's. She takes a satisfying sip and Eric is about to do the same, but he checks himself just in time and quietly puts it back down.

"Mmm," Edith says, appreciating the warm feeling already running through her ancient body. "It's medicinal, you know."

"Of course."

"No really. When I asked my doctor what I could take for these headaches, he said, "Take whisky.""

"I wouldn't mind a doctor like that."

"Of course he's useless in every other department."

Eric is about to carry on with the paper when Reg appears once more in the doorway, his cap still on his head and, looking, by the deepening colour of his nose, as if he has found Bridie's latest hiding place for the Scotch.

"Morning, Edith."

"Who's that?"

"It's Reg."

"Oh, Good Morning, Reg. Where's Tyson?"

"He ran off."

Eric starts to say something but Edith, having perhaps turned her hearing aid down too much, cuts in on him.

"I don't think you should let him off the lead, Reg."

"He'll find his way back," Reg grins, showing a gap in his teeth; the result of having had a good seeing-to outside a pub recently.

"Yes," Edith replies, "after he's terrorised the local children."

Reg moves unsteadily into the room.

"I was wondering if you could let me have a small advance, Edith."

"Weren't you paid yesterday?"

"Yes. But it's been an expensive week. Hedda hasn't been very well. I've had to get her medicines and things."

"Oh dear."

Having heard all this before, Edith turns her blind but unerringly accurate gaze upon Eric.

"Will you pass me my purse, Eric? How much d'you need, Reg?"

"Well, I think er ... twenty pounds ought to do it."

Eric hands Edith her purse, and she expertly selects by size the correct notes. As she does this, Reg moves closer to Eric and casually picks up his glass. It is one of Reg's ways of getting back at Eric – treating him as if he isn't there. Eric pretends not to notice anything. Reg raises the glass half to his lips, and then adds, "Better make it thirty. Just to be on the safe side."

Edith takes another note from her purse and, just as Reg is about to take a sip, she checks him with, "What's the matter with Hedda?"

Reg pauses.

"Oh … women's trouble I think."

"Ah," she says, and thinks how clever Reg is in his lies, choosing those which discourage any further questioning. He raises the glass once more to his lips, and again is checked by Edith.

"Well here you are," she says, holding out the notes. "I do hope she's better soon."

"Thanks, Edith," Reg says, stuffing the notes quickly into his pocket as if someone is about to mug him. The glass is again on the way to his lips, and Eric has almost stopped breathing. Finally it is there and half the contents disappear in one draught. Reg smiles again at Edith and starts to say, "Well, see you tomorrow," when his expression changes. He shoots a look at the glass, and then at Eric, who appears to be suddenly fascinated by something in the paper. Without a further word Reg leaves the room. There is silence for a moment, then Edith turns to Eric and asks, "Has he gone?"

"Yes," Eric replies, a look of pure joy upon his face.

Edith sips her drink and reflects how she always feels a sense of relief when Reg leaves.

"You've mixed it just right," she says.

"Yes, I think I did."

Edith puts down her glass and sits back in her chair.

"Well, I think we'd better get on. Bridie will be telling me lunch is ready soon," but as Eric turns to the next page there is a sudden and furious barking from outside, followed by an agonised cry.

"Ah! You bastard!" Reg shouts from the garden, trying to extricate his calf from Tyson's jaws.

Eric closes his eyes and thinks, "This has been a perfect morning."

"I think Tyson is back," says Edith.

Eric looks across to her and studies her face. Is it possible, he wonders, that she is relishing the moment too? It is sometimes hard to read her thoughts, for the glass substitutes where once her eyes had been tell him nothing.

"He did it again you know," Eric says.

"Who? What?"

"Reg. He picked up my drink again, and drank it. Right in front of me."

"The gall of the man! Why didn't you say something to him?"

"It's alright. I don't think he's going to do it again."

*

Barbados. The balcony of my hotel room.
August, 1981. Evening.

I shall never be clean again. I have bathed, I have showered, I have dived into clear (so I am told) rock pools and I have swum in the Caribbean, which the hotel manager tells me is aquamarine. Not bad for an old blind lady. I have done all this and I still feel dirty.

I curse that insane nurse for recommending this place, and I curse myself for taking her advice. To be fair to her she did not recommend I took that man with me. Quite the reverse. "The blind leading the blind" was how she put it. But anyway I had to have some sort of guide and Unity refused to accompany me. In spite of her curious ways she would have been ideal for the job. Both as a nurse (so-called) and someone who knows the island. This is another little mystery. She speaks of Barbados in such glowing terms but shows no inclination to return here. She hasn't been back once since she left. So I ended up with a very poor substitute. Said man is no more capable of telling me that the sea is aquamarine than he is of describing the view from my balcony. I must rely on strangers for that, and my imagination, which has become most fertile since the war. I smell the air, I feel the breeze and the heat, I listen and I remember. If someone says, "Look – flying fish!" (odd thing to say to a blind person but they do) I have an image of it in my mind.

Things hadn't gone so badly until the night before last. The flight was comfortable though long. S.M. (Said Man – I can't bring myself to use his name), still grumbling about having to lug my Braille machine around, was starting as he meant to go on, and making the most of the free on-board drinks. Unity had suggested taking the banana boat.

"Banana boats is luxury travel," she said, but I didn't relish so long a journey, particularly with S.M.

The hotel seemed clean and well-run and the food is good. It is just as well I like fish as that is the staple diet here. The bar has a bewildering array of rum-based cocktails, which I shudder to think of now, as I believe that's where it all started to go wrong.

Although the island is independent now, there is still an old colonial feel about the place. I am treated with deference, though perhaps that's less to do with being white than being rich and elderly. We have visited some beautiful spots, so I am told. There is a spectacular view out to sea from a place called Hackleton Cliff. I am fortunate in having found a driver who is rather more lucid than S.M. and can not only describe a scene well but can tell us something about its background and history. They speak a kind of pidgin English here, which I am used to hearing from Unity. It may be limited but it is remarkably expressive.

We walked a lot the day before yesterday, and I could feel the sun taking its toll on my scarred face, even though I had put on the cream the dermatologist prescribed and was wearing a broad-brimmed straw hat. I felt quite enervated when we returned to the hotel, but a little siesta and then a long soak in the bath set me up well enough for the evening.

We had a leisurely dinner on the terrace of the hotel's restaurant. Flying fish again – they have an infinite variety of recipes for it. My glass was never allowed to be empty and I could feel it going quickly to my head. Perhaps the sun that day had something to do with it. Then S.M. insisted on buying me a cocktail. When it comes to spending someone else's money his generosity knows no bounds, though he was managing, as he knows he can, to be quite entertaining. He does have a way of charming, though as the empty glasses pile up this can easily tip over into a mawkish sentimentality, and I have no time for that whatsoever. Stage three, if he gets that far, is something really rather unpleasant. He has a chip on his shoulder. He feels that he should be doing better in life but he expects it just to be handed to him on a plate. I have no time for that either. You make your own luck. Fortunately on this particular evening, or unfortunately as I view it now, he was still on stage one. It was very pleasant, sitting out on that balmy night, but two or three cocktails later – I was starting to lose count – I told him I simply had to turn in. He didn't try to dissuade me, and dutifully saw me to my room. I said goodnight and as soon as I got through the door I kicked off my shoes and flopped down on the bed. And then I heard his voice, soft and close to me now. I was startled, as I thought I had heard the door close and I assumed he was on the other side of it. He asked me if I would like a cigarette and for some reason I accepted. A few minutes later I felt his hand on my leg. I stiffened at first, but then I found myself relaxing. Neither of us said a word.

I would like to blame it all on the drink, but I promised to be honest with myself here. No dissembling, no self-delusion. What after all is the point in deluding oneself?

The truth is that in all the years since my blinding,
I have had only brief and dissatisfying affairs. I
seemed to attract all the wrong sort of men, the worst
being those who took pity on me. The best of them
was the one who was blind himself – only the blind
understand the blind – but he was also the kind
who believes that the man should bring home the
bacon. As I was far more capable of bringing home
the bacon than he, and he knew it, there was clearly
no future for us. That side of my life then, since the
war, has been both frustrating and disappointing, so
when S.M. made his none too subtle overture I was
susceptible. Throughout it all though I remained
outside it, as though I were merely an observer. I felt
like a bystander witnessing a road accident. That isn't
to say I didn't enjoy it, even though S.M. was clumsy
and insensitive. There are times when I have yearned
to be touched, and in that way, but so many assume
that if you are blind and getting on a bit you can't
possibly have such feelings. So there I was, looking
down upon us with a mixture of emotions (one of wry
amusement, for there is something fundamentally
comic about copulation) but even though I was
experiencing a rare physical pleasure there was a
voice in my head saying to me, "You will regret this."
Which I did, immediately.

For S.M. it was all over rather quickly, which left me feeling less than satisfied, and then the feelings of self-loathing and self-disgust began, and the sense of having been sullied. And then, as he dozed off beside me and began to snore, I found myself wondering how this would affect our relationship, such as it is. I had not the remotest intention of repeating such a folly, not with him, but I knew that something would be altered all the same. And as I lay there, thinking about it all, I realised what it would be. Nothing would be very different for me – I have been foolish before and consigned it to history – but S.M., I was convinced, would get it into his head that from now on he had some sort of hold over me. That I would feel, in effect, in his power.

How to describe a day in the life of Tyson? It is very simple and straightforward, because they all follow a pattern, but it is hard to define just when that day begins, as it isn't clear when the previous one ends.

When Bridie has shut up the house for the night, having let Tyson out in the garden to do any final business, and the Mistress has been transported up to bed, Tyson waits until he hears Bridie's door close, and then he pads up the stairs, his claws tapping on the bare boards, and into Edith's bedroom. She always leaves the door open in anticipation of this. Tyson climbs onto the foot of her bed, settles himself down and has doggy dreams about fights in which he gets the better of a German Shepherd, and then copulates with that nice-looking black retriever next door. Or Bridie gives him a double-helping of pedigree chum. Or he finds himself taking a chunk out of Reg's leg. And throughout all this REM activity, he remains his mistress's loyal sentinel, guarding her against any harm.

Then, early on, when he hears Bridie turn on her radio and start moving around, he pads back down the stairs. The stairs are no longer so easy for him. He has rheumatism now in his hind quarters, added to which his eyesight has started to cloud over. He patrols the old house from room to room, checking for unfamiliar scents that might indicate an intrusion. By the time Bridie comes down in her dressing gown, bleary-eyed and yawning, he is standing by the French Windows looking expectantly out into the garden.

"Morning Tyson," she says and he wags his tail. As he looks up at her, he sees her mouth twitching at the corner and he knows he has dominion. Bridie struggles with the door, which is another part of the routine.

"Oh, this damn door!" she says, and then he's out into the garden, putting down markers as he relieves himself, staring into the low, morning sun and feeling his pupils contract, and sniffing about to discover which creatures have visited in the night.

'That fox has been in again.'

Then he's back to the kitchen, where Bridie is sitting at the table with a cigarette in one hand and a coffee in the other, trying to jump-start her brain. He gives her another expectant look.

"Oh, Tyson. Give me a chance to wake up, will you?"

But that's not good enough, so now he drills into her with his look, forcing her to get up and open a tin, and almost before his dish has touched the floor, he's onto it, and she has to step smartly out of the way.

He loves that first meal of the day. The sweet scent in his powerful nostrils, the even sweeter taste on his long, flexible tongue, and that gloriously satisfying feeling as it passes down his gullet and travels on to his rumbling tum. He is always careful to leave plenty of bits around his muzzle to lick off later at his leisure. Then it's back to the garden to see if that moggy's come in yet.

He's in luck, and she only *just* gets away this time, tail all fluffed up, claws working furiously up the high fence. He watches her bottom disappear over the other side and thinks, again, 'I wish I could do that.' Then it's another circuit of the garden and the selection of a little spot in the sun where he gives his genitals a good lick.

'What a grand way to start the day!' he thinks, but it's all spoilt by the arrival of his bête noir; his nemesis; Reg.

'There he is, standing in the doorway, eyeing me uncertainly. Well, you're right to look uncertain, mate, because as you can see, Bridie hasn't put me on the lead.'

'Bloody Bridie!' thinks Reg. 'She's supposed to put him on the lead and tie him up to the radiator.'

They continue to watch one anther. It's a battle of nerves, and both have a pretty good idea whose is going to snap first, but just for good measure, Tyson curls his lip and emits a distinctly threatening growl.

"You little runt!" says Reg, to hide his humiliation, and turns away. But it's all the same to him really. He still gets paid, even if doesn't walk the dog. He's not going to try and get him on the lead. He's not paid danger-money, after all.

Watching him go, Tyson is thinking, 'This is turning into a brilliant day! Three victories already. First, getting Bridie to feed me when she wanted to finish her fag, then seeing off that cat, and now, besting Reg. Again! How can I top that?'

Well, you're about to, Tyson, because here comes Eric.

'Great!' thinks Tyson, as he hears the bike on the gravel path on the other side of the house, and he's skidded over to the front door even before he's heard the key go in the lock. Then it's lots of jumping up and down, and funny poses with head lowered and keen eyes.

'Look at me, Eric. I'm about to spring up and give you a nip.'

"Tyson – you funny old mutt!" and with that he gives him lots of hefty pats on his strong back and pulls his ears and Tyson is beside himself.

"Where's your tennis ball, Tyson?"

'That's a good idea. I'll just scoot off and get it.'

The day shifts on to late afternoon, and Tyson can't believe his luck, for Eric is still there. Normally he goes just before lunch, but this week Edith's afternoon reader is away and Eric has offered to stand in for him. He is waiting for her now to return from the lavatory, and to keep himself amused, he has, gripped between his knees, a round, empty biscuit tin, while in each hand he holds a large, wooden knitting needle, and as he chants, he drums the needles rhythmically on the tin.

"One bright day in the middle of the night,
Dang dang dagger dagger dang dang dagger dagger
Two dead dogs got up to fight.
Dang dang dagger dagger dang dang dagger dagger
Back to back they faced each other,
Dang dang dagger dagger dang dang dagger dagger
Drew their swords and shot each other.
Dang dang dagger dagger dang dang dagger dagger."

Watching and listening to this dead-dog-doggerel is a real-life canine. Attached by his leash to the radiator, Tyson looks on eagerly, convinced that this is all being done for his very own entertainment. The ancestors on the wall look down disapprovingly. Eric launches into a repeat of the refrain but in the same moment becomes aware of the figure of Edith standing in the doorway. He stops abruptly.

"Oh ... hello, Edith. You were quick."

Hearing that nonsense rhyme again, which she still remembers vaguely from her childhood, her mind goes, instead, to the Blitz, and London ablaze, when there had been many bright days in the middle of the night. She shuffles into the room on her Zimmer.

"I didn't realise you were there," Eric adds awkwardly.

"No. Is it dark in here?"

"Getting that way."

"We're going to need a light on then."

"Yes," Eric replies, putting down his drum and sticks and going to the standard lamp behind Edith's chair. He clicks it on but its glow illuminates little more than the immediate area, leaving the rest of the room still in gloom.

"Here," he says to Edith, and helps her into her chair. Then begins the ritual of wrapping her in rugs and shawls. Try as she might, Edith just can't get the cold out of her old bones. She yearns for summer, and to feel the warmth of the sun on her sightless face.

Eric kneels down to adjust the footstool and is immediately enveloped by a rug thrown by Edith to cover her legs. Oblivious, she continues, "Eric, would you put the cushion on my right foot. It's like ice."

"Sure," comes the muffled reply, and then Eric emerges and does as instructed.

"Better?"

"A little. I think we'd better have the windows closed."

"They are. Here – I'll sort out your head cushion," and he moves to behind the chair. "Alright?"

"Just down a little. ... That's better. Eric, do you think you could massage my shoulders? They're so stiff."

"Sure," and he begins very gently to knead the ancient shoulders, whose bones feel as fragile as a bird's. Concluding that the show is over, Tyson lies down and stretches his back against the skirting board beneath the radiator. Edith closes her glassy-blue eyes.

"Mmm," she murmurs, and for a moment all is silent, save the measured ticking of the old clock.

"I enjoyed your little ditty," she says dreamily.

"Oh ... just some silly school thing."

""One bright day in the middle of the night." I like that."

"It's just a nonsense rhyme."

"No," Edith replies, "it makes perfect sense. I've had bright days, in the middle of the night. ... I liked the drumming too."

"Ah... I used to be a drummer," Eric recalls, "in the cadet force. I was a bugler first. Which worked out as long as I just played with the other buglers. But then I had to do a solo one day, on parade, and they decided to make me a drummer after that."

Eric's hands continue to unravel and untie the knots in the old lady's sinews, and Edith thinks back to a time when her body was supple and strong, and she stood proud and erect on the concert platform, looking out at the myriad faces in the darkened auditorium, awaiting the rise of the conductor's baton.

Suddenly, from the darkening garden, a sweet and mournful tune is heard, as a blackbird just beyond the window flings his last song against the closing of the day, and Edith is projected still further back in time, and she is standing nervously before her classmates, reciting the words of Thomas Hardy that she had learned by heart the evening before. She recites them again now, with perfect recollection.

> ""At once a voice arose among
> The bleak twigs overhead
> In a full-hearted evensong
> Of joy illimited,
> An aged thrush, frail, gaunt and small,
> In blast-beruffled plume,
> Had chosen thus to fling his soul
> Upon the growing gloom.""

There is still music in Edith's voice, Eric thinks, as he too recalls a classroom, and his English master, David Giles, sitting up on the dais, chalk dust on his gown, intoning that very same poem, in such a way as to hold the attention even of the distracted adolescents before him. Rummaging in his memory, for he too studied Hardy, Eric picks his way through, a little less certainly than Edith, the next and last verse of the poem.

""So little cause for carollings
Of such ecstatic sound
Was written on terrestrial things
Afar or nigh around,
That I could think there trembled through
His happy good night air
Some blessed hope whereof he knew
And I was unaware.""

Edith smiles.

"You told me you had a rotten education."

"I did," Eric replies, recalling how his old school, Bancroft's in Essex, even in the 1960's, bore an astonishing resemblance to that in "Tom Brown's Schooldays."

"The worst of it is," Edith continues, "it's just an unpleasant, grating sound to me."

"What is?"

"Birdsong. Or music come to that. You get no pleasure from it when your hearing's like this. Funny way for an opera singer to end up."

Eric remains silent, finding nothing to say in reply to so bleak a statement. All he can do for the old lady in that moment is to try and ease the stiff and aching muscles.

"Mmm ... you have healing hands."

"Good."

"Did you come on your bicycle today?"

"Yes."

Edith sighs contentedly again.

"Mmm. That's much better. Thank you. I could almost have a little nap now."

Eric returns to his chair, taking care to avoid Tyson, who being woken from his doze might conclude that he is about to be taken for a walk he doesn't want and decide to bite the nearest foot. He hasn't forgotten how he was deceived the night he was abandoned in Battersea Park and now, anyone given the task of walking him has to approach with extreme caution. Eric sits and picks up Edith's current book, Beryl Bainbridge's account of the Titanic disaster, "Every Man for Himself," and opens it at the marker.

"How long does it take you to cycle here?"

"About three quarters of an hour. It's a nice ride. I go across the heath."

"I wouldn't want to do that in the dark. ... I used to enjoy cycling. Of course there was much less traffic in those days. Not many people had cars in the thirties. Or forties. You had to be quite well off."

Eric looks up from the book

"Did *you* have a car?"

"Lots. Not all at once, you understand. My favourite was the Armstrong Siddley Hurricane. We went all over Europe in it."

"We?"

"Me and my sister. Of course that was after I lost my sight."

"You drove after you lost your sight?"

"Of course not. My sister did the driving. Though there were one or two occasions. I drove on a beach in Spain. There was no one else about. I scared the living daylights out of her. Got it up to seventy."

"Crikey."

"That was during the days of Franco."

Eric regards her face for a moment. In the confined glow of the standard lamp her thoughts seem more readable. She *is* back on that beach, racing across the sands of her darkened world, her hair wild behind her, her sister screaming at her side.

"How did you lose your sight?"

"Haven't I told you?"

"No. You sort of started once but we got interrupted."

"It was in the war. I was driving an ambulance during an air raid. I was a Fanny you know."

Unable to suppress a smile, Eric attempts to keep it out of his voice.

"Were you?"

"Yes. You know what that is, don't you?"

Eric does, but can't immediately remember its meaning, in the context that Edith is using. She prompts him.

"First Aid Nursing Yeomanry. Used to drive an army truck as well. A three-tonner."

Eric is impressed. First an Armstrong Siddley, now a three-ton truck.

"Gosh," he says.

Eric doesn't just look old-fashioned, he sounds it too, and often uses words like "gosh" and "crikey."

"Anyway, on this particular occasion, I got too close to a landmine. Or it got too close to me. They were sea mines really, but they used to drop them from planes as well. On the end of parachutes. That way they didn't make a crater, and there was terrific lateral damage. ... Fiendishly clever when you think about it."

Edith finds herself reliving that night, more than fifty years before, when her world went dark forever, and she wonders yet again what became of the nurse who was with her in the ambulance. Though she had tried to find out soon after, in the confusion of war, and the turmoil within her own life, she had had no success. So she assumed that she must have been killed, so devastating was the explosion, but she couldn't help but wonder.

What neither she nor Eric knows, nor will ever know, is that they are, just then, in one of those peculiar moments of confluence which happen very occasionally; for the nurse is none other than Eric's own aunt, who had indeed survived and is living out her retirement in a cottage in the Brecon Beacons. She herself relives that night from time to time, in nightmarish detail, for she had been so traumatised by the event that she never allowed herself to speak of it, and each ended up believing the other died that night.

So Eric and Edith sit silently for a moment, quite unaware of the connection between them.

"Well," Edith goes on, "even if you survive the blast from one of those things, you can literally be sucked into the vacuum that follows. So, I shouted to the nurse to get under the truck, and we dived down beneath it, scraping hands and knees. Then I told her to grab hold of something, and we both of us gripped the axle. Then I saw that she was shaking violently, as if she had delirium tremens. I was about to say something to her when she darted out and sprinted away. I shot out after her and was just making a grab for her when the mine detonated."

Eric tries to conjure up the horrific scene.

"The funny thing is, Eric, I never heard the explosion; because I was instantly deafened. I just saw it all happen, as if I was watching a silent film. The truck was plucked up like a matchbox toy and hurled over on its side, and the very last thing I saw on this earth was the nurse's uniform being stripped from her body as the blast caught her. Then the fuel tank exploded, and I just saw a vivid, blood-red film ... And then total blackness."

Eric stares at her. The nightmarish picture she has painted is almost unimaginable to him

"And that's how I lost my peepers."

The matter-of-factness in her tone is all at odds with the enormity of what she has said, and Eric is completely at a loss.

"I don't think I'd know how to carry on," he murmurs.

"Worse things happen at sea," she continues, as though she is recalling having once got a bit of grit in her eye. "They soon sorted me out at St. Dunstan's. That's the rehabilitation place down near Brighton, but of course the career was over. In opera, that is. But I carried on in concerts. And making records."

"You made records?"

Eric is continually having to revise, upwards, his impression of Edith. Here is someone who has clearly packed a considerable amount into her life, even after being so severely disabled. Of course the money must have helped, he reflects. Old money too he guesses, looking at the ancestors on the walls. Edith has all the self-assurance of the *grande dame*; of someone who has never had to consider cost.

"Yes," she continues, "there's an old set of 78's around here somewhere. I find them hard to listen to now."

Edith then presses a button at her side which, as well as raising the chair-back slightly, seems to return her to the present.

"Shall we carry on with the book?"

"Yes, I've got it here."

He leans towards the little pool of light.

"We're up to page 140. Er ... "I grew cold cowering in the shadows of that room reeking of lavender. In spite of the ghastly nature of my predicament – any moment I might be discovered – I burned with a jealousy so fierce that I had to clench my jaws to keep my teeth from grinding. Not that I would have been heard. How foolishly I had deceived myself in thinking that I desired more than a casual intrigue of the sort often described by more fortunate men – for now, listening to those voices which rose and fell and started up again with horrid definition, I shuddered with revulsion. It wasn't the words themselves that shocked me – "I want your lovely prick.""

Eric comes to an abrupt halt and, his breath held, throws an alarmed glance at Edith. Her head has lolled forward and she appears to have dozed off, but just to reassure himself, Eric calls her name. There is no response. Intrigued himself by the story now, Eric continues, aloud, for he knows that if he stops, she will probably wake up.

""It wasn't the words themselves that shocked me – "I want your lovely prick, nor his reply – "Show me your lovely cunt ...""

Again he casts a glance at Edith, but she doesn't appear to have stirred. He goes on.

""... but the context in which they were used. Such expressions belonged to anger, mockery, contempt. How foul...""

"Oh dear," Edith cuts in, rousing herself. "I fell asleep. It must have been your massage."

"Not to worry," Eric says with considerable relief.

"Can we go back a bit?"

Panic seizes him.

"Er ... why don't we just carry on?"

"No, I'll only get confused then."

"Right. ... Er ... I'm not sure how far back to go."

"I remember something about "burning with jealousy.""

Eric looks despairingly at the text. He has no choice but begin again, but when he comes to the awkward bit, his normally clear voice becomes, for Edith, indistinct.

"What was that? I can't hear you."

He is forced to take another run at it. This time he keeps the volume up but rattles it out at such speed that each word collides with the next.

"Eric – you're going much too fast. I missed that completely."

He has to admit defeat, and makes a mental note that when they move on to another book he is going to inspect it minutely first, word by word. He resumes, his articulation impeccable this time.

""It wasn't the words themselves that shocked me – "I want your lovely prick" – nor his reply – "Show me your lovely cunt," but the context in which they were used.""

Not daring to look at Edith and staring fixedly at the page, Eric ploughs on to the end of the paragraph.

""I shamelessly pressed myself against the jam of the door and timed my groans with theirs. It was over for me quicker than for them, and I was left, a blind voyeur, scrabbling for memories to blot out the continuing din of their beastly coupling.""

Eric pauses and holds his breath. The silence in the room is absolute, and it seems that even the clock has stopped and is waiting.

"I'm sorry," he says. "I didn't realise it was ... that sort of book."

The silence continues. Edith stares before her, her face once more a mask, then breezily she says, "I'm enjoying it. I like her directness."

Eric starts breathing again, and the clock resumes its ticking.

"And of course there's the personal interest," she goes on.

"Personal interest?"

"Yes. My uncle was First Officer on the Titanic."

She has just done it to him again – lobbed in with pure nonchalance something utterly extraordinary.

"Your uncle was First Officer on the Titanic?"

"Yes – didn't I tell you?"

How could they have got to page 140 without her telling him something like that, Eric wonders.

"In fact," she goes on, "he ended up as Second Officer, because the Chief First Officer – of the White Star Line – who was going to retire, decided to stay on, just for the maiden voyage, so my uncle became Second Officer."

"Did he survive?"

"Yes. Miraculously. He was the one Kenneth More played in that film."

"Oh yes," Eric recalls. "Er ... "A Night to Remember.""

"That's the one. He was a remarkable man, my uncle. A cousin of mine got married to a bad sort. He wasn't at all interested in women. Quite the opposite, in fact. She was dreadfully unhappy but couldn't get out of it. So my uncle went along one night with a ladder and hauled her out of the bedroom window."

"Yes. A remarkable man."

"He wrote a book about his life."

Eric wishes that *he* had the ability to write a book, because it seems to him in that moment that he has an ideal subject before him.

"I used to have it here. But now we can't find it any more. Things have a way of disappearing in this place."

"Do they?"

"Yes. Just look around the walls. There were some magnificent pictures here. Family portraits. An engraving of my great grandfather at a military banquet with the Duke of Wellington. After Waterloo."

"And it's ... just gone?"

"Yes. Along with a lot of other things."

"What other things?"

"Oh, jewellery for instance. I had some very precious items. Things that had been in the family for generations."

"And you've no idea where they've got to?"

"None."

Of all the fantastic things the old lady has told him that afternoon, that last is the only one that Eric does not believe. He scrutinises her face again. It tells nothing it does not want to tell, but he wonders if she isn't at that moment thinking of a very likely suspect within the household.

As he watches her, the blank look becomes one of discomfort, and Edith starts to shift about in her chair.

"Are you alright?" Eric asks.

"I'm just massaging my bladder."

"Ah."

"If I can just put it off a little longer. ... Oh, it's so tedious. I've only just *been*. Don't ever get this old, Eric."

Eric promises not to.

"And I was perfectly alright until they *fixed my hips*. What a fix! Now I can't get anywhere without the Zimmer. It's galling to be this helpless."

"I don't think I'd describe you as helpless, Edith," and Eric thinks again about the power of money. Without it, Edith would probably have died years ago, forgotten and neglected in an old folk's home. But here she is, her little contingent of helpers about her, living in one of London's most exclusive quarters.

As Eric is thinking this, Tyson, though fast asleep, lets out a series of strangled yelps. He is having a dream, and in this dream, while still attached by his leash to the radiator, he has leapt through the nearby open window and is now suspended just two feet above the ground, turning slowly on the lead and being steadily throttled. This is not pure fantasy. In his waking life, Tyson regularly makes a bid for freedom through that tantalisingly open window, forgetting every time that he is still attached to the radiator, and each time he only saves himself from a good hanging with a furious, strangled barking which eventually brings someone to the rescue. The last had been Eric, who approached the thrashing creature with trepidation.

"Oh, is Tyson here?" Edith asks.

"Yes. He's by the radiator. I think he's having a bad dream."

"Poor old Tyson. ... He didn't damage Reg too badly did he? The other day?"

Eric smiles as he recalls the incident.

"No, just superficial stuff really. Though he did have to have a tetanus jab."

"Reg or Tyson?"

Edith smiles, and thinks for a moment.

"I think he must have had a difficult childhood."

"Reg or Tyson?"

The old lady giggles like a schoolgirl.

"How did you come by him?" Eric continues. "Tyson I mean."

"Battersea Dog's Home."

"Ah."

"He's had a go at *me* once or twice," Edith says.

"Has he? ... Yes. Me too."

"I'm sorry about that, Eric."

"It's alright. I've learnt to move quicker than him. Just."

"Reg of course doesn't have that ability. Moving quickly I mean. So it's particularly unfortunate Tyson has developed such a … taste for him. He seems to have taken to *you* though," she adds.

"It's just because I make a fuss of him."

"We've grown old together," she reflects. "That old mutt and I. Reg, on the other hand … well, it's no wonder Tyson hates Reg, the way he treats him. Did you know that on one of his so-called walks this week, which often entails Tyson being tied up outside a pub, Reg got so drunk that he forgot what he was doing there, and just staggered off home, leaving the poor dog tied to a post outside."

"Yes. I heard something about that."

"It was a neighbour who found him. And one of the coldest days of the year apparently."

"Yes. It was pretty cold."

Edith's expression clouds again.

"Why do I keep him on?" And then, in answer to her own question, "I don't know. There's something helpless about him really."

Eric maintains a diplomatic silence. There are points on which he and the old lady simply don't agree.

"He's quite harmless, of course," Edith adds.

Eric looks again at the book, thinking that if he carries on with the reading he might move them off the subject, but in the same moment Edith shifts uneasily in her chair again.

"I really don't think I can hold it off much longer, Eric. Could you help me to the Stannah?"

"Sure," says Eric, as Edith's chair hums into life. The noise wakes Tyson, who looks about him, bewildered for a moment, but then relief sweeps over him as he realises that he is not being hanged after all.

"Oh dear," Edith sighs as she grasps the Zimmer, "I think I may have left it too late."

Eric guides the Zimmer and its sorry cargo across the floor to the foot of the stairs.

'No,' he thinks as they go. 'Better not to get that old.'

*

February, 2002. Another endless winter.
Evening. Downstairs.

I am on the deck of the Titanic, in a ball gown and a
fur coat, waiting to be put in a lifeboat. Our uncle is
there of course, keeping everyone in order. He is being
very cheerful, but I can see the grim expression he is
hiding. He knows there aren't enough lifeboats.

And you are there too, Sis, also in a fur coat, and you
have the head of my dog. I have never seen the head of
my dog, but I have felt it, so I know what it looks like.
You are being very calm and stoical, which I don't
think you would have been if you had really been
there. I recall your fondness for histrionics. Why I was
the one to take to the stage and not you I don't know.
Anyway, we are put in a boat – Uncle sees to that
– and lowered towards the inky sea, where people are
bobbing about and crying out. As we go down we hear
the orchestra on the deck playing "Nearer My God to
Thee." (I wonder if they really did that? I know Uncle
said they did, but then he always liked a good story).

How on earth did Uncle survive it? I can't see him
getting into a boat while there were others who
couldn't, but then I remember him saying there had
to be a crewman in every boat, so perhaps that's how it

came about. I know he describes it all in his book but I can't remember it now. I have forgotten so many things. I am regressing. Going back to a time before I knew anything.

Anyway, Sis, I'm afraid this dream doesn't turn out too well. As we are clunking down the side of the ship, which looks like a great black cliff in the darkness, I am standing in the prow, singing along with the orchestra, and getting everyone else to do the same, when suddenly one of the ropes gives way and we are all pitched out. The icy water takes our breath away, and as we sink beneath the surface, I see your face in front of mine, your dog's face, and you give me that look of yours, and you say, "Well what have you gone and done now?" And as you sink still further, leaving me behind – you are a bit overweight in this dream, Sis – the last thing I hear you say is, "And I'd only just bought this coat."

That's when I woke up. Which I think I must have done deliberately, as I wasn't much enjoying the dream by then. And I lay there for a while shivering, and I thought to myself, 'That's all that's left to you now, Edith. Dreams.' Sad, isn't it, Sis. Pathetic really. You were lucky to go when you did. You were spared all that. Let me tell you, there is nothing worse than being dependent on others. It saps your self-esteem. And have you seen those "others?" Yes of course you have. I felt you about this afternoon. You were having a little nose around. I heard you muttering, "What's happened to all the pictures? Where's Ma and Pa, and Grandma and Grandpa, and Great Grandma and Great Grandpa?" You did go on a bit, Sis.

Well, I can tell you. We have the dog walker to thank for that. Did you know, I have a dog walker who is a felon? He is also a drunk. In addition, I have a housekeeper who is neurotic and a nurse who is insane. My dog is aggressive and unpredictable – though he seems to defer to the venerable old girl and doesn't bite her that often – and as for the reader … well I haven't really worked him out yet. He seems fairly normal, but I don't suppose he'll remain so if he stays here much longer. And that's it, Sis. That's my motley crew. My Fred Karno's Army. That's what I have to show for ninety plus years on this earth. I can't see, I can barely hear, and I can't walk, except with the help of the Zimmer. My hips are buggered, thanks to that so-called specialist. The only thing that hasn't happened to me yet is incontinence, and I have had one or two close calls in that department. So you see Sis – you really are much better off out of it.

Unity Geest bursts from her doorway onto the street. Unity Geest always bursts from her doorway, for she is always late, whether she is on her way to work, going to meet a friend, attending a service at the Unity Church or simply going shopping. She is forever finding something else to do. "Displacement activity."

She hobbles halfway down the street, clutching her bag, which seems about to spill its contents onto the pavement, stops, mumbles an oath to herself, and hobbles back the way she has just come. This is another part of her routine. She seldom leaves home without immediately having to return to collect something that she has forgotten. Back at her doorway, she is then unable to find her keys. They are usually in her bag, unless she has left them inside, but cluttered as her bag is, they can be hard to find. Her frustration rising, she empties its contents onto the street and, on hands and knees, fishes around. Finding them, she unlocks the door and dashes back upstairs to her flat.

This is the council flat to which she moved soon after her arrival in Whitechapel all those years before. She looks uncertainly about the room, having by now forgotten what it was she came back for. It is a chaotic scene. Hanging above the sink are bra, tights and knickers, that she hand-washed the previous night, and in the sink are unwashed breakfast things that she just dumped there in her dash out of the flat. The bed is unmade.

Evenings are a calmer time for Unity. It is then that she takes stock of the day, and attempts to get some order back into her disordered life. She washes out her smalls, which are anything but, prepares herself a meal, and generally tidies up while waiting for it to cook. All this to the accompaniment of gospel singing, played louder than her neighbours would like, on her Ghetto Blaster. She then leisurely eats her meal, washes up, and sits by her window reading the Bible, or a romantic novel. Romance has hardly figured in her life, and never will now, she knows, so she lives it out vicariously in those paperbacks. Sometimes she stands on her eighth-floor balcony looking out over the roofs of London, and imagines herself back on top of Hackleton Cliff, gazing out over the Caribbean. Occasionally, she goes to the pub on the corner to meet a friend from the church, but as most of them are teetotal this doesn't happen very often. She then kneels by her bed and says her prayers, always remembering her estranged son and her mother who, she supposes, will be dead by now. Then she snuggles between the sheets and sleeps an innocent sleep until the alarm clock shatters her peace, and she leaps up, cursing herself for not having set the alarm to go off earlier, and runs around like the proverbial headless chicken.

Still unable to remember what it is she has returned for, Unity dashes out, this time forgetting to take her keys with her, and hurries down to the corner of the street, just in time to see not just one but two buses pulling away.

Fifteen minutes later she is still standing at the bus stop, an anger rising in her. When her bus arrives she is the first on.

"You's supposed to come every ten minutes," she growls at the conductor. He gives her a weary look, for Unity has become a well-known figure on that route.

"An' why," she goes on, working herself up still further, "you always goes along in twos and threes? What's the matter? You get lonely or somethin'?"

The conductor gives her a ticket. Unity rummages in her bag, looking for her purse, realising, in the same moment, that she has left her keys indoors. She looks angrily at the conductor, as if it is somehow his fault.

"I get to the bus stop in good time – I know when you's supposed to be there – and what do I see? Three buses, all the same, jus' pullin' away together."

Already, Unity has adjusted reality to fit in with the story that she will tell the Mistress when she arrives. In this story, her lateness has become punctuality, and two missed buses have become three.

For the rest of the journey she conducts a conversation with herself about the inefficiency of London Transport, the traffic congestion, which, though no worse than usual, is, apparently, "somethin' shockin' today; and gonna make me even more later." Her fellow passengers, also used to Unity's diatribes, continue to look at their papers or stare out of the window, as if there isn't this demented woman among them, talking to herself for the best part of half an hour.

So, by the time Unity arrives at Edith's, a full three quarters of an hour late, she has worked herself up into a lather of self-righteous indignation, not just over London's public transport and its congestion, but over the sorry state of the world in general.

One of Edith's clocks is chiming twelve. It has, for her, been an endless winter, as are all winters for her now. The cold is always there, in her bones, and she can sense, if not see, the darkness of the days. She feels as if she is in Death's waiting room, and has been there for some time, but no one has come through to say, "We're ready for you now." She so wants to hear those words, but she fears them also, and this is an acute dilemma for her; both to yearn for and be terrified by one and the same thing.

"Wake up, my girl! I try turn you. Wake up!"

Unity gives the Zimmer a sharp tug and twists it round, and Edith is rudely brought back to the mundane present and the routine reality of her morning exercise; back and forth, back and forth across the hall floor, the boards creaking beneath her creaking bones, dragged along on the chariot of her walking frame.

"Unity. Stop jerking me!"

"I no jerk. You jerk," and another clock begins chiming twelve.

In the sitting room, Bridie looks from the doorway, across which Edith and Unity intermittently pass, to Eric, and smiles a knowing smile, even though he is looking down at the newspaper. Bridie is sitting proudly on the Mistress's brand new chair, which has just cost Edith almost four thousand pounds at a shop in Wigmore Street (not far from her old haunt, the Wigmore Hall) that specialises in items for the disabled. She thinks about the salesman there, a man of about her own age, though not as well preserved in her opinion, and what he said to them – herself, Edith & Eric; that the chair could do everything but sing to you. She purses her lips and is about to confide a little something to Eric when the mournful sound of a saxophone floats in from a distant part of the house. Bridie gives a theatrical sigh.

"Why that man can't practise at home I've no idea."

To Eric, Reg's ability to play the saxophone is his one, redeeming feature.

"I quite like the sound of the saxophone," he replies, attempting to keep on the more neutral ground of the instrument rather than the person playing it, but Bridie is not to be diverted.

"Why she keeps him on is utterly beyond me. He can't even walk the dog without creating a major incident."

"Why does she keep him on?" asks Eric, voicing a question he has asked himself many times.

"Well ... I don't really know if I ought to tell you this ..."

Eric waits, for clearly she is going to.

"Well ... just between you and me ... we think he has some sort of hold over her."

Eric is intrigued.

"What sort of hold?"

Her eyes twinkling, Bridie leans forward in the chair.

"Well … it might just be a rumour, you understand, but when her sister died, she came into a lot more money, and she decided to go away for a while, and she took Reg with her, because she needed someone to look after her – the blind leading the blind if you ask me – and they went off to the Caribbean, because Unity had told her what a beautiful place Barbados was, and apparently, one night, they both had a little too much to drink, and well," and here she becomes a little coy, which she is rather good at, "you know how one thing can lead to another."

Eric does, but he can't imagine it between two such disparate people.

"Reg and Edith?"

"Not a very likely couple, I'll admit. And it may just be tittle-tattle. But then …"

Eric is almost dumbfounded.

"Reg and Edith!?" he repeats, with still more incredulity.

Bridie leans closer to Eric.

"Edith has led a very sheltered life," she says.

"I thought she was pretty experienced," Eric replies, thinking of the various tales she has told him.

"Not in *every* way," Bridie sums up, tapping the side of her nose.

From the hallway, over the wailing of the saxophone, comes the sharp, authoritarian tone of the Mistress.

"Unity! Stop jerking me!"

Edith feels tired. Her day has hardly begun and she is weary already; and she feels her authority draining away. As if in confirmation, Unity snaps back, "I no jerk – you jerk!" and then she continues to herself, as if Edith isn't there, "Oh she really playin' me up this day!"

Pushing herself up on the walking frame, Edith says, "When I am present, kindly do not refer to me in the third person."

For a moment Unity is confused.

"What you talkin' about – third person? There's jus' two of us."

"Never mind."

"You really give me disdress today."

Now it is Edith's turn to be confused.

"What dress have I given you?"

"No, disdress – you give me disdress!"

Edith thinks for a moment.

"Why should I give you this dress?" she asks, genuinely perplexed. "I've only just put it on."

"What's the matter wit' you. You no speak the Queen's English?" and with that, Unity gives another sharp tug on the frame, more to express her exasperation than to project her mistress in any particular direction.

"Don't jerk!"

"One day I give you a real good jerkin,' my girl. Yeh – you just be jerk chicken when Unity finish with you."

Partly because the phrase "Jerk Chicken" is unfamiliar to her, and partly because everything she says seems to elicit another aggressive and perplexing response from the other side of the Zimmer, Edith decides to remain silent. In the sitting room, where conversation has been suspended for the duration of the floor show taking place in the hallway, Bridie looks away from the door and, tapping the arms of the chair, says to Eric, "Do you like the new chair, Eric?"

"It's very impressive."

"It ought to be – the amount she paid for it."

But it isn't the chair that Bridie wishes to discuss.

"D'you remember the salesman?" she asks, her eyes twinkling again.

"The one with the bad breath?"

Bridie seems a little put out by this.

"Did he? I can't say that I noticed. Anyway – he asked me out to dinner."

"*Did* he?"

Eric wonders when the salesman found the opportunity to do this, with himself and Edith also present. He recalls also that the salesman had a distinctive paunch, as well as bad breath.

"I think he wanted to get chummy," Bridie continues. "Anyway, I said, "No." … Well, I've enough complication in my life."

As Unity, the Zimmer and Edith pass across the doorway once more, they hear the nurse saying for the umpteenth time, "I fed up wi'dis job. I go back to Barbados."

Edith is fed up too, with hearing that veiled threat.

"Well, why don't you?" she shoots back. "Nobody's forcing you to stay."

Unity stares at her, open-mouthed. She wasn't expecting that. When she talks of going back to Barbados, she wants people to say, "Oh, don't do that, we'd miss you so much." They never do, but it's what she wants to hear.

While Unity is stunned into silence, Edith presses on.

"I'm sure we'll all be able to manage without you."

The clock in the hall ticks on, and then decides that *its* time has come to strike midday, though it is by now a quarter past. Still struggling for a response, Unity blurts out, "Well, we all know about *you* an' Barbados."

"What?" Edith calls back, just as Tyson adds a chorus of barks to the chiming clock, and the echoing saxophone, which has become maudlin in tone. Unity chuckles to herself.

"Oh yeh! We know all about that."

"I can't hear a word you're saying. Where's Tyson?"

"He's in the garden, Edith," Bridie calls out, adding then to Eric, "Probably wanted to get a bit of peace and quiet."

"Good Morning, Bridie," Edith calls back.

"Good *Afternoon*, Edith," Bridie corrects.

"Yes, we're very late again," Edith replies, as much to Unity as Bridie.

"No, I've enough complication in my life," Bridie resumes to Eric. "That daughter of mine – she'll be the death of me."

Eric looks up from the paper.

"What's happened?"

"She came round in a cab last night. A cab! And she's on Social Security! You can imagine who ended up paying. And she threw up in the back of it, she was that drunk. I had to pay double."

Eric has met Bridie's daughter, Emily. She has, he thinks, inherited her mother's highly-strung quality, and more besides. She seems unstable. She can be quite charming to you in one moment and vitriolic the next. She is as unpredictable as Tyson.

"Mind you," Bridie goes on, "she hasn't got an easy life. That special school her Tom's at. Do you know what the headmaster said to her?"

Eric has also met Bridie's grandson, Tom, who has been diagnosed autistic. To Eric he seemed a perfectly normal little boy, whose only real handicap is his mother.

"What?" Eric asks.

"He said, "What you need is a really good poke.""

"Really?"

Eric is starting to take an interest in the headmaster.

"I ask you – is that a thing for an educated man to say?"

Out in the hallway, Unity is chuckling again. Like a dog that has just found a juicy bone and isn't about to relinquish it, she presses on.

"Oh yes. We know all about you in Barbados."

"I don't know what you're talking about. I think you'd better take me to my chair."

As she says this, her long pants slide into view, below the hem of her skirt.

"Your knickers is comin' down."

"Oh dear," Edith replies, reflecting on the indignities one has to suffer in old age. "Can you pull them up for me? Somebody's taken the elastic out of them."

Edith genuinely believes this. Unable to see, or hear properly, what is going on around her, she has moments of paranoia.

"Now, why anybody do that?"

"I've no idea," Edith replies, adding darkly, "Strange things happen in this house."

"You tellin' me!" and Unity hitches up the wayward knickers.

"Thank you."

As they appear in the doorway, Eric begins preparing for the old lady.

"This woman can't keep her knickers on," Unity murmurs, loud enough for Bridie and Eric, but not for Edith to make out.

"What?" Edith says.

"An' we know she no keep them on in Barbados."

"What!?" Edith says again, for it infuriates her when she feels that her impairment is being taken advantage of.

"Unity, I don't think we wish to hear that story now," Bridie cuts in, and then adds quietly to Eric, "That's what I was telling you about."

"Why is everyone whispering!?" says Edith, who is getting thoroughly exasperated. "Eric," she continues, "could you do the chair for me? I don't think I'm ever going to get used to it."

"Sure," says Eric, picking up the new remote control. It has a confusing array of buttons, but he's been rehearsing with it each day since it arrived.

"You got more money than sense, my girl."

Talk of the new chair reminds Bridie of what she has not yet imparted to Unity.

"Did you know that salesman asked me out? The one who sold us the chair."

"No!" Unity exclaims.

As she says this she leans forward, bends her knees and slaps her hands on her thighs.

'She's got a good line in pantomime gestures,' thinks Eric, but Bridie is less impressed.

"Well, I don't know why you're so surprised."

"He really got the hots for you!"

""Got the hots?"" Edith queries, having just been mechanically lowered into the chair.

"Is that alright?" Eric asks her.

"Just let it down a little more, would you?"

The new electric motor hums.

"That's better."

"I'll go and get your drinks," says Bridie, stepping through the doorway, displeased that news of her ability still to attract has failed to impress.

"Thank you, Bridie," Edith calls after her. "Oh dear, we're so late this morning."

"Yes, we'd better get on," Eric replies. "I'll just finish your blankets," and he tucks them in under Edith's knees.

"I've just been opening my bowels," Edith informs Eric.

"Ah. ... Have you?"

Edith regularly gives him such rudimentary information, and he never knows quite what to do with it.

"See you later, Edith," and with that Unity steps into the hallway and clatters across the bare boards towards the kitchen, in the hope that Bridie will offer her a Scotch. Edith pauses for what she judges to be long enough and then says, "Has she gone?"

"Yes."

"Thank goodness for that. If ever someone were inappropriately named. Unity! The woman's totally fragmented. I keep finding her in corners talking to herself."

"I once knew someone called Serena. She was anything but," Eric says. "Totally neurotic in fact. Is it true," he goes on, "that Unity's surname is Geest?"

"That's correct. As in the bananas."

Eric chuckles.

"Are you sure she hasn't made it up?"

"Why would she do that?"

"It just sounds so unlikely."

He tries it again.

"Unity Geest. ... I think I quite like it though."

"Yes. Well ... thanks to Unity Geest we're running late."

"Yes."

Taking his prompt, Eric settles into his chair and flicks open the paper. Just then Bridie comes breezily back.

"Here are your drinks, boys and girls."

"Oh, thank you, Bridie," Edith says, as the housekeeper places one by Edith and one by Eric, and then sails back out. Eric has only just begun reciting the headlines when another figure appears in the doorway.

"Morning, Edith."

Eric looks up. Reg is clutching an envelope and looking craven.

'He's after something,' thinks Eric.

"Oh Lord! What is it now?" Edith wails.

"It's Reg," says Reg.

"What is it, Reg? We're very late."

"Won't take long. I just wondered if I could use the phone. It's just a local call."

"Yes, of course. But use the phone in the next room."

"Right. Thanks."

Reg hovers for a moment, then sidles over to Eric.

"D'you think you could read her this letter?" he says, proffering the envelope. "It's from Hedda."

Eric has not had the pleasure of meeting Hedda, but knows precisely who she is – Reg's girlfriend. The idea of Reg having such a thing as a girlfriend Eric finds incongruous.

"Don't *you* want to read it?" Eric replies, not wanting to get involved in this.

"No, I'd rather you did."

Reg places the envelope on Eric's side table and is about to go when he notices Eric's drink.

"How are you today, Edith?" he says, suddenly very genial, and at the same time picking up the glass.

Eric watches him steadily.

"Oh fine, Reg. How are you?" says Edith, quite unaware of the charade taking place.

"Fine," Reg replies.

He raises the glass to his lips, but then something seems to stir in the fog of his brain. The glass hovers.

"We're running a bit late, Reg," Edith reminds him.

"Right," he says, hesitating still. Eric continues to watch him.

"Right," he repeats.

There is a further pause, and Edith senses that something is going on.

"In the next room, Reg. Use the phone in the next room."

"Right. Yes. ... Yes. I'll just go and make that call," and finally relinquishing the glass, he scuttles from the room, leaving Eric smiling after him.

"Let's get on, Eric."

"Yes. Er ... Reg has given me a letter he wants me to read to you."

"Dear Lord! I don't know why I bother to buy a newspaper."

"D'you want me to leave it?" Eric asks eagerly.

"No. Go on – read it."

"OK."

Taking a penknife from his pocket, Eric slits open the envelope. This is one of his little idiosyncrasies, inherited from his father. Envelopes should not be opened roughly with thumb or finger. He scans the childlike hand before him.

"It's from Hedda. ... "Dear Edith, I do hope you are well. The reason I am writing is that I feel I have to express my feelings about Reg's situation with you. Now that you have cut his hours down, as he no longer reads for you, obviously he is less well off financially. In addition, I understand that you have given him an annuity, in recognition of his long and faithful service to you. This, of course, is no more than he deserves, but I wonder if it is as <u>much</u> as he deserves.""

"What!?"

"D'you want me to carry on?"

Eric had been right not to want to become involved with this.

"Certainly."

Throughout the recitation, Eric has heard the low murmur of Reg's voice into the phone in the next room. Suddenly the voice is raised.

"I said I want the *international* operator!"

Eric glances at Edith, wondering if she has heard. 'This local call,' he thinks, 'is going to cost her something.' But the old lady's expression remains impassive and unreadable. Eric resumes the unwanted task.

""When you consider just how much he has done for you over the years ...""

"I've already given you the number!" Reg shouts from the other room, clearly getting quite worked up.

"What's going on out there?" Edith asks.

"It's Reg on the phone."

"... Carry on," Edith instructs, but Reg's voice breaks in again.

"It didn't work. That's why I'm talking to you!" Reg shouts.

"Is he trying to communicate *without* the phone?" Edith asks dryly.

Eric ploughs on.

""I'm sure you will feel he should be properly rewarded and that, perhaps on reflection, ten thousand pounds a year is not sufficient.""

Eric stares with incredulity at the scrappy piece of paper before him. He had no idea Reg was receiving this ex-gratia payment. 'What on earth for?' he wonders.

The raised voice is heard again from the next room.

"The number I've just given you is in Catalonia. That's Spain in case you didn't know."

"Go on, Eric," Edith says, keen to get it over with.

"Yes. Sorry. ... "I know Reg told you too about all the extra expense we have had lately. Anyway, I hope you don't mind me saying all this to you, but I felt it only right, particularly as Reg doesn't always speak up for himself in the way he should.""

Eric hadn't noticed Reg having any problem in the speaking-up-for-oneself department, and he glances again at Edith to check her reaction. Reg's voice sings out, all oily bonhomie now.

"Hedda! Is that you? ... It's Reg. ... I said it's Reg!"

How galling it is for him that the woman with whom he has been sharing a bed for the last twenty years hasn't recognised his voice.

Edith says wearily, "Is there much more of this ... *letter*?"

"No. Nearly there. ... "I do hope I'll have the opportunity to come and see you again soon. All my love -""

"Hedda!" Reg shouts.

""Hedda,"" Eric concludes.

Reg becomes more placatory and quieter, but he is still audible to Eric.

"I was just phoning to see how you were. See how you're coping with all that Spanish sunshine."

"Is that it?" Edith asks.

"Yes."

"Yes, I know it's winter there." Reg's voice is rising again. "It's frigging winter here too. ... Well thank you and fuck you!"

Edith winces, and the phone in the next room is slammed down. Eric hears Reg stamping through the hallway and off to a more distant room. Moments later the saxophone is echoing through the house once more, this time with a sharp and angry edge to it. In response, Tyson begins howling outside. Edith reaches for her Scotch.

"Paddington Station would be more restful than this," she says.

*

February, 2002. Late evening. In the living room. Still cold. Or is it I?

I see little grains of sand, issuing minutely one by one through the neck of the timer. There is little left in the top and the bottom is almost full. People don't understand the value of time. Perhaps I didn't understand its value until I realised it was running out. If that so-called nurse keeps me waiting one more time I have determined to sack her. No one else would have her — she's as mad as a bag of frogs. My sister asked me why I put up with it.

"And why on earth," she said, "do you tolerate that man?"

Meaning Reg of course. I do wish she'd leave me alone sometimes. She bossed me around enough in life, and she's still at it. I couldn't think of an answer. Not one that she would understand.

"It's all about loyalty, Sis," I started to say, and immediately trailed off. I don't think it means anything to her. She was loyal to me, of course, but that's different. She wouldn't think of being loyal to a bunch of menials, as she would put it. But I do. They've all had twisted lives. That's something I can empathise with. I don't know so much about Eric, but I know something about the rest of them. Reg, with that chip on his shoulder; Unity, so insecure she borders on the paranoid; Bridie, only loved once and she's been looking for someone else ever since; and Tyson, twice abandoned, so no wonder he doesn't trust anyone.

"Well, Sis," I say, "I believe in standing by people."

She gives me that look again. The other one. The one where one of her eyebrows goes up and there's a smile on her lips that could curdle milk.

"They're hardly your sort," she says.

Oh dear – here we go again.

"Sis, there is only one thing worse than a snob, and that's a dead snob."

This seems to throw her, and I have a rare moment of sisterly silence. Needless to say it doesn't last long.

"Edith," she says, "I think that man has some sort of hold over you."

She won't leave it alone.

The eyebrow, I notice, has gone even higher. I would smack her if she existed. I am about to say something lame like "I don't know what you're talking about" when it suddenly occurs to me that she was probably there! She's everywhere after all – Ubiquitous Sis – so she was probably on Barbados, looking down on the whole sordid business. This gives me further pause for thought. What else has she seen me doing?

Anyway ... I'm damned if I'm going to operate on her level.

"Sis," I say, "I simply can't think of another way of putting it. I believe in standing by people. Even people like Reg. Whatever he's done."

"But Edith, we know what he's done." (So she was there!)

I am silent. What can I say? She's done it again. She's managed to have the last word.

As with Tyson, so with Reg it is hard to discern when his typical day begins, because it isn't clear when the previous one ended.

He is usually slumped on the sofa, fairly drunk, and staring bleary-eyed at whatever happens to be on the television. It doesn't matter much what it is, and in the morning he will have no recollection of what it was. Unless, perhaps, it was a jazz programme.

His experience of jazz these days is vicarious. He never really got back into it after prison. He had lost most of his contacts, and by the time he came out other musicians had taken his place. Additionally, he found himself shunned by so-called friends who found his pathetic attempt to rob a post office an act of incredible stupidity. On top of that, but unbeknown to him now, his girlfriend, Hedda, will soon take herself off to live in Spain, and will make no pretence that it isn't to get away from him.

Stretched out on his sofa now, if he could but grasp it, Reg would know that he was seriously depressed. If he were to take himself to a psychiatrist he would be clinically diagnosed as such, and treated, and perhaps the treatment would alleviate his depression, but it wouldn't tackle the underlying condition: the personality disorder, which is untreatable.

Reg is a psychopath, in the psychiatric sense of the word, in that he is out of touch with his emotional side, and he feels no sense of responsibility for his actions. This doesn't necessarily make him dangerous, to others, but he is a danger to himself, in that the depression is causing him to neglect himself, and his physical health is suffering. His heavy drinking has caused his liver to take on the consistency of an old shoe, and his smoking has left him with a rasping cough and a shortness of breath. He has little exercise, save when he succeeds in taking Tyson for a walk, and very often that ends prematurely, with the dog tied up outside a pub.

Around him now, as he starts to doze off, there are discarded take-away containers, empty lager cans and overflowing ashtrays. Beyond, in the kitchen that hasn't been cleaned for weeks, the sink is piled high with unwashed dishes, mugs and glasses.

His eyes are closed now, his cheek is pressed against a cushion, his mouth has fallen open and saliva is dribbling out. In three or four hour's time the need to urinate will wake him, and he will open his eyes and stare about uncomprehendingly for a moment, wondering where he is. The television will still be on, and as he takes in the squalor about him, he will say, "You've really got to get a grip, Reg."

But he can't. He hasn't got the willpower, and although he has the inclination, it is sapped by the belief that this is all somebody else's fault – Hedda's, Eric's, Edith's – anyone but him.

Between nine and ten in the morning, long after it has got light, he will stagger back to the lavatory, then into the kitchen, where he puts the kettle on and splashes water on his face, then he will sit at the uncleared table, and puff on his cigarette, between sips of coffee and lager.

He will be late for work and the old lady will chide him. He will smile and shrug it off, knowing that she couldn't bring herself to get rid of him. He is set up there for life, though with regard to himself and Edith – by far his senior – it is no longer clear who will survive whom.

"You've really got to get a grip, Reg," he says to himself again, as he makes his unsteady way home.

... It is now evening at Edith's. The windows of the main living room have not been cleaned for some time. Bridie has more or less given up the unequal struggle against the accumulation of grime; and anyway, she reasons, what does it matter, if the Mistress can't see it anyway?

Still, the windows glow dully in the moonlight, casting a suffused glow into the darkened room. Outside, the lawn is bathed in a ghostly, blue light, as are the heights of Hampstead Heath beyond, where a solitary walker looks out over the myriad street lamps of the city. In the garden all is quiet and still, save for an old, lame dog-fox, foraging about on the frozen earth, struggling to survive another winter.

Isolated and alone in her four thousand-pound chair, Edith wonders if she even wants to survive another winter. Why *does* she have to live so long, she asks herself.

Tiring of the negativity of her thoughts, she reaches for the little transistor at her side and clicks it on. She recognises the music instantly. It is one of Strauss's "Four Last Songs," this one entitled, "At Dusk," or, more accurately, she reminds herself, "In the Sunset Glow."

'Very apt,' she reflects, recalling the time that she sang these songs herself, and even made a recording of them. The quality of sound from the radio is poor, and she hasn't quite got it on the station, but the music remains sublime. She can even identify the singer – Lucia Popp.

'Such a funny name,' she thinks.

Attempting to improve the reception she turns the little, knurled tuning wheel but only succeeds in making it worse. Frustrated, she turns the radio off and picks up a sheaf of Braille from the table. How long the evenings seem to her when the house is empty.

"I was enjoying that," a voice cuts in from the shadows.

Edith freezes. She recognises it straightaway.

"Reg. ... What are you doing here?"

He strikes a match and lights a cigarette, illuminating for a moment his bloodshot eyes and discoloured nose, then he puffs the smoke in Edith's direction.

"I just thought I'd drop in for a chat."

Edith suppresses a shiver.

"You're here every morning, Reg. Plenty of time to chat then."

He sits back and sips the whisky he has just helped himself to in the kitchen, moving as quietly as a cat.

"Well, you know how it is. I don't like to disturb you. And there are so many people around. You can't really have a cosy little chat."

"What did you want to chat about?"

Reg chuckles to himself and flicks some ash onto the floor.

"What did you want to chat about, Reg?"

"Oh, just this and that." He stretches out his legs. "Old times. How's the new reader by the way?"

"He's been coming for a while now."

"But he's still new, isn't he. I mean I was your reader for what – well, years, wasn't it."

"He's very good. He gets here on time and he's sober."

Reg chuckles again and raises his glass.

"Oh, cheers by the way."

Just for Edith's benefit he slurps his drink noisily.

"You know I don't like you helping yourself here. If it's offered to you that's another matter."

"Well, if I waited to be offered these days. I mean there was a time when we'd have a little drink together. Shall I get you one now?"

"You don't know when to stop. Thank you. No."

Reg draws again on his cigarette, one eye squinting in the smoke.

"We go back a bit, don't we, old girl?"

With the cigarette clamped between his teeth, he is beginning to sound like Humphrey Bogart.

"A bit," she replies, thinking that there must have been a time when he wasn't so contemptuous. Her kindness towards him, she realises now, has made him despise her.

"I do like your new chair," Bogart goes on. "Must have set you back a bit. I mean I heard it was something like four grand. What on earth does it do? ... You must have money to burn."

"You get enough of it. I'm not particularly enjoying this *chat*."

Reg draws in his legs and leans forward, more ash falling to the floor as he does so.

"Well, you see, I don't think I do. Get enough, if you see what I mean."

Edith can feel his closeness, and can smell his breath and the unwashed clothes. Pressing herself further back into her chair, she says, "I don't think I do see what you mean."

"Well, it's just not easy making ends meet these days. What with Hedda and all that."

"Surely, Hedda's perfectly capable of looking after herself. She's a grown woman. And you're not even married after all."

"But you know how it is. A man likes to take care of his woman."

"While *this* woman takes care of the man."

Reg lets out a sigh of frustration. He never seems to be understood.

"Come on, Edith. I've done a lot for you over the years."

"Everything you do you do for yourself."

"Now that's not very nice."

Not taking his eyes off her for a moment, he takes a slow sip of the whisky.

"It's not very appreciative. After all ... I'm the one man who's made you feel like a woman."

"The *one* man?" Edith bursts out. "You have an inflated opinion of yourself. And a distorted opinion of me. What exactly do you want?"

Reg turns the glass around in his hands. Why does she have to make things so difficult for him, he asks himself. Why does he have to spell everything out?

"It's this business of the payment. And the annuity. Like Hedda said in her letter. I thought we might have had heard something from you about that."

"What about the payment? And the annuity?"

"Well, to put it bluntly, I just don't think it's enough."

"What could you possibly mean?"

"It just doesn't ..."

Edith cuts him off.

"I couldn't let you carry on as a reader. You were drunk most of the time. Barely able to read. And your language was foul."

"Oh, I think you're being ..."

"I've given you an annuity of ten thousand pounds. For as long as you live. Not a bad reward for doing your job so badly you had to be sacked."

Reg rises from his chair and begins pacing about. Edith can sense him moving but can't quite work out where he is. It has been years since she has been alone in the house with him and she feels acutely vulnerable.

"And there's another thing I wanted to talk to you about."

His voice, she can tell, is coming from the direction of the window now.

"Hedda's going away again."

"Is she?"

"Yes. You know she's got this little place in Spain. Well … she's thinking of moving there."

'To get away from you,' thinks Edith, but she doesn't want to provoke him, so she simply replies, "Is she going for good?"

"Looks like it, yes."

He sounds genuinely crestfallen and Edith feels sorry for him.

"And you're not going with her?"

"No. I don't think she wants that," and then he adds quickly, making light of it, "You know women. They can be very funny."

"What has all this got to do with me?"

Edith senses that he is moving around again.

"Well … the thing is … I don't think I'm going to be able to keep the flat on – on my own – and I was just wondering … you know, just until I get myself sorted out … I was wondering whether I could possibly move in here."

The voice has moved closer again, and Edith is holding her breath. She can just make out the ticking of the clock.

'What time is it?' she wonders.

She looks towards him; or to where she thinks he is.

"I don't think that would work, Reg."

"I don't see why not. Just for a month or two."

The voice has come closer still. Clutching for a response, Edith says, "I don't think Bridie would be very happy about it," but she has chosen badly.

"Pardon my French, but fuck Bridie!"

She can smell him again. A stale smell, of whisky and cigarette smoke.

"You know I don't like you talking like that."

"She's just the fucking housekeeper after all!"

"Reg!"

"I mean whose house is this for fuck's sake!?"

She can hear the anger being spat out in that foul word, chosen deliberately, she knows, to offend her. She feels something rising in her throat and tries to swallow. When she judges that her voice might be steady enough she says, "I think we had better leave it there."

She hears the chair creak next to her, as Reg sits and leans towards her.

"I don't know," he says. "I just don't seem to be coming across somehow."

"You've made yourself perfectly clear."

"No. No. I just don't think you're getting the point."

He sits back in his chair again and looks coolly at her – he has a facility for switching abruptly from mood to mood – and he can see the fear in the old woman's face. He drains the whisky from his glass and carefully places it on the table.

"I really do like your new chair," he says.

"... I think it's time you went home."

"I'll go when I'm good and ready."

The evenness of his tone is more frightening to Edith than the anger.

"Bridie will be back in a minute," she says.

Reg smiles.

"I don't think so. You see I saw her go out. She didn't see me of course – I made sure of that. All done up to the nines she was. Looked like she was going to make an evening of it."

Reg rises from his chair.

"I'm really impressed with this new gismo of yours," he says, running his hand along the top of Edith's chair. She feels his fingers brush against her hair.

"Apparently it can do everything but sing to you. It probably even does that. Now," he goes on, picking up the remote control, "I wonder what would happen if I pressed this button here."

The electric motor hums. The chair-back slowly reclines, while the footrest rises. In just a few seconds Edith is lying horizontally, rigid and helpless.

"Put the chair back as it was."

It isn't her customary, strong voice, and it seems, to her, to be coming from someone else.

"I must say," Reg says, smiling down at her, "you look ever so comfy."

"Put it back as it was."

"I take back everything I said about it," he goes on, glancing at the various buttons on the control. "I think it's been worth every penny."

From a room seemingly far away, Tyson lets off a short volley of barks.

"Don't worry," Reg says, "I made sure he was safely shut in. I know you don't like him roaming about."

'Where *is* Tyson?' Edith wonders; he sounds so far away. Reg leans down close, his face almost brushing Edith's.

"Does this remind you of anything?" he says softly.

Edith shudders but remains silent. Reg smiles again, enjoying the power he has in that moment. He looks again at the remote control.

"Now ... what does *this* button do? Shall I try it?"

He presses it. There is a low humming sound and the chair starts to vibrate.

"O-oh! Your own personal masseur. Now, that is what I call luxury."

He watches her quietly for a moment, scheming his next move.

"Won't be a tick," he goes on cheerily. "Don't go anywhere, will you."

Over the hum of the vibrating chair, Edith can just make out the sound of his footsteps on the bare boards in the hallway. She holds her breath and strains to listen.

... Nothing. The footsteps have receded. She lies like that for a few seconds more and then gropes about for the remote control. Finding the connecting cable she gives it a tug and hears the control hit the floor. She pulls the cable towards her until the control is in her hands. She presses several buttons until she finds the one that turns off the massage function. She lies motionless for a few moments, listening for the sound of returning footsteps, but all is silent. She presses the buttons again and the chair hums, bringing her slowly back to the upright position. She sits still and can feel her heart pumping fast. Her lungs are working hard too, and she feels sick.

'Come on, Edith,' she says to herself. 'You've got through two world wars – you ought to be able to get through this.'

Recalling exercises from her singing days, she breathes deeply and steadily and gradually her breathing becomes less erratic and more controlled. Tyson barks again and Edith tries to locate the sound.

'Where *has* Reg put him?'

The bark is muffled, as if from behind a closed door.

'So,' she thinks, 'he can be of no use to me now.'

She reaches out for the phone, but it is closer than expected and she sends it crashing to the floor. She holds her breath and listens, fearful the sound will bring Reg scuttling back, but all seems quiet still. With a supreme effort, for her old body has little flexibility now, she half rolls out of the chair until she finds herself, painfully, on hands and knees on the floor. She moans quietly and feels about for the phone. Finding it, she puts the receiver to her ear, trying as she does so to remember Eric's number.

'Assuming he is in,' she thinks, 'how long would it take him to get here?'

Impecunious as he is, he has a car, she knows that. She is about to dial when she hears Reg's voice, soft and mocking, coming from the doorway.

"Did you want to use the phone, Edith? Why didn't you tell me?"

Edith freezes, and in the brief silence, Tyson barks again.

"Woof woof woof!" Reg calls back. "Tyson, you mad old bastard! One day I'm going to put you in a sack and throw you in the pond! ... Now then, who was it you wanted to phone? I'll help you."

He comes into the room and places two drinks on the table.

"Oh, I got you that drink by the way. I thought you might be ready for it now."

He smiles down at her.

"Had a little mishap, have we? Here, let me give you a hand."

Edith shudders at his touch, but allows him to haul her into the chair. Reg picks up the phone and puts it back on the table.

"So, who did you want to call? I'll dial it for you," he says, with no intention of doing so.

"It's alright," Edith's voice quavers. She makes an effort to control it. "I've changed my mind."

"Are you sure?"

"Perfectly sure."

"Here's your drink," and he hands it to her.

"Thank you."

'I could do with it,' she thinks, 'but I must keep sharp.'

Reg sits and raises his glass to her.

"Cheers."

Edith shakily puts the glass to her lips. He has mixed it strong, but she feels it steadying her.

"Nice massage?"

Without waiting for an answer, he goes on breezily, "Now, what were we talking about?"

"I can't remember."

"Oh, I know. That business of me coming here to live. For a bit."

Reg takes a gulp of his drink.

"Look, don't feel you've got to give me an answer straight away. You just have a think about it. Take your time."

"Alright," Edith replies, also with no intention of doing so.

"But the money," he presses on, "I think we ought to talk about that. You see, I've been thinking – suppose we just up it, from ten to say fifteen pounds an hour."

"Why don't you go and get yourself a job?"

"I've got a job. Working for you."

"A proper job."

"No no – I'm quite happy as I am, thank you."

He gulps his drink again.

"And then there's this business of the annuity. Why don't we do the same thing there. Up it from ten to say fifteen thousand a year. I think I could just about manage then."

"I'll think about it," she lies.

"That's right. You think about it."

She shifts uneasily in her chair.

"I need to go to the lavatory."

"Right," he says, putting down his glass and getting up from his chair. "I'll help you."

"No, it's alright. I can manage on my own."

Edith feels for the remote control and presses a button. The seat of the chair rises and tilts forward.

"Is the Zimmer there?"

"I'll just get it," Reg says, and places it before her. "There. It's right there. In front of you."

"Thank you."

She leans forward, takes hold of the frame and hauls herself up, but Reg is still holding it firmly from the other side, preventing her from moving.

"No … the thing is," he resumes quietly, his face just a few inches from hers, "I do want you to take me seriously. I don't want you just to *say* you'll think about it, just to get rid of me. I mean, we both know I'm not the kind of person you can get rid of that easily. No. I really do want you to think about it."

Edith detests people standing too close when talking to her. "Invading my space," as she puts it. Reg is doing it now and she finds her repugnance even stronger than her fear.

"The annuity, Reg. My will. It can be changed, you know."

"Well, that's exactly what I'm talking about," he comes back brightly, not getting her drift at all. "I just want you to make a little change. It's very simple."

"I might not change it the way you want me to."

Reg looks steadily at her.

"Oh, now ..."

"You could end up with nothing, Reg. Or suppose I say the annuity lasts just as long as *I* live. You might not want to harm me then."

She has just made another error of judgement.

"That's not a very sensible thing to say. It's not very wise. I mean, just consider the situation you're in at the moment. Here we are, just the two of us, in this big old house. This big old *detached* house. I mean, you don't hear the neighbours, do you. And they don't hear you – that's the important thing. And the thing is, you've given me this annuity – which is only what I deserve, after all I've done for you – for the rest of my life. So, if something was to happen to you now ... well ... I'd still be alright, wouldn't I. So, d'you see what I mean? It's not really very sensible for you to talk like that."

Edith feels him release his grip on the Zimmer, and a moment later his voice is coming from further away. She breathes out. His proximity has almost made her retch.

"You've really got me thinking now," he is saying. "I mean why should I take a chance on it? Like you say, I could end up with nothing."

Edith can feel her heart beating fast again, and her bladder loosening. She takes a deep breath.

"No, Reg. I wouldn't do that to you. You know me. And I know you need my help."

"I do *not* need your help!" he growls. "I just want what's due to me." Then he checks himself and continues more evenly. "I'm just not sure I trust you any more, Edith."

"You can trust me, Reg."

He goes over to the window and looks up at the moon. Life has dealt him such a bad hand, he thinks. He could have had a career. Made some real money. It might have kept him on the straight and narrow. Out of trouble. But here he is, more or less penniless, dependent on a ninety-year-old, blind woman, and with a girlfriend who is about to leave him.

"You bastard!" he says, still looking up to the sky.

Edith is holding her breath. He turns back to face her.

"D'you know what I'm going to do?" he asks.

"...What?"

"I'm ...".

He pauses and, looking about the room, his eyes settle on Edith's chair.

"I'm going to try out that new toy of yours. I could do with a massage. This has got me all tense."

He sits in the chair and rests his head back.

"Yes," he goes on, "I'm going to sit here. Have another cigarette. Finish my drink. And just think it all through."

In the dim, eerie light, another match flares and Edith smells the tobacco smoke as it drifts towards her. She hears the electric motor whirr as Reg adjusts the chair, and then the low hum as the massage button is pressed.

The moon has shifted to behind the stark, black branches of the old oak in the garden. Edith doesn't dare move. She stands stock still, feeling his malevolent presence just behind her.

"I mean, it wouldn't be difficult, would it," he continues. "Little old lady … little crippled old lady … all alone in the house … takes a tumble on the stairs."

He glances up at her.

"I thought you wanted to go to the loo."

Slowly and warily, Edith begins to move towards the doorway.

"Mind those stairs, won't you," he calls after her.

*

April, 2002. Still feels like winter.

They don't know that I am watching them. They think it's the other way around. The old assumption again – that the blind don't know what's going on around them.

The dynamics in this household are fascinating. Mundane but fascinating. Reg is still seething at being demoted to dog-walker, even though he's had plenty of time to get used to it. He could always go and get himself a proper job, as I often point out to him, but he doesn't. He knows which side his bread is buttered. I suspect he's unemployable now anyway. The funny thing is he seems to blame Eric as much for his lowly status as he does me. It isn't so much what he says... I just sense it somehow.

I wish he <u>would</u> take himself off. I no longer feel comfortable with him around. (Did I ever? ... Well, the curious thing is I did. I used to enjoy that roguish side to him).

Then there's Bridie and Unity, sparring all the time. But again it's more what is unsaid than what is said. Bridie doesn't believe for one moment that Unity's a proper nurse. I don't think we ever did see her certificate, and as for her testimonial ... well

...who ever heard of a consultant talking in Pidgin English? I can't chuck her out though. She's probably unemployable too. And I do believe in standing by my decisions – even the bad ones. Within reason. And all considered, they do just about muddle through their jobs; with the exception of Reg, that is.

So ... who does that leave? Tyson. Well, he's mellowed a bit with age – like his mistress, though Bridie is still terrified of him. She needn't worry. He's more of a threat to Reg. Which is hardly surprising.

Eric must be wondering what on earth he's got himself into. Dear, normal Eric. I still haven't quite worked him out. Or is it that there isn't anything _to_ work out?

Anyway – when I think about them all, I find myself recalling something Sis said to me many years ago. That I seem to go for people in whom I see something of myself, and I'm not sure that she wasn't on to something. There's Unity, trying to hang on to a sense of time because she's not quite _in_ the world, and ungovernable because of it. Well, I can relate to that. And then there's Bridie – stubborn, and giving off a sense of being able to cope with anything life throws at her, rising to any situation, with her instincts rather

than her brain. I certainly recognise that in myself.
Isn't that how I got blinded in the first place?

Even Tyson, when I come to think about it, is myself.
All that forward tugging, wilful, unpredictable, even
aggressive when he chooses. A survivor – pushing his
snout into the hollows of my body, feeling me, sussing
me out as if with his hands, like a blind person.
And on top of that, left at the wayside. Which is not
altogether different from finding yourself suddenly
blind, and suspicious of all dependency.

What is most curious, when I consider them all, is
that perhaps Reg is the most like myself (though not
to outward appearances). He's manipulative. So sure of
himself – on the surface – but never quite in charge
of his life. Plausible and composed, but you never
quite get the truth from him. There's an evasiveness,
as though he's protecting himself, because, like me, he's
basically weak and needs to hide it. By the same token,
he has a nose for others' weakness. As I did for my
sister's.

And Eric? The seemingly straightforward Eric. The
one person in the household who's different. Someone
who just seems normal. Someone who's not like me.
Superficially he might seem so. What would you

call him? Lower middle class? And what would you call me? Upper middle class? But very different backgrounds, and I suspect he's a Guardian reader, if he reads a paper at all, and not a dyed-in-the-wool Telegraph reader. And he brings me all that. All of it. Events, adverts, killing, wars, obits, etc. – everything that's happening to all those other people – the distrusted world, to which, through his calm tones, I feel I can again relate.

But when I think, that with all the money I have, I could have had a really top-flight team. And then I think to myself, well maybe you've just hired this lot so you can suffer and endure that too?

…What do _you_ think, Sis? You're the one with the bird's eye view.

The sun shines brightly on the windows, emphasising their grimy state. Through the glass there is an illusion of summer, but outside the air is crisp and the trees still bare. Tyson snuffles around in the undergrowth, catching the scent of the fox from the night before, and feeling intimations of spring in his stocky body.

Bridie watches him from the French Windows, which she has just opened with more than the usual difficulty. Over the winter the wooden frames have swollen, causing the doors to stick on the threshold. She is dressed smartly and soberly, and certainly does not look as if she is about to undertake any housekeeping duties. She watches the mist rising from a part of the lawn, as the shifting sun gets to work on a patch of frost, and thinks about the night before.

Turning from the garden, she steps back into the room. The sun has dazzled her and it takes a moment for her vision to adjust to the darker interior, but then her eyes settle upon the record player resting on a table in a corner of the room. It is a relic of the 1960's, and it took some time for her to find for her mistress a machine capable of playing those old 78 rpm discs of hers. She goes over to it and raises the lid, then she opens the case containing the records, selects one, places it on the turn-table and lowers the stylus arm onto it. The needle finds the groove, and after a moment or two of crackling, Edith's voice can be heard, from sixty or so years before, high-pitched and mournful, intoning one of a series of "Negro Spirituals" she had recorded. Recognising his mistress's voice, Tyson looks up from his snuffling.

The voice is vigorous and vulnerable at the same time, and as she stands listening to it, Bridie sways slightly to the rhythm. Then she turns and walks back to the French Windows and surveys the bright garden again, where Tyson has resumed his inspection of the undergrowth. She takes a packet of cigarettes from her pocket and lights one. She thinks again about the events of the previous night.

Watching her from the doorway behind is Eric. He also is listening to the record, but is taking in too the unexpected sight of Bridie in a dark suit.

'She could be going to a funeral,' he thinks.

He hesitates, not wanting to break in on the moment, but when the record comes to an end he steps into the room and calls across, as if he has just arrived, "Morning Bridie."

She looks at him, startled.

"Oh! Eric. I didn't know you'd arrived," and she turns quickly away again.

"No. Just now," Eric says, coming across the room towards her, the piece of tape still tied around his trouser cuff.

"Everything's topsy-turvy today," Bridie says, still looking away from him.

Eric comes up beside her.

"Is it? … Well …"

"But it's a beautiful day all the same."

"Yes," Eric says, following her gaze across the garden. "That was Edith, wasn't it?"

"Yes. She's very crackly."

"You can still make out she had quite a voice."

Bridie draws on her cigarette.

"Well … it seemed appropriate. To play it today."

Eric is about to ask her why, but he decides not to and says instead, "That's a very smart outfit."

"Oh, this," Bridie says, smoothing the skirt down over her ample hips. Eric waits for her to continue, but she remains silent.

"D'you think you could let me have one of those?" he goes on, indicating her cigarette.

"Yes, of course. I didn't know you smoked."

"Oh yes. I've got all the usual vices."

He takes the proffered cigarette. Bridie clicks her lighter and holds it up to him. Her hands, he notices, are trembling slightly, and when he looks into her eyes, he sees that they are reddened, and the skin around them puffy.

He takes a drag on the cigarette and then asks, "Are you alright, Bridie?"

"Of course. … Alright as anyone might be. In the circumstances."

Eric isn't sure if he is being invited to enquire what those circumstances might be. He decides he isn't. At that moment, Tyson, who had disappeared around the side of the house, reappears, and seeing his bespectacled friend, comes scooting over towards him, his tail wagging, a smile playing across his dangerous jaws. Eric steps into the garden and bends down to greet him, rubbing him behind the ears and giving him some hefty pats on the back.

"Tyson, you funny old mutt!" he says as usual, and turns to grin back at Bridie. But she is no longer there.

Eric goes back into the sitting room, with Tyson playing about his feet, hoping for a game. Bridie isn't there either. He goes over to the record player, turns it off and stands listening for Bridie's footsteps.

... Nothing. It is as if she has been spirited away. Eric begins to feel uncomfortable. There is something not quite right about the atmosphere in the house; something out of the ordinary.

By now, Tyson has found his chewed-up tennis ball, slimy with his spittle. He drops it at Eric's feet and looks at it expectantly. Eric picks it up smartly, only just avoiding the dog's sharp fangs as he goes for the ball also, and then flings it through the open French Windows. Tyson's legs work frantically as his paws seek purchase on the wooden boards, like a character in a cartoon strip, then he shoots after it, clearing the threshold and the step down into the garden in one bound. The ball lands deep in the undergrowth.

'That ought to keep him occupied for a while,' thinks Eric.

He stands listening again to the silence of the house. He can't even hear a clock ticking, and he is just about to go off in search of someone – anyone – when he hears the familiar, low hum of the stair-lift. Almost in the same moment he hears footsteps in the hallway, and Unity calling up the stairs, "I here, Edith!"

Eric checks his watch. Unity is on time. Something out of the ordinary *is* happening, he thinks.

"What?" Edith calls out, as the chair makes its descent.

"I here! Unity here!"

The chair jerks to a halt over the last stair, which it doesn't always do. Sometimes it stops five or six stairs up, and Edith rises imperiously and reaches out for the Zimmer, only to find herself toppling forward, clutching at nothing but air. Many a time have Unity, or Bridie, or Eric, made a heart-in-the-mouth leap up the stairs to catch their precipitating mistress.

Edith raises the arm of the chair.

"Is the Zimmer there?"

"It here. Jus' to the right."

Edith's mottled old hands fold around the frame and she hauls herself up.

"That's it," Unity says.

Edith's morning exercise begins again, up and down the hallway, and as Eric watches from the doorway, he notices that Unity is guiding the Mistress more carefully and gently than is her custom. Bridie appears from the kitchen and walks across the hall.

"Mornin' …" Unity begins, but Bridie sweeps past, acknowledging neither Unity nor Edith.

"Who are you talking to?" Edith asks.

"Bridie."

"Oh, Good Morning, Bridie," Edith smiles.

"She gone."

"Ah."

Edith doesn't seem surprised.

"I think we'll dispense with the exercise this morning, Unity. I'm not really feeling up to it."

"OK. You the boss."

Eric smiles. Some character transformations appear to be taking place this morning.

"Just take me to my chair."

"Right-o," says Unity, and Eric steps aside as she guides the frame through the doorway.

After the usual "Good Mornings" etc., Eric informs Edith what a "spiffing day" it is – another of his anachronistic phrases – and this leads to a discussion on whether or not Edith should be wheeled out into the garden. Eric thinks that she is looking particularly frail and worn, and seeing a bruise close to one eye, concludes that she must have taken a fall since he saw her yesterday. He tries to dissuade her from going outside, while Unity mutters in his ear, "She no good this day," but Edith becomes more adamant.

"I just want to feel the sun on my face," and so coat, scarf, mittens, muffler, hat and rug are gathered.

"What time is it?" Edith asks, as she is being bundled into the above.

Eric looks at his watch.

"It's only half ten."

"Ah – we're in good time today."

"I get the early bus. Get up early," and then Unity adds quietly to Eric, "Doan know why I bother goin' to bed."

"It makes such a difference," Edith goes on, as her arms are guided into her coat sleeves, but Unity is continuing her murmured conversation with Eric.

"What's the matter with Bridie?"

"I don't know."

"Why she dressed like that? She got an appointment?"

Eric shrugs and positions the wheelchair.

"The chair's just behind you, Edith," he says. As she tumbles back into it, Edith asks, "Is the cushion there?"

This kind of thing happens regularly. Edith, in her dark world, is often not quite tuned in to what is happening in the bright world around her. With a dexterity acquired from considerable practise, Eric grabs the nearest cushion and slips it smartly into the diminishing gap between the wheelchair and the rapidly descending bottom.

"Yes," he says.

He kneels and puts Edith's slippered feet onto the footrests.

"Wrap the blanket around them, Eric. They're like blocks of ice."

As he is doing so, Bridie marches in, all cold efficiency now, and stands just inside the doorway.

"I've made your drinks and left them in the fridge. As I *shan't* be here later on."

"Ah – Good Morning, Bridie."

Edith's tone sounds a little forced.

"And how are you today?" she continues, but sounding fearful of the answer she might get. In the event she gets none.

"Would there be anything else?" Bridie asks, in a way that suggests she isn't offering anything else.

"Well ... if you're about to go ... somewhere," Edith says, "there's something you ought to know first."

"I think I know just about everything I need to know."

"Really," says Edith. "I wish I did."

There is an uncomfortable pause, then Edith asks, "What about lunch?" to which Bridie replies with a cold smile, "It's in the dog."

"Oh dear," says Edith.

It isn't the first time Tyson has got to her lunch before her. Having relished the moment, Bridie continues, "I've made you something else."

"Yes?"

"Sausages," and with that she turns around, adding, as she steps into the hall, "with arsenic sauce."

"Lovely," Edith replies, not having quite caught the last bit. Unity looks quizzically at Eric, who then breaks the awkward silence with, "Here – let's get you into the garden. I'm just putting the papers onto your lap."

"Right."

Edith gathers them in her mittened hands.

"Bridie ..." she starts to say.

"She's gone," Eric says, as he manoeuvres the wheelchair.

"What did she say about the sausages?" Edith asks him.

"Er – with parsnip sauce," Eric improvises.

"Oh. That's unusual."

"OK. Just tipping you back. Get you over the threshold."

At an angle of forty five degrees, Edith says, "They made such a mess of this. It was easier to get out before they had it altered."

"Who had it altered?" Eric asks, easing the wheels as gently as he can over the awkward step.

"The Disablement Access Officer," Edith replies.

"You want a hand?" Unity asks, but Eric tells her that they can manage, and so Unity says her goodbyes and leaves.

In direct sunshine for the first time in months, Edith tilts back her head and closes her eyes. She can no longer see that red glow the sun makes through the lids, but she can imagine it, and she recalls girlhood trips to expensive and exclusive resorts, long before the mass market for such things began. She sighs contentedly.

"Is that alright?" Eric asks her.

"Wonderful."

Eric goes back in and gets his jacket and a chair, and when he returns Edith is still basking quietly in the sun's regenerating rays. The air is undoubtedly crisp, but she looks well enough muffled up, he judges, as he pulls his jacket on and sits to her side. A jet drones high above them, seeming only to accentuate the peacefulness of the moment.

"Is the sky very blue?" Edith asks, her head still inclined, her eyes still closed.

"Yes. Just a few fluffy bits. High up."

"It's been such a long winter. You've no idea how it can affect you. When you can't get out. That house can be very oppressive. And it's not just the cold. Or the damp. Or lack of air. I can *feel* the darkness."

Eric closes his eyes and tries once again, as he has done so many times in Edith's company, to imagine a world without light, but it is impossible. Seeming to know exactly where he has positioned himself, Edith turns to him and asks, "Was Bridie wearing her dark suit?"

"Yes."

"I thought so," she says. "That's her interview outfit. She'll be going to the agency. She's handed in her notice again. She does it two or three times a year."

It takes Eric a moment to absorb this, then he asks, "You don't think she'll go then?" He can't really imagine the house functioning, or dis-functioning, without Bridie. Highly-strung as she is, she seems to him the glue that holds it all together.

"I don't know. I'm not too sure this time. She is very upset."

"Yes," he says. "I think she'd been crying this morning."

"Yes. I thought so. When I heard that choked, tight voice. Tears and rage. And then sweetness and light. I think she's a little unhinged you know."

Eric has begun to wonder if they aren't *all* a little unhinged. He thinks of that motto he has seen in souvenir shops; "You don't have to be mad to work here, but it helps!" Always with the exclamation mark. 'It wouldn't be out of place on a wall here,' he thinks, and then asks, "Why has she handed in her notice?"

"Oh … she says she's not prepared to put up with Reg being here any more."

'What has he done now?' Eric asks himself.

"It's perfectly true," Edith continues. "His behaviour recently ... he's become rather ... unpredictable."

Eric is aware that the old lady is choosing her words carefully.

"And she wants you to get rid of him?"

"Yes. But I can't be dictated to like that. *I* have to decide how this place is run. And I don't know what Reg would do, left to his own devices. He's quite helpless really."

Eric thinks of one or two so-called helpless characters *he* knows; the sort who know exactly how far they can go in playing on the kindness of others.

"He's become rather ... dependent," she continues, "and perhaps that's my fault. But I've seen him through a lot. And one feels an obligation. I used to visit him, you see, when ..."

She trails off.

Eric waits for a moment, and then prompts, "Yes?"

"Eric ... this is just between you and me."

"Of course."

"Well ... I used to visit him when he was in prison."

Eric is intrigued but not entirely surprised.

'Now, what would all that be about?' he asks himself. 'Theft? Embezzlement? Child molesting? No, not that. Reg is a lot of things but not that. Assault? Possibly. After he's had had a few drinks.'

The option he doesn't consider is armed robbery.

"He had no friends, you see," Edith continues. "Or rather what few friends he had simply deserted him. Even Hedda wouldn't have anything to do with him. But I'd known him for some time. And ..."

Again she trails off. Eric watches her quietly. She seems to be rewinding the years, and revisiting times and places that she hasn't been to for a long time. Suddenly she remembers the hat in her lap.

"Oh I must put this on. The sun doesn't smile on me any more."

"Doesn't it?"

"No. Not after I got myself blown up. They pretty well had to rebuild my fissog. It's mostly scar tissue. Perhaps it's just as well I can't see it."

Eric regards her for a moment.

"You look pretty good to me."

Edith smiles self-consciously. She suddenly seems coquettish, and Eric can't repress a smile himself. Feeling his eyes upon her, she quickly changes the subject and quips, "So ... Bridie's bridling. She refuses to go to the bank with him any more."

"To the bank?"

"Yes. They usually go together, to draw cash for the week. And she says it's just too embarrassing. Having him standing there next to her, in front of the cashier, with a can of beer in his hand, at eleven in the morning."

Eric smiles again as he conjures up this image.

"Couldn't she just go on her own?"

"No. Reg has to sign the cheque. He's the only one, other than me, who's authorised to draw money out of my account."

"Is that wise?"

"Probably not. But I can't go myself. And Reg persuaded me that would be the most sensible thing."

'I bet he did,' thinks Eric, recalling also how Bridie had told him that Reg had some sort of hold over Edith. He can't work out whether it is a measure of Reg's guile, or Edith's gullibility, that an ex-convict can persuade a wealthy woman to let him have access to her bank account, and he speculates again on the possible reasons for Reg having gone to prison in the first place.

"If he could only control his drinking," she continues. "It's got much worse recently. He's a completely different person when he drinks."

"Is he?"

Eric is unable to make the comparison. In all the time he has been there, he isn't sure that he has ever seen Reg sober.

"Oh yes. He can be quite ... disturbing."

It suddenly occurs to Eric that he hasn't seen Reg that morning.

"Where is he today?" he asks.

"We decided he should take a few days off."

"So, who's going to walk Tyson?"

At the sound of his name, and the word "walk," Tyson looks up sharply. He has settled himself on the grass between Eric and Edith, and is enjoying the novelty of being with them in the garden for the first time that year. However, he is not in the mood for a walk. He goes for a walk when *he* chooses, and if someone is about to impose one on him they had better look out.

"Oh, we'll manage somehow," Edith replies. "Bridie refuses to take him. Even if I gave her danger money, she said."

So Eric offers to take the dog himself, but aware of the challenging look Tyson is giving him, he avoids using the word "walk" again. Edith readily accepts the offer, then adds, mysteriously, "but now I'll have to think of a more permanent solution."

"What d'you mean?"

"Reg isn't coming back."

"... But I thought he was just taking a few days off."

"That was the arrangement last night. Reg phoned this morning to say he wouldn't be coming back. He'd had enough, he said. ... Well ... that wasn't exactly what he said. He was rather unpleasant. I think he was still drunk from last night. Anyway. He was flying out to join Hedda in Spain. He was phoning from the airport. Considering she'd probably gone off to get away from him, she's in for a pleasant surprise."

None of this is making sense to Eric.

"But if that's what Bridie wanted ... why has she gone off to look for another job?"

"She doesn't know anything about the last bit. I took the call from Reg in the bedroom. Bridie was downstairs in the kitchen. And I've only just seen her myself. You heard. I tried to talk to her. But she wasn't being very receptive."

"So, you're not just minus a dog-walker. You're minus a housekeeper too."

"Possibly. But I think when she hears Reg isn't coming back, she might think again."

Another plane is droning overhead. Eric looks up and wonders if Reg is staring, red-eyed, out of one of its windows. It is a relief to think he won't be seeing any more of him, and yet, he thinks, his antics have certainly added a bit of colour to the place. He looks back at Edith, who seems to have drifted into another of her reveries, and it strikes him that in spite of Reg's unconscionable behaviour, she is probably going to miss him.

The drone of the aircraft fades away, leaving an air of utter stillness about them. Eric continues to study the broken and noble face of the old lady, when suddenly she raises her eyes to his and murmurs, "Death comes in the silences."

He finds himself held yet again by her unseeing gaze, and knows, at the same time, that she *is* seeing something. He can think of nothing to say by way of reply.

'Is she quoting from something?' he wonders.

"I'm terrified of it," she continues. "Which is preposterous, for someone of my age. I really ought to have come to terms with it by now … that we don't carry on forever."

Over the years, Edith has learned, or has had to learn, to be strong and self-sufficient. True, she depends on the ministrations of others, but they, in turn, are dependent upon her, to greater or lesser degrees. Sometimes though, in her dark and remote world, she craves to speak simply from the heart, and to let down her guard and confess her concerns and fears. Although she does this in her diary, it is not the same. Bridie is perhaps the closest she has to a confidante, but she has to be careful what she says to her. Sensitive and basically kind though she is, she is also emotional, volatile and superstitious, and there are certain subjects that are better avoided with her housekeeper. It occurs to Edith now that Eric, with his apparent detachment, is not a bad substitute. They have shared a lot of time together now, and the reading of papers and books has led on to much discussion between them, and though often their opinions have been at odds, she feels, nevertheless, an accord with him.

"Bridie's impossible to talk to when she's like this. Not that I could tell her about last night."

"What happened last night?"

"Well ... to begin with, Reg turned up."

She grimaces at the recollection.

"He wasn't very ... pleasant. And then, later on, Bridie came back, and Reg was still here, completely in his cups, and there was quite a scene. You see, Bridie wasn't expected until much later. I think she'd been stood up. So she wasn't in the best of moods."

"Oh – she's er ..."

"Yes. I think she's walking out with someone," Edith says, supplying her own anachronism. "Or thought she might be. And that's how all this came to a head. With Reg."

She breaks off and appears to repress a shudder. Eric is about to ask if she wants to go back in when Edith continues.

"Anyway, after Reg had gone, she gave me an ultimatum. That either he went or she did. She was very upset. Beside herself, you might say."

Eric is beginning to understand Bridie's conduct earlier on, but can only wonder at what Reg has done to precipitate it.

"One thing that did come out of it though," Edith goes on, "which is perhaps for the best. Before Reg went, she insisted he left his key."

"What – for here?"

Eric is astonished. Reg, he considers, is the last person to entrust with your house keys.

"Yes. She said it simply wasn't on for him to come round and let himself in any time of day or night. I'm not sure she wasn't thinking more of herself than me. Anyway, this is all academic now. Reg has resolved everything by taking himself off to Spain."

Edith pulls her coat tighter around her, and Eric thinks again to ask if she wants to go back in, when she picks up the thread of her story.

"But it wasn't really that I was thinking of just now. It was what happened later."

Eric waits for her to go on.

"Well – we finally got to bed. But I couldn't sleep. Not for a long time. Eventually I fell into a very fitful sleep; and then I seemed to hear something and I woke up. And I just lay there, straining to hear whatever it was. ... I had the distinct sensation that there was someone else in the room. I was paralysed with fear. I lay absolutely still for I don't know how long, and then I got that feeling in my bladder, and I knew I couldn't ignore it for too long. I shifted around, trying to make it go away, and suddenly a voice said, very softly, "Come on – I'll take you there." And I thought, I know that voice, but I couldn't quite place it. And I felt two hands taking mine, very gently, and I said, "Bridie is that you?" and the voice said, "Fancy you mixing me up with Bridie!" and I opened my eyes, and I saw my sister, in the moonlight, looking down at me, smiling. My sister. Who's been dead for more than twenty years. But it was my sister the way she was before I lost my sight. From more then fifty years ago. And she just raised me gently up. "Come on," she said, "we don't need that silly old walking frame," and she walked me along the corridor, never taking her eyes off mine for a moment. I felt weightless, and I was seeing again, and hearing everything clearly. And then we got to the bathroom, and she lowered me onto the lav., and then she just sat on the edge of the bath, and we chatted, about all the old times. It was like we were little again. We just chatted and chatted and chatted, I don't know for how long, and then she said, "Come on – I'll take you back to bed," and I seemed just to glide along the corridor, and then she was pulling the bedcovers back and tucking me in, and I closed my eyes and felt a light kiss on my forehead, and I could feel a most delicious sleep coming over me, but before it did, I heard her calling softly from the doorway, "Everything's going to be alright now. Everything's going to be alright, but you have to take care." And then there was silence. This beautiful … velvety silence. And I didn't know another thing until I woke up in the morning."

Eric watches her quietly. During her story he had felt the hairs rising on the back of his neck.

"Were you …" he starts to ask, but Edith cuts in.

"No. I was not dreaming. There is absolutely no doubt in my mind whatsoever. I was fully awake"

"No," he says, "I was going to ask if you weren't frightened."

"Not in the slightest."

'Why do those sort of things never happen to *me*,' thinks Eric. 'It's always somebody else.' And yet there is no doubt in his mind that Edith believes completely in what she has just told him.

"And you didn't say anything to Bridie?"

"Oh no. I couldn't have told Bridie about it. She'd have had the heebie-jeebies. She already thinks this house is haunted."

"I just can't believe you weren't frightened."

"There was nothing frightening about it. It was such a comforting presence."

There is no doubting that, thinks Eric, looking at her now, positively glowing.

"I think that's why I didn't recognise her voice at first. I should have done because she comes to me quite often now. But this was different. I could actually feel her touch me this time. My hands in hers. Her lips on my forehead."

Eric watches her quietly. He simply doesn't know what to make of all this.

"But there," she goes on, "it seems to have left me ... reflecting on mortality."

She smiles, and then, seeming to decide that it is time to revisit her more practical, no-nonsense self, she says, brightly, "Well, Eric, we'd better get on. We've made such an early start. It would be a shame to waste it. Who knows – we might even get to page two today."

"Yes." Eric reaches for the papers on Edith's lap. "What's happened to Unity?"

"Well ... let's just say she's had a little talking to. And it's been pointed out that she can't take her position here for granted."

Eric unfolds the paper.

"Well ... it seems to have worked."

"For now," she says. "She's really become so unreliable.

There was that time recently when she was off sick. Said she had the flu. For four weeks. Who has flu for four weeks? No one believed her."

They should have, for Unity was, indeed, very sick, but not physically. She had been found standing on the tube platform at Whitechapel, a place she normally avoids. She was dressed only in nightdress and slippers, and she was staring at the rails, wondering which was the live one. She could have saved herself the trouble and just flung herself from her balcony. But she didn't really want to die; she just wanted help. The police came quickly, and she found herself in the psychiatric hospital in Hackney, under section.

Edith turns her face towards the sun again, though she knows that it is against doctor's orders and that she will probably pay for it later.

"What are the headlines?"

Squinting in the glare of the light reflected from the paper, Eric scans the front page.

""BLAIR ACCUSED OF EURO FUDGE.""

Edith sighs. It is all so predictable.

"I don't think so."

""TEA DRINKERS PROTEST OVER TOWN HALL'S PC TIPS?"" he queries, noting as he does that Tyson has taken a chunk out of the page, and with it most of the story. Edith, however, hasn't responded, and as he looks up he sees that her thoughts have drifted elsewhere again.

"Edith?"

"I was just thinking," she replies after a moment. "My sister. Coming to me last night. You asked me if I'd been frightened."

"… Yes?"

"There was one thing. It didn't so much frighten me. It gave me pause for thought. What did she mean when she said, "But you have to take care?""

Eric had wondered about that too. It sounded enigmatic; as if it might have more than one meaning. He is agnostic about the whole thing. If Edith believes that her dead sister returned to her, then for her, at least, she did. But detached and incredulous as he is, he can't help but feel that there was something ominous about the sister's last words.

*

November, 2002. Winter just begun and already it seems interminable.

Sis came to me again last night. Her visits are becoming more and more frequent. I wonder if that means something? How long has she been dead? ... I can't remember. I try to keep on top of time but it gets harder and harder. The years just bleed in to one another.

God! All that rivalry between us. The epic rows. How did we keep it up? It got into everything. Even her getting married. I might have been happy for her but she wouldn't let me. She had to present it to me as some sort of victory.

"No one's interested in *you*," she said.

"That's how much you know, Sis."

She didn't know the half of it. I hadn't any trouble attracting men; I just hadn't attracted the right ones. And underneath it I knew she was making that assumption again – that losing one's sight equals losing one's sexuality. Anyway – I couldn't hold myself back.

"Sis, the man you're about to marry is a wastrel. So don't present him as some sort of triumph over me. Or a trophy, because he's not my idea of a catch."

Smoke coming from her ears now. I press on. I'm starting to enjoy myself.

"It's just as well he's inherited some dosh, because he isn't capable of _earning_ a living. His idea of a working day is careering around the countryside on the back of some nag with a bunch of cronies as feeble-minded as himself chasing after animals considerably brighter than they are. The unspeakable in pursuit of the uneatable, as Wilde had it.

End of sisterly relationship. For the time being. Then one bright day, brainless husband, no doubt none too sober, attempts to jump a hedge as high as his horse. Said horse, being more intelligent that its rider, refuses at the last moment, leaving rider with no choice but continue the jump alone. End of hubby. Sis then finds her so-called friends don't quite cut it when it comes to comforting a grieving widow. She also finds that blood is thicker than water, and back she comes. But she's still a dreadful snob. More so after her brief spell as Lady of the Manor.

"The trouble with you," I tell her, "is you've got a superiority complex."

""People in glass houses," Edith," and I know the look she's giving me.

"There's nothing complex about it in my case, Sis. It's simple. I _am_ superior. I'm a sight more intelligent than most people I know." (God! What an ego I had then!) "But your sense of superiority has got nothing to do with intelligence and everything to do with class."

"Don't forget, _Little_ Sister, we're from the same class. I seem to remember you being pretty pleased with yourself when you drove that bus during the General Strike. There was no doubt then which class _you_ came from."

"It was nothing to do with class! I simply wasn't prepared to see the country brought to its knees."

Etc., etc., etc. The rows and the bickering went on, but something had changed. We seemed to have an understanding now. A tacit one. An acceptance of the differences between us.

Anyway ... getting back to the visitation. Or the dream. Whatever it was.

Soon after she came back to live with me, we went on holiday. To Spain. This was the Spain of Franco.

Someone Sis admired.

"Franco," she told me, "has put this country on its feet again."

"But can't you see the fear in people?" I said. "I can and I'm blind."

Remembering she also admired Mussolini and Mosley, I had a little game with her.

"Sis," I said. "What d'you think of Toscanini? You rate him as a conductor, don't you?"

"Yes," she said warily, not knowing where this was going.

"You know what he called Mussolini? He didn't call him The Great Dictator – he called him The Great Delinquent."

I'd tripped her up and she was silent for a moment. Bliss! But it didn't last long.

"Just because I admire him as a musician, doesn't mean I agree with everything he says. And what are you getting at anyway? Are you trying to tell me I'm some sort of Fascist?"

I said nothing. What's the point? It was all water off a duck's back. I was wasting my time. So I decided to sit back and conjure up a picture of the country around us. Let her get on with the driving. Which was galling for me. Because she was a bloody awful driver and I had been a good one.

Anyway, come the evening, we found ourselves running along the coast, and I got her to drive on to the beach. You could do that sort of thing in those days. And then I made her move over and I got behind the wheel. It was the Armstrong Siddely Hurricane and we had the roof down. I jammed my foot hard on the gas and let her rip. My headscarf got torn off in the slipstream, and I could feel the offside wheels clipping the waves, which is how I kept her on course. Above the wind, all I could hear was the roar of the engine, and Big Sis screaming at me to stop. So I jammed my foot down even harder. And for one brief moment I had my power back!

Edith sits on in her chair, in the glow of the standard lamp, her fingers typing another line of Braille. As usual, there is no need for the light to be on, but she likes the place to be lit during these long, dark evenings, particularly when there is no one else in the house. She is just reaching the end of a page when the phone makes a clicking sound. She reaches across for it and puts the receiver to her ear.

"Hullo?"

She can hear nothing at the other end, and is wondering if her hearing aid is playing up again when she recalls that when Bridie's daughter, Emily, phoned just a few minutes before she had no difficulty in hearing her. She told her that Bridie would be out until late and that there was no point in her calling back or coming round tonight. Emily tires her, with her silly, juvenile behaviour and incessant wheedling. She is always wanting something, and this runs counter to Edith's strict code of self-sufficiency.

She says "Hullo?" a couple of times more and taps the receiver but can still hear nothing. She holds the receiver down for a second or two and listens again. There is no dialling tone; just a sound of emptiness, or of a wind, in her imagination, moaning distantly over a darkened field. She puts the phone down and thinks for a moment. The clock ticks on and her long-dead ancestors stare out from their portraits. There are times, for her, when the house feels more like a sepulchre.

She fiddles with the control on her hearing aid and it emits a thin, high-pitched whine that makes her wince. Beyond the closed, connecting doors, in the adjoining room, Tyson looks up. Edith adjusts the control again and the whining subsides, but Tyson's ears are still cocked. He has heard something else, in the further recesses of the house. He looks up to the ceiling. A moment later he hears it again and lets out a volley of barks. Edith turns her blind gaze towards the doors.

"Tyson, what is it?"

Under all this, a low humming has begun, which the old lady can't hear, and in the dark hallway, the empty stair-lift begins slowly to ascend the stairs. She calls again.

"Tyson, what's the matter? ... Tyson!" And then, to herself, "Oh, Bridie, why on earth did you shut him out there?"

She pushes her table aside and, feeling around for her Zimmer, she calls a third time.

"Tyson! Tyson – be quiet!"

Tyson obeys but remains listening intently. He has heard the hum of the stair-lift, but this is not a sound out of the ordinary to him. Edith listens intently too but now all seems quiet again. She thinks to get up and let Tyson in through the connecting doors, but she isn't sure that they aren't locked. If they are, she wonders, on which side is the key? If it is on the other side, she will have to go out and enter the adjoining room from the hallway. Just thinking about it tires her.

She is about to resume her Braille when, fingers poised above the keyboard, she hears something that transfixes her. The hum of the Stannah has started again, and though she can't hear that, what she can hear, echoing eerily through the house, is the sound of a saxophone.

Tyson is barking again. For him, that sound means just one thing and he loathes that thing. For a moment, Edith is motionless, as she listens to the mournful wailing getting closer, then she makes a grab for the phone and starts dialling.

Gliding down through the darkness, he has a faraway look on his face, as if borne along not just by the stair-lift, but by the ethereal music he is making. First one flight – turn – then the next – turn – and then the next. His timing is perfect; the refrain finishing just as he reaches the ground floor. He steps from it and walks towards the doorway, through which light spills from Edith's lamp.

Standing in the doorway, he sees Edith tapping the receiver, frantically trying to get a dialling tone. In the same moment she stops and looks up, instinctively knowing that he is there, watching her.

Tyson is still barking. She looks towards the sound and calls out, "Tyson! It's alright! Everything's alright! Tyson!"

The dog obeys, but he is not reassured.

'Everything is far from alright,' she thinks.

"That's better," Reg says from the doorway. "Could hardly hear myself think."

Edith puts down the phone.

"I think you might find that phone's out of action. Why don't you phone up and report it?"

He chuckles and steps into the room.

"Reg, what on earth are you doing here? You're supposed to be in Spain."

Ignoring her question, he says softly, "Has anyone ever told you you've got beautiful eyes? Shame they're just an old pair of marbles. I knew a bloke who had a glass eye. D'you know what he used to do? When you weren't looking, he'd pop it out and slip it in your drink. Always got a laugh. What a character he was."

As he is saying this, Reg unclips his saxophone and places it on a chair.

"Did you like my little serenade by the way?"

"What are you doing here? When did you come back?"

Edith is talking to herself. On sneakered feet, Reg has slipped silently out of the room. A few moments later he is back, a bottle of whisky in one hand and two glasses in the other. He chuckles again.

"Bridie makes me laugh. She keeps finding new hiding places for the whisky, and I just keep finding them."

"She'll be back soon."

"Edith," he says as he pours the whisky, "you're telling me porkies again. I heard you talking to Emily. You said Bridie won't be back till late."

"How long have you been here?"

"I was listening to you, on the extension. That was just before I pulled the cable out of the wall."

Edith quietly digests this.

"I only told Emily that to stop her coming round."

"No, it's just you and me, Edith. Just the two of us."

"Eric will be along shortly."

Reg laughs and puts one of the glasses on Edith's table.

"Your drink's just by you," he says, settling himself in the chair opposite.

"He will," she repeats, knowing that the more she insists, the more it sounds like a desperate lie.

"I know what hours that little pratt does here, and it's not evenings."

He sips his drink and stretches out his legs.

"How did you get in without a key?"

"Well, this isn't exactly the Bank of England, is it. Also – and I'd been meaning to mention this to you for some time – you really shouldn't leave that ladder in the garden. I mean, it's just asking for trouble."

"... What have you come here for?"

Reg feels in his pockets for his cigarettes.

"Well, now ...," and he trails off.

In spite of her fear, Edith suddenly feels very tired. Tired of her narrow, proscribed life; tired of people wanting things from her; tired of being so dependent; tired of the struggle just to get up in the morning.

"What on earth has happened to you, Reg?"

"I don't think I'm with you, old girl."

He places a cigarette in his mouth and strikes a match.

"You never used to be like this."

Reg inhales deeply and then blows the smoke in Edith's direction.

"Like what?"

"Like ... this."

"You're not making yourself very clear. You see, I'm just the same old Reg. Same old chummy Reg. No. ... I'd say if anyone's changed it's you. I mean – you haven't been exactly friendly to me. Not recently. Chucking me out on the street. That's not very friendly, is it."

"I didn't chuck you out on the street."

"You did. You knew I needed somewhere to stay. Just for a while. But you turned me away."

"You told me you were going to stay with Hedda in Spain."

"Yeh ... well ... she wasn't very pleased to see me."

'You can't have been too surprised,' Edith is about to say, but she thinks better of it.

"You really ought to take more responsibility for yourself. A man of your age."

Reg shifts in his chair.

"Now don't start getting all pious with me," he says, taking another drag on his cigarette, "because you know that really does get on my tits."

Edith can hear an incipient anger in his voice.

"Alright. Alright," she says.

He looks at her steadily for a moment.

"Would you like a cigarette?"

"You know perfectly well I haven't smoked for years."

"Just to keep me company."

"Reg, puff away all you like ..."

"I said just to keep me company."

There is an insistent, boyish whine in his voice, which is now coming from beside her, only a few inches away. Edith stiffens.

"Here, Edith. I'm holding the packet out to you."

Slowly, tentatively, she reaches out her hand and the packet finds it. She pulls a cigarette out and holds it awkwardly in her arthritic fingers. She doesn't quite know what to do with it.

"Just put it in your mouth. It's not going to bite you."

His voice is coaxing and threatening at the same time.

Edith puts it between her lips and then smells the sulphurous odour of the match as Reg lights it. He returns to his chair and watches her for a moment, smiling.

'How comic she looks,' he thinks.

He sits back contentedly, relishing his feeling of dominion. As if reading his thoughts, Edith says, "You're humiliating *yourself*, Reg. If you only knew it."

His smile fades, and she hears his voice, tight and toneless.

"You're doing it again. You're getting all pious."

Smoke from the burning cigarette drifts up into her nostrils and makes her cough.

"D'you want me to come over and give you a little pat on the back?"

She feels her throat constrict and her chest tighten. She is doing her best to repress another cough, fearing that he will indeed come over and give her a little pat. The seconds tick away, and when eventually Edith feels sufficiently in control to speak without betraying her fear, she asks, "Why do you hate me?"

"Hate? That's a very strong word."

"It's a strong emotion. And it consumes you."

"Oh, hang on," Reg cuts in, reaching for the bottle. "I'd better top myself up. I can feel a speech coming on."

Whatever Reg does tonight, and she feels certain that he has something ghastly in mind, Edith is going to have her say, even if it means placing herself in still greater jeopardy.

"It's very simple," she begins. "You've grown to resent me, because of all I've done for you. And I really find myself wondering why now. But over the years I've given you a lot of support. And remember, I was the only one who stood by you when you were in prison."

Reg shifts again in his chair.

"Now, you know I don't like talking about that part of my life. It's very painful to me."

There is a mocking but dangerous tone to his voice, but Edith continues undeterred.

"I've always helped you, whenever Hedda's kicked you out. I've helped you out of endless scrapes. I settled the bills you ran up and couldn't pay. And all your little ... peccadilloes here, I've pretended not to notice. The missing jewellery. The family paintings. That must have taken some gall – walking out of the house with a life-size portrait under your arm. But the thing is, in doing all this for you, I've simply made you resent me. And now that resentment has turned to hatred.

Reg's voice hisses into her ear, giving her a start.

"I don't hate you. I couldn't be bothered."

His eyes fall on the un-smoked cigarette in her hand. Much of it has turned to ash, which now falls onto the sheets of Braille on her lap. He looks at it for a moment, his head cocked on one side.

"You don't seem to be enjoying your cigarette very much. You ought to be more careful, you know. There's a lot of flammable stuff around here."

He starts moving around the room, a plan forming in his mind.

"What's the difference between flammable and inflammable?" he asks, himself as much as Edith. "Don't they mean the same thing?"

Edith feels her bladder loosening.

"I think I need to go to the lavatory."

Reg stops pacing and looks at her, as if he had forgotten that she was there.

"Yes. ... You probably do. Well, go on then. We don't want any little accidents, do we."

He takes the remains of the cigarette from her and stubs it out. Then, placing the walking frame before her, he says, "There. The Zimmer's right in front of you."

Edith pushes aside her table, operates the control to raise the chair seat, and then tentatively reaches out for the frame. Just as she feels it, Reg whips it beyond her grasp and she topples forward, crashing painfully onto her knees.

"Oh!" she calls out.

Tyson barks again, more agitatedly this time.

"Oh dear – you just missed it. You really have got to be more careful."

"Are you trying to kill me?"

"Now what kind of a question is that?"

Reg is standing right over her now.

"Tell that mutt to shut up. He's getting on my nerves."

"Tyson! Be quiet! Everything's alright!"

She tries to sound calm, knowing that if the dog senses her fear he won't stop. The barking ceases.

Reg circles around the pathetic figure of the old woman on all fours.

"The Zimmer's just in front of you," he says, but makes no attempt to help her. Edith crawls forward, finds the frame and somehow manages to haul herself onto it. She makes her way to the door, blundering into one or two things along the way. Reg chuckles. She shuffles across the hall, finds the stair-lift and begins her ascent.

In the living room, Reg settles into her chair, picks up her untouched drink and resumes his train of thought. He hears the Stannah reach the top of the stairs, and the ancient feet shuffling across the floor towards the bathroom. Then he hears a sound that he hadn't been expecting – a key in the lock of the front door.

Reg can be surprisingly agile when the need arises. In the time that it takes the front door to swing open and close again, he has leapt noiselessly across the room and concealed himself behind the living room door. He breathes in sharply as he catches sight of the tell-tale saxophone on the chair, but he resists the temptation to go back for it, as he hears footsteps coming across the hallway.

Eric stops at the foot of the stairs. Noting that the chair-lift isn't there, he calls up into the gloom of the landing area, "Edith! It's Eric!"

In the darkness of the adjoining room, Tyson recognises his voice He snuffles at the crack beneath the door for a familiar scent, and waits for his friend to come and greet him.

Eric isn't surprised to receive no reply. He knows that if Edith is in one of the upstairs rooms she probably wouldn't hear him.

Edith has by now locked herself in the bathroom, but she knows that a locked door will offer her little protection if Reg's anger spills over. She sits on the lavatory, her heart still pounding and her brain racing as she tries to work out what to do next. She knows that she has to play for time. Her only hope is that Eric will arrive soon, for she really had been expecting him. It is true that he doesn't normally come round in the evenings, but she has been fearful of being left alone in the house at night since her last encounter with Reg, even though she supposed him to be a thousand or more miles away. So when Bridie announced her intention to go out, she had asked Eric to come round and read to her out of hours; but really all she wanted was the reassurance of his company.

Suddenly, from below, comes a cacophony that penetrates even her deafened state.

Eric has walked through into the living room, where the first thing he notices is the saxophone glinting in the light of the standard lamp. He has hardly taken this in when someone pounces on him from behind, sending him flying forward into a small table. This in turn shoots across the room and crashes into the doors that connect to the adjoining room, resulting in a furious barking from the other side. Eric finds himself pinned to the floor, wedged between a pair of knees, with his assailant attempting to smash his head against the wooden boards.

Although Reg has the advantage of surprise, Eric has the advantage of being a good twenty years younger, and is able to resist the attempts to crack his head on the floor. He rears up and feels the grip on his neck loosen. At the same time, the scissoring knees slip around him, bringing into his inverted view the crotch of a pair of jeans. Eric jabs at it hard with his right elbow and hears a sharp intake of breath. The weight upon him becomes limp, and as his attacker rolls off, Eric finds himself looking down into Reg's blotchy and contorted face. His eyes are narrow and bloodshot, giving him the look of a vampire, but before Eric has time even to ask himself why is this man here at all, Reg is on his feet again, kicking wildly at Eric's crouching body. He springs up and just manages to avoid a punch to his head. Then the two of them begin dancing around the room, Reg throwing and generally missing with a rapid series of kicks and punches, while Eric attempts to keep as much space, and furniture, between them as possible.

In his rage, Reg seems tireless. Some of his wild blows begin to find their mark and Eric knows that he has somehow to incapacitate him. He needs a weapon, and springing to another part of the room he finds an apt one.

Grabbing it by the neck, just below the mouthpiece, Eric wields the saxophone and brings it into sharp and satisfying contact with the side of Reg's head. Reg jerks to the right and slumps to the floor, where he lies stunned. Breathing heavily, Eric stands looking down at him, the saxophone hanging down at his side, a slight dent now in its bell.

As he watches him, Eric begins to get his breathing back under control. In his stupor, Reg shifts and twitches and Eric wonders if he should give him another whack, but he can't bring himself to do it. His public school background gets in the way – "You don't hit a man when he's down," and all that stuff. Looking about the room he sees the glass of whisky miraculously still intact on Edith's table. He steps over to it and downs it in one.

Suddenly he becomes aware of Tyson's urgent and insistent barking. Until then he has been focused solely on the need to subdue his opponent. Having achieved that, he thinks of Edith, and wonders if Reg has done something to her. He calls in the direction of the dividing doors, "Tyson! Tyson! It's alright! Quiet down!" and then runs out into the hallway and calls from the foot of the stairs, "Edith!? Edith!"

There is silence for a moment, and then a small, frightened voice answers, "Eric? Is that you?" Edith has slipped out of the bathroom and has been standing, trembling, at the top of the stairs, listening to the pandemonium below.

"Hang on!" Eric calls back. "I'm coming up!"

He bounds up the stairs two at a time and finds her, very shaken, clinging to the balustrade around the landing. He does what he can to steady her and gently gets her onto the stair-lift.

"You just sit there and hold on. I'll operate it from downstairs."

He runs back down to the bottom and presses the start button. Hearing the electric motor hum and the chair begin its descent, he steps quickly back into the living room to check on Reg.

As the lift descends, Edith takes some slow, deep breaths and tries to restore some equilibrium. As the chair reaches the second turn of the staircase, she hears Tyson barking again.

She presses the stop button and the chair comes to an abrupt halt.

"Eric!" she calls. "Are you there?"

She can't hear a reply, but she can hardly hear herself above the furious barking that resounds about the hallway. She presses the start button. The chair jerks down two or three more stairs then comes to a halt. She presses the button again but nothing happens.

"Eric? Am I at the bottom?"

She feels disoriented. Tyson's barking seems to be echoing right inside her head.

"Tyson! Be quiet!"

Edith presses the start button one more time, but still nothing happens. She decides that she must have reached the bottom.

At the foot of the stairs, Reg takes his finger off the stop button and waits. He looks up the first flight of stairs to the landing, where he has brought the lift to a halt, and smiles.

'That,' he thinks, 'would be an unpleasant fall even for someone half her age,' and he quietly watches as she pulls herself up from the chair.

Finding flat floor and not stairs beneath her feet, Edith is reassured. She feels around for her walking frame but of course cannot find it, so she shuffles forward until suddenly there is nothing beneath her. With a gasping moan she pitches forward like a felled tree.

In the living room, Eric lies face down and motionless, a trickle of blood behind one ear and a lens in his glasses cracked. He has often thought of himself as one of those people who never miss an opportunity to miss an opportunity, and had he been conscious now he would have been cursing himself for not having delivered that decisive, second blow when he had the chance. Reg, for his part, had not missed the opportunity. It had cost him another dent in his prized saxophone but he reckoned, as he watched Eric drop like a sack of potatoes, it had been worth it. He then kicked the inert body hard in the kidneys.

"I've been wanting to do that for some time," he growled, and kicked him again.

As Edith falls forward now, the adrenaline courses through her and everything seems to go into slow motion. She is gliding down through space with the sensation that in this, the last moment of her life, she has all the time in the world. She hears her sister saying to her again, "But you must take care," and Edith thinks, 'Too late for that now.'

Reg steps smartly up the stairs. Gripping the banister firmly in one hand, he braces his left arm and gathers Edith up with his right. Cushioned and pressed against his chest, she breathes out, "Oh Eric – thank God!" Reg backs down the remaining few steps and then lifts her up into his arms. He is out of breath but still manages to say, "Lucky for you I was there. That could have been very nasty."

Edith freezes, and is as stiff as a board as he carries her back to the living room.

"What have you done with Eric?" she gasps, just as Reg is, in fact, stepping over him.

"Would that be Eric the Unready?" he chuckles. He then puts her down in front of her chair and presses the button for the seat to go down. Compliant, Edith sinks into it.

"That's it," he goes on. "Let's get nice and comfortable."

He pours himself another slug of whisky, takes a gulp and sits down, still breathing heavily.

"What have you done with him?" she asks again.

"You really are a crafty sod, aren't you. You told me he was coming, knowing I wouldn't believe you. That really was clever. Only it hasn't done much for you. Because now I've got a sore head and I'm not in such a good mood."

"If you've hurt him ..."

Edith trails off, knowing that she isn't in a position to be making any threats.

"Yes? What?" Reg prompts. "What exactly are you going to do?"

He takes another gulp of whisky, looks about the room, and then adds, "No. I think what's more relevant now is what *I'm* going to do."

He lights a cigarette, draws on it deeply and flicks the still-burning match in Eric's direction. Edith smells the smoke again.

"What *are* you going to do?" she asks.

"D'you think it's a bit cold in here?" Reg asks, looking first at Edith, then across to Eric. She doesn't reply.

"I do," he goes on. "Unseasonably cold, I'd say."

He reaches down and places the waste-paper basket in front of him, then he gathers up the Braille sheets scattered about on the floor, and with the cigarette clamped in his mouth and one eye squinting against the smoke, he begins tearing up the paper and dropping it into the basket.

"What are you doing?" Edith calls out.

"Don't you miss those big old open fires? I do."

For Edith's benefit, Reg is holding the paper close to her ear and tearing it noisily. She can only just discern it, but well enough to know what the sound means.

"If something happens here, Reg ... don't you realise, you're the first person they'll come looking for?"

Reg is quite absorbed in his task now.

"I'm not sure I really care, old girl."

"Of course you do. You've still got a life ahead of you. It's different for me. My life's more or less over."

He smiles.

"I don't know about more or less."

Edith remains silent for a moment. She is trying to make a decision. She has, she believes, one last card to play, but she can't be sure how he will react. She hears another sheet of paper slowly being torn across. 'What is there to lose?' she thinks.

"I think you ought to know, Reg ... I've changed my will."

The paper-tearing stops. Reg's smile fades as he stares at her.

"No. No. ... You've fooled me once already tonight."

"I mean it."

"No. You wouldn't do it. You haven't got it in you."

"Haven't I? After everything you've done?"

"Yeh, but some people are like that. They'll take anything. They even get pleasure from it. And you're one of them."

"I wouldn't bank on that, Reg."

"No. You feel too responsible. You wouldn't cut me out."

"I haven't cut you out. Just cut you down."

Reg continues to stare at her.

"What d'you mean?"

"The annuity. I've changed the terms. It's no longer for as long as you live. It's for as long as *I* live," she lies.

The cigarette, forgotten in his mouth now, is largely ash.

"So, you see," Edith continues, "you have a vested interest ... in my well-being."

The ash falls from his cigarette into the waste-paper basket.

"Edith ... I don't believe you. People like you – they need to think they're doing good. Makes them feel better. And I'm your little good deed."

Edith looks back at him, her expression inscrutable. Reg feels as if something has been wound up tight inside him, and that it is about to snap. He looks at the paper, still half-torn in his hands, as if surprised to find it there, then he looks at the old woman.

"I'm so – tired – of you – trying – to manipulate – my life."

His words come out in a robotic monotone. With his eyes fixed on her, he slowly tears the sheet of paper in his hands. He drops it in the basket, picks up another piece, tears it across and drops that in too. And another. And another. Each piece is, for him, a year of Edith's life. A year less. But he doesn't know how literally true that is; that he has in his hands much of the diary that she has so meticulously kept since she was blinded, and in which she has so fulsomely expressed herself. He presses on, taking her back to zero, to before she was born. It is the only way to expunge her from his life.

Eventually, the ritualistic destruction is over. Edith listens hard, but can hear nothing. All seems silent, then something else seeps into her senses. A smell this time. Smoke. And she knows that it is not the smoke of a cigarette.

In the same moment, though further away and on the other side of a door, Tyson's more powerful sense of smell catches it too. He puts his snout to the bottom of the door. He knows that smell. Sensing danger, he gives four or five sharp barks, then presses his nose again to the gap beneath the door.

Reg steps across the room and kicks the door hard.

"Shut the fuck up!"

The door rebounds painfully onto Tyson's nose. He springs back, barking furiously. Alarmed by the smoke and enraged by the blow, and the sound of that hated voice, he begins throwing himself against the doors. Reg laughs, bends down, grasps the cable of the standard lamp and rips the plug from its socket. The basket and its contents are well ablaze now and he wants to get the full effect. He picks up the whisky bottle and scatters the contents about the room.

Through a kind of fog in his brain, Eric is listening to it all. He has been listening, motionless, for some moments, but now the increased sound is stirring him further towards consciousness. The pain in his head is severe, and he is finding it hard to connect his thoughts. He knows that he is probably concussed, but nevertheless, in the last few seconds he has put together a plan.

Not trusting himself to stand, he rolls quickly over and gets himself onto all fours. Reg has positioned himself close to the French Windows. With the fire burning so close to the living room door, he reckons he will have a safer exit into the garden, and avoid too any curious neighbours who might be coming up the drive to see what is going on. From this point, however, the place where Eric lies is obscured to him.

Suddenly, on the other side of the blaze, Reg sees a figure scuttling like an enormous insect from one side of the room to the other. He has hardly taken in that it is Eric before the figure reaches up to grab the handle of the connecting doors. But Eric's run of bad luck is not yet over, for the doors are locked and the key is on the other side.

By now, Tyson is in a lather of fury. He is unable to see what is going on in the next room because, although the doors are glazed, heavy drapes have been pulled across them, so he tears savagely at the material and with just two or three hefty tugs, the old, worn fabric comes away from the curtain rings and falls to the floor. In the same moment, Eric, recoiling from having pushed so hard against an immovable door, falls onto his back. Reg starts towards him, for he knows what will happen if Tyson gets into the room, but as he does so, Eric kicks out with his right foot and smashes the glass in one of the doors, opening up a large gash in his calf.

"No!" Reg shouts. He spins around and leaps back towards the French Windows.

Tyson springs into the room. Teeth bared, gums slobbering and wild-eyed, he looks like the Hound from Hell. Clearing Eric's prone figure in just one bound, he comes skidding to a halt just before the fire. If he is astonished by the spectacle before him he does not show it, and as soon as his eyes fall on Reg he does not hesitate.

*

December, 2002. Early evening. In the other living room.

Well … I've only got myself to blame. Reg was a self-induced nemesis. God knows I'd had enough warnings. From Bridie. From Unity. From Tyson (he had him sussed). Even Eric hinted at it.

But I knew it all along myself. I knew he was irredeemable. Why I let him get away with it for so long I just don't know.

I've been taking a good long look at myself. Through my glass darkly. And the face I see looking back at me looks foolish. So it's time I think to smarten myself up. Get a little bit sharper. Maybe tougher too. (Though perhaps not too tough, or poor old Unity Geest would be out on her ear).

God … Do I have the energy?

Oh, Sis! I wish you'd give me some good counsel. But you only turn up when <u>you</u> choose. As in life, so in death.

No, that's not fair. All those years you gave up for me. I haven't forgotten that. But it wasn't so bad for you, was it, Sis? It got you back on your feet again also. Yanked you out of that miserable, wallowing widowhood. So aren't you grateful to your little Sis just a bit?

And we had some fun, didn't we? We certainly got about a bit. Not just up and down this country, but on the Continent too. Milan, Rome, Madrid, Barcelona, Paris, Berlin, Hamburg. The X Sisters! We had some nerve, didn't we?

Lord! ... It hasn't been such a bad life.

I'm getting some things done around here, Sis. I neglected the place after you died. You really did knock the stuffing out of me for a while.

Anyway – I'm starting with that room. It was in a state already. Reg just added the finishing touches. I thought I'd go for Primrose. Something bright and hopeful. And something that will wash over those reminders of the unhappy past. Like the gaps on the wall where You-Know-Who carted off the old portraits. Well ... some of them _were_ pretty grim, weren't they.

Another service Reg has accidentally done me – though he's been a bit premature – was to burn my diary. It was in my will that it should be burned after my death. But as I haven't yet popped my clogs, here I am bashing away at it again. It's helped me a lot over the years. Helped me make sense of things. Helped me plan, and get my life back. Helped me look at myself and work things out. As the saying goes, "A life unexamined is not worth living." (I bet you don't know who said that, do you, Sis).

And I've confided in it. I said things there that I wouldn't have said to a living soul. It's been a friend to me, and that's something, because darkness is a lonely place. I know just what Anne Frank meant when she started her diary, "I hope I will be able to confide everything to you, as I have never been able to confide in anyone, and I hope you will be a great source of comfort and support."

Well … my diary was all that.

Perhaps it's just as well you weren't around today, Sis. I went for a walk. Or rather Eric walked and I got pushed. He wheeled me through the woods on the edge of the heath, where he tells me there are some funny goings-on. "Man on man" is how he put it. That's the bit I don't think you'd have approved of. Not so much him saying it, but the fact that it was going on at all. And in Hampstead! I think he wanted to shock me, but people forget that we old people have seen it all before.

We went on into the park and he found a bench in the sun, and parked me alongside it. We had another chapter of Sassoon. He writes about an England that doesn't exist any more, and it's one I recall and remember fondly. Well, most of it anyway. Then it was back through the woods, (more man-on-man sightings, Eric told me. There are some advantages to being blind), and when we got back there was a Cornish Cream Tea, which I think Bridie provided as much for herself as anyone else.

I'm turning in early, because I'm pooped.

Unlike Unity's journey to work, Bridie's couldn't be simpler. She only has to step out of her bedroom and she is there. This, for her, is the drawback. Living over the shop, she never seems to get away from it.

Her favourite time of day is late evening, if it is not one of those evenings when she has had a little assignation, (and they have become fewer and fewer, and never seem to lead to anything). After the Mistress has been put to bed, she pours herself a Scotch, lights a cigarette, sits herself in Edith's chair, reclines it a little, presses the massage button and closes her eyes. She sighs – a long, satisfied and contented sigh – and contemplates the day; or perhaps her life. If it is the latter, the feeling of contentment doesn't last long, for it raises too many issues, such as her daughters, whose problems always seem to become her problems. She had begun motherhood with the idea that once they were grown up they would be off her hands.

'How wrong can you get,' she thinks.

She might think wistfully of her late husband, and consider how different her life would have been had he not died so young; an event for which she still blames herself. Or she might think of all the opportunities she has had since to remarry, and wonder why she didn't take any of them.

"You're too damn fussy, Bridie, that's your problem," she says, once more.

Sometimes, she distracts herself with a little television, but she has become bored with it; so much of it seems as repetitive as her life. Eventually she will get up, check the place is all locked up, put out the downstairs lights and climb the old wooden stairs.

Her next most favourite time of day is the moment just after she has clicked shut her bedroom door behind her, and feels she is now truly un-get-at-able. Even Tyson can't trouble her now. She climbs into bed, and in the intimate glow of her bedside light, continues her latest romantic novel, living vicariously the life she might have had. Then, assuming the Mistress has no little "emergency" to be attended to during the night, she drifts into sleep, and has occasional wistful dreams, again along the lines of *what might have been*.

In the morning, the whole damn thing begins again. Early morning tea in bed for the Mistress, attending to the dog while trying to keep as much distance between them as possible, then all the trickery involved in getting him on the lead without it all turning nasty, the arrival of the other troopers in the Mistress's little army, the preparation of Edith's breakfast tray, also to be taken in bed, the inevitable unpleasant exchange with the dog-walker, (now history), the preparation of the Mistress's lunch (which secretly Bridie enjoys), and then sparring with the "nurse," always in inverted commas as far as Bridie is concerned.

Etc., etc., etc.

"I think I need a drink," she says, (Unity isn't the only one in the household who talks to herself), puts down her recipe book and goes to the fridge, where a chilled bottle of Chablis awaits her.

It is barely half past eleven.

That day is bright. It is early spring, and the birds in the garden are busy collecting material for their nests. The old oak tree is coming into leaf and the sun shines through it, casting a spindly shadow across the lawn where a solitary chair is placed. The French Windows have been thrown open, partly to let out the strong smell of paint, for the living room is transformed. Against one wall is propped a pair of step-ladders, and most of the furniture is under dust covers. Fresh, new paint-work glows in the midday sun that streams through the un-curtained windows. There is an atmosphere about the place of regeneration. Like the curtains, the dark, old portraits have also been removed and not yet re-hung, and there is a feeling now of space, which the cluttered, neglected room has not had since the house was built. Eric is pottering about, carrying a box of light bulbs and singing to himself in a cod Scot's accent.

"Oh dear little Flo, I love you so,
Especially in your nightie.
When the moonlight flits
Across your tits,

Oh Jesus Christ Almighty!"

Bridie watches him quietly from the doorway. She takes a sip of the Chablis. She is in a particularly good mood.

"Good morning, Eric," she says, her eyes twinkling.

Eric looks up sharply and colours slightly. He doesn't know whether to apologise for the mock Scot's accent or the word "tits." It occurs to him also in that moment that this is a house in which people have an uncanny habit of appearing in rooms silently and without warning. His mind rushes back to his early days there when he opened his flies, in this very room, and squirted that secret ingredient into his drink, knowing that Reg would be the recipient. Had someone been observing him then?

He colours still further.

Bridie, mellowed by the wine, continues to regard him quietly, a flirtatious smile on her lips.

"Morning, Bridie," Eric says, hastily resuming his light bulb duties. "I just thought I'd fill in while waiting for Edith."

He turns his attention to a pair of lights halfway up the wall. In doing so, he exposes the crown of his head to Bridie's view, where an area two inches by one has been shaved clean but is now partially re-grown. In the centre is a scar, pinkish-red, with four or five stitches. Bridie takes on a pained look and draws in her breath sharply.

"It still makes me wince, Eric. Looking at that scar."

"It doesn't really hurt any more," he replies, untwisting one of the bulbs. "It just throbs occasionally." He shakes the bulb by his ear, discards it and takes another from the box. Bridie watches him and takes another sip.

"I think you'll find the standard lamp has gone as well," she says.

"Right."

He twists in the bulb and goes over to it. Bridie crosses to the Mistress's record collection and rummages through it.

"The number of bulbs we get through here," she says. "Edith should have shares in Osram."

"The wiring looks pretty old."

"My dear, the place is a positive death trap."

"Tell me about it," Eric replies, thinking more of the event that provided him with the gash on his head than the wiring. Having changed the bulb, he clicks it on and off.

"I mean, just look at them," Bridie continues, indicating an old, brown, Bakelite switch by the door. "They're antiques."

Having selected a record and placed it on the turntable, she helps herself to one of the chocolates that had been meant for Edith, and then proffers the box to Eric.

"Chocolate?"

"No thanks."

Unity can be heard, clumping down the stairs, bickering, as usual, with her mistress, who is not far behind on the Stannah. Edith is looking particularly smart this morning, and in spite of the tedious exchange she is having with Unity she has a bright expression on her face. As she reaches the bottom, she calls out, "Is the Zimmer there?"

"Of course the Zimmer here," Unity replies, planting it truculently in front of her.

Being a special occasion, Unity has arrived sporting a spectacular Afro hair-do. It adds six inches to her height and no one is fooled by it.

Bridie pops another chocolate in her mouth and listens to them arguing as they go back and forth across the floor.

"It's business as usual out there," she says to Eric.

On the third circuit of the hallway, Unity informs Edith, "This job doan mean nothin' to me."

Determined not to be sucked into the nurse's ill humour, Edith smiles back at her.

"Then it must mean something."

Unity looks at her suspiciously.

"What?"

"You just used a double-negative. Which makes it a positive. If the job doan mean nothin' to you, then it must mean something."

Unity looks even more suspicious.

"What you doin'? You tryin' to discombobulate me?"

Edith bursts out laughing.

"Oh, Unity! The things you come out with."

Felling that she is being ridiculed, Unity's anger erupts. She rips the wig (which had cost her half a day's wages) from her head and flings it to the floor. Had Edith been the only person around to see it (or not) Unity might have got away with it, but unfortunately for her, Tyson is walking across the hallway at that moment. When his clouded vision sees what appears to be a miniature poodle scooting across the floor his first instinct is to pounce on it. Grabbing it in his jaws, he gives it a vigorous shaking, to break its neck, and then, his tail raised in victory, he struts into the living room, so that he can demonstrate to Bridie and Eric that he does his job about the place and repels intruders. All three seeing-humans are staring at him open-mouthed, as he settles on his haunches in a corner to complete the annihilation of the uninvited guest. Knowing better than to try and retrieve her wig, which has become, now, Tyson's trophy, Unity remains in the hallway and tries to contain herself.

Attempting to repress an incipient hysteria, Bridie says to Eric, "It certainly wasn't like this in my last position."

Attempting to do the same, Eric asks, "Where was that?"

"Aldeburgh. In Suffolk"

"I know Aldeburgh. Nice place."

"It is."

In spite of the suppressed laughter, Bridie starts to get that dreamy look in her eyes again.

"Beautiful house," she goes on, "and a very English gentleman. Perfect manners. He proposed to me, you know."

Eric has anticipated this response. Though he believes her, these reminiscences of Bridie follow a pattern.

"What happened?"

"He died on me. Literally."

"Literally?"

"Yes."

She sits in the Mistress's chair and sips her wine, Unity's misfortune forgotten for a moment.

"He was an old colonel. Bit of a cheeky monkey really. We'd gone out for a drive. He had a lovely old car. Called her the Duchess. The roof was down. We were sitting at a junction, waiting, even though there wasn't another car in sight. He had this funny habit of waiting until something was coming before pulling out. I think it was his idea of sport. So I was sitting there with my eyes closed, waiting for the car to lurch forward, and then there'd be all that hooting from behind. And suddenly I heard this car shooting past, so I opened my eyes and looked at him. ... He'd slumped down in his seat, so that his eyes were on a level with the dashboard, only they didn't seem to be seeing anything any more. ... Well, how I got him home I'll never know. I waited for a few moments. I could hear the old engine ticking over, but nothing or no one appeared, and there wasn't a house in sight. And then I just knew what I had to do. Gently as I could, I pulled him towards me, and after a struggle he tipped over against me, pinning me against the passenger door. I managed to get my arm free and reached outside for the door-handle. I gave it a turn, but with the weight of both against it, the door sprang open and I fell out onto the road. I picked myself up, and then I hauled the Colonel a little further across and closed the door to stop him tipping out. And then from the other side of the car I managed somehow to move his legs across to the passenger side. And as I was doing this, I remember a car went past, but it didn't even slow down. Can you imagine that? Only in England, I thought. And throughout it all, I could hear this strange sound; something between a wail and a whimper, and I suddenly realised it was coming from me. Well ... I sat in the driver's seat, and as I gripped this great big steering wheel, I was thinking of my husband. Because that's sort of how he died. In a car crash. Years before. I was driving, and I'd never got behind the wheel again. So ... I took a few deep breaths and told myself, "You can do this, Bridie." I just about managed to get it into gear and let up the clutch and we jumped forward like a kangaroo, but I managed not to stall it, and soon we were cruising along. We must have just looked like a couple out for a drive. Which we were of course. Only one of us was dead. I knew that already. His body was already cool when I put him in the passenger seat, and looking at him as we were driving along, I could see that he was already a bit grey. Because normally he had quite a ruddy complexion. Liked his whisky did the Colonel. So we drove along, and the funny thing is, Eric, I was feeling quite calm. You'd have thought I'd have been a bit flustered, getting behind the wheel again after all those years, and with a dead body next to me, but I wasn't. I think the Colonel would have been proud of me. Anyway, I got us back to Aldeburgh, and I remember, as we were driving along, one of the Colonel's old friends waved at us, and then just froze and stared while we hiccupped past. We must have been quite a sight – what with the Colonel's head slumped against the window, and just the top of my head above the dashboard. Anyway, he hurried after us, as fast as his stick would let him, and caught up with us outside the house, just as I was trying to get the Colonel out. Which is just as well because I never could have done it on my own. Well, we just about managed to get him inside, and lie him down on the old leather sofa. Then this old friend, another ex-army type, poured us a couple of stiff drinks, while I dialled the doctor's number. But that was just a formality.

And I was still feeling quite calm. Sad, but calm. But the other old boy was pacing around and saying "Shouldn't we cover him up?" and I just said "No. There's no need," but sort of softly, as if I was afraid of waking the Colonel. And I looked at him, and I saw that his hair was all blown about, so I knelt down beside him, and took the comb from his top pocket, where he always kept it, and just ran it back, strand by strand, and there was that old boyish face again. The one that used to wink at me."

Bridie sips her drink.

Perhaps it is the Chablis that has allowed Bridie to tell this tale, but then she is usually well-oiled. Perhaps it is something about Eric – his reserve, and his apparent ability to listen – that tends to inspire confidences. Eric, for his part, has been enrapt. He has always admired Bridie. In spite of her neurotic side, and the volatility that seems always to be lurking just below the surface, he has always felt that there is a strength there, albeit a not always dependable one. She has certainly demonstrated that strength in her story, and his admiration for her has just been raised a few notches.

"Well bloody done, Bridie! You showed a lot of courage."

She smiles. It is an embarrassed smile, but a proud one also.

"But I wouldn't have married him, anyway, if he'd lived." She is trying to get away from the vulnerability one feels after confiding something so personal. "I don't believe it's wise to mix business with pleasure. He did leave me comfortable though."

Eric realises too they need to move it on.

"You've had a lot of proposals in your time."

"Yes. Yes, I have. And broken one or two hearts, I have to say."

She sounds proud of the broken hearts.

"My daughter said, "Well of course he wanted to marry you. That way he gets your services for nothing. And a few more besides." She can be very cynical – Emily."

Throughout the tale, Eric and Bridie had become so drawn in to one another that they had forgotten the Unity/Tyson/wig incident. They are rudely brought back to it as Unity's ample bottom appears in the doorway. It is a bottom whose principal purpose is clearly to be sat on. Still in a state of shock, she is silent as she reverses into the room, drawing her mistress after her. She turns her head briefly, avoiding the corner in which Tyson has reduced her wig to shreds, and reveals, above a crumpled face, a close-cropped head of grey hair. In that moment, both Bridie and Eric's hearts go out to her, and it suddenly occurs to Eric that Unity must have been wearing wigs for years. For her part, Bridie is quick to appreciate that Unity needs be left alone for the time being.

"Good Morning, Edith," she says, as she has said every morning, barring vacations, for almost the last two decades. The usual greetings and enquiries are gone through, the only unusual contribution coming from Edith, who has, apparently, "had a particularly good night."

"It's a beautiful day out there," Eric tells her, and Edith says that she would like to sit in the garden, which he has anticipated by bringing in the wheelchair and placing a chair for himself on the lawn. Without the need for coats, Edith is quickly prepared.

"I like your outfit," he says to her. "Very nice."

"It ought to be," Unity says, forcing herself towards recovery. "Took her long enough to choose it. She got more clothes than Debenham's."

"I don't shop in Debenham's," says Edith archly.

Bridie whispers something in Unity's ear, which seems to work its magic, for Unity smiles back at her.

"I'll just go and get on with your lunch, Edith," Bridie calls across the room, giving Eric an exaggerated wink at the same time.

"Right-o," Edith calls back. "What is it?"

"Salade de Coquilles St. Jacques et Saumon Sauvage Marine a l'Aneth."

"Ah …" Edith replies uncertainly. "Sounds very nice."

"Let's hope so," Bridie says, giving Eric another wink.

"See you later, darling," she calls over her shoulder as she heads off towards the kitchen. Unity follows, but stops in the doorway and bends down to rub the back of her leg.

"God, my popliteal's giving me grief this day!" and she hobbles off.

Eric manoeuvres the wheelchair over the step.

"Did Unity just say "popliteal?"" asks Edith.

"I think so."

"How on earth would she know a word like that?"

"I don't know. What does it mean?"

"It's the area just behind the knee."

"Crikey!" says Eric. "We've got a word for everything," and then, on reflection, "Well – she is a nurse."

A derisive snort from Edith.

He wheels the chair onto the lawn and positions it facing the sun. Edith basks silently in its regenerating glow.

"Oh yes. ... That's the ticket," she says softly.

Eric picks up the papers from her lap and sits down adjacent to her.

"Eric," Edith asks, as the clock in the living room begins to chime, "are you still getting those headaches?"

"Not so much now."

The chiming stops and Edith asks, "Was that eleven o'clock?"

"No – twelve."

"Oh dear," she sighs. "What *can* I do with Unity?"

Eric has one or two ideas but keeps them to himself. The old lady sits quietly, drinking in the sun and feeling great relief at having put another long winter behind her, plus an attempted murder.

"It seems awfully quiet without Tyson," she says. "... I wonder how long they'll keep Reg in hospital."

"Apparently they've still got a few skin grafts to do."

"They've done so many already. It's all taken from his bottom, you know."

Eric does know. It is keeping them all much amused in the household.

"I do miss that mad old coot," Edith goes on.

"Reg?"

"No, Tyson. ...Why did he run off like that?"

"It's just as well when you come to think about it. Like I said before, if he hadn't run off, they'd have probably put him down."

"Yes."

"Personally, I'd have given him a medal."

Edith is about to respond, but Eric goes on quickly, "Of course, if you'd told the police what really happened ..."

"I couldn't have done that. Reg would have been back in prison, and I don't think he'd have survived it this time."

Eric remains silent. If Reg is anything, he thinks, he is a survivor. But he is aware too that he, Eric, had the opportunity to tell the police what really happened, but instead went along with Edith's version of events; which was that the fire had been started accidentally by Reg with a cigarette butt, and that Tyson had attacked him in the garden that night because he had mistaken him for an intruder. The police appeared to believe the respectable, old lady.

"I know you think I'm mad," Edith continues.

Eric starts to say something but Edith cuts in.

"Bridie certainly does. She told me yesterday that I was one sandwich short of a picnic; that the lift, in my case, didn't go to the top floor; and that I was, in fact, knitting with only one needle. I told her I thought I'd got her drift."

Eric smiles but remains thoughtful.

"What are you going to do if Reg comes back?" he says.

"He won't."

"How d'you know that?"

"He wouldn't dare. He knows he's got off lightly. He won't want to push his luck. He's too shrewd."

'He's certainly that,' thinks Eric.

Another clock in the house begins chiming twelve.

"We ought to get on, Eric. It's not that long to lunch."

Eric unfolds the paper.

"OK ...The main picture is ..."

"D'you know ... I don't think I want to hear what's in the paper. I'm tired of it. Tired of what's going on in the world."

"... D'you want to carry on with the book?"

"Have you got it with you?"

"It's in the house," Eric says, rising from the chair. "I'll go and get it."

"Has Bridie brought the drinks yet?"

"Not yet. Shall I go and get them?"

"No, it's alright. She'll bring them soon."

Eric goes off towards the house.

"Bring those chocolates Bridie gave me," Edith calls after him.

Eric goes into the living room and finds the book they have been reading. He picks up the box of chocolates and goes back out to the garden.

"Here you are," he says, proffering the box. Edith feels about and selects one.

"There don't seem to be many left," she says, and pops a chocolate into her mouth. "Help yourself," she adds.

"Thanks," says Eric, only to find they have all gone.

"Mmm – lovely," he lies, making it sound as though his mouth is full of succulent chocolate.

"They're nice, aren't they?"

Eric opens the book, but is immediately interrupted by a female chorus.

"Happy Birthday to you,
Happy Birthday to you,
Happy Birthday, dear Edith,
Happy Birthday to you."

Unity's voice is practised and assured, from all her gospel singing at the Unity Church. Bridie sings as richly and lyrically as she speaks, while Eric, who has joined in on the second line, is less sure of himself. He has played many leading roles in musicals, but a long time ago, and his singing is rusty now. There is the usual applause at the end, and calls for Edith to make a speech, which she politely declines.

"How did you know it was my birthday?" she asks.

"Edith," Bridie says, "we've celebrated it every year for ..."

"Twenty years," Unity prompts, though it is pure guesswork, "and each year you ask the same question."

"Anyway – here's a little bubbly to mark the occasion," says Bridie, who doesn't need any excuse to open a bottle. She hands Edith a flute of fizzing champagne from the little, silver tray she is holding, distributes the rest, and then raises her glass.

"Here's to you, Edith. Many Happy Returns."

"I sincerely hope not," says Edith, and raises her own glass. "Here's to friends present ... and friends absent."

"Now, Edith," says Bridie, "I hope you're not expecting us to drink to that psychopath who nearly burnt the house down."

"I was thinking of Tyson actually."

"Oh, that psychopath," Unity chimes in.

Unity and Bridie exchange knowing looks.

"I'll drink to that," Eric says quietly, and they all do.

"Where you think he get to, Edith?" Unity asks. Bridie answers for her.

"Now don't you worry about Tyson. He knows how to take care of himself."

"He must be starving by now," says Edith. "If he's still alive."

"Now I hear he take a little pack-lunch with him."

Unity winks at Bridie and tugs the lobe of her ear. The two women giggle. Eric smiles too, for it is also a source of much amusement that a chunk of Reg's right ear disappeared in his tussle with Tyson. What, they all wonder, has become of it?

When, on that fateful night, the enraged dog leapt into the room, Reg stepped smartly out into the garden, but not smartly enough to prevent Tyson shooting out after him before he had the chance to close the door. Eric, still unable to stand, had managed to smother the flames with a rug, crucially before the fire had spread to the areas that Reg had sprinkled with whisky. In a state of shock, Edith had been sitting rigidly in her chair, immobile as a statue, but she seemed to be intact, as far as Eric could tell, and was still breathing.

Outside, there were growls, barks and shrill, human cries, but when eventually Eric crawled to the French Windows and looked out, all was still, and though the night was dark, he could see enough to ascertain that Reg and Tyson were no longer there. He crawled back into the room, poured the remains of the whisky into a glass, and administered it to Edith's cold, white lips. It was an hour or so later, apparently, that Reg had turned up at A&E at the Royal Free Hospital, minus part of his ear.

Unity presses on with her routine.

"*Ear-ear* – what's all this then?"

"No don't!" and Bridie bends forward, slapping her thigh.

"What we got *ear*, little doggie?"

"Stop it!"

Fuelled by the champagne, Bridie is becoming more helpless with each awful pun.

"Unity, that's not in very good taste," Edith says, not realising that she has just provided her with her next line.

"That's what Tyson say – "*Ear*, this doan taste too good!""

Eric glances at Edith. She is trying to look stern and disapproving but isn't quite succeeding. Bridie lurches off towards the house.

"I'll just go and get us that bottle," she calls back. "I think we might need a little top-up."

Edith waits until she feels Bridie is out of earshot and then murmurs to Eric, "How much has she had?"

"Oh come on, Edith," Unity says, "we're celebratin'. You jus' wait to see what we got you," and she gives Eric a conspiratorial wink.

"I hope you haven't been spending a lot of money on me," Edith says, as she does every year. In spite of her protestations, she enjoys these little celebrations.

"We aint spent nuthin," Unity replies, and Edith looks a little disappointed.

Bridie reappears and tops everyone up.

"I jus' been tellin' Edith," Unity says to Bridie, "we got her a little somethin'."

"Well, just a little something," Bridie says. "That was supposed to be a surprise."

"Really, you shouldn't have," Edith says, also as she does every year.

Bridie looks at Eric.

"Well ... I suppose now's as good a time as ever."

Eric nods and walks back into the house. He returns a few moments later and positions Edith's present at her side, as the other two look on in anticipation.

"Just reach out your right hand," Bridie says. "It's just there."

Edith does as instructed, and finds her hand instantly washed by a long, slobbering tongue.

"Oh, no!" she cries, unable to hide her disappointment. "You haven't got me another dog!"

"Not *another* dog," Bridie corrects.

Edith sits quite still, taking this in. Then she slowly bends forward and takes the furry head in her hands. Methodically, she feels first the ears, then the muzzle, the strong, squat neck and the powerful shoulders. He feels thinner than before, and his coat doesn't feel as sleek, but it is unmistakably he.

"Tyson," she whispers.

Not used to being the centre of attention, and after some time away from humans in general, Tyson finds it all rather bewildering. Nevertheless, he gives his reply by way of a series of unhygienic licks across his mistress's face, having just spent a few minutes in the kitchen cleaning his private parts.

"You couldn't have got me a better present," Edith says quietly.

Bridie, always ready to raise a toast, proposes another to Tyson, and all raise their glasses. The Mistress, of course, requires some explanation, and Eric duly gives one.

He had found Tyson a week or so before, as he cycled home. He hadn't recognised him at first, for he had lost weight, his coat was matted and his eyes were dull. He looked dejected and weak, and he was on the other side the heath, several miles away. Little wonder then that he hadn't been able to find his way home, and they could only speculate on how he had got there.

At the end of his exposition, Eric feels that he has been back in one of the several Agatha Christie plays in which he has had the misfortune to perform. They always seemed to end up in the library of a country mansion, where the sleuth would tie up all the loose ends of the mystery. Eric feels that he is very much back in that library.

"But why didn't you bring him straight here," Edith asks, "and let me know that he was alright?"

"That was my idea," Bridie says. "I thought, let's save it for your birthday."

"Also," says Eric, "he was in a bit of a state. I wanted to take him to the vet and have him checked out. And get him clipped, and generally feed him up."

"You've done all that?" says Edith. "I must owe you something."

"That's alright," says Bridie, "I took it out of the housekeeping."

Suddenly, Unity's face clouds over.

"What happens if the police come back?"

"Why should they?" Edith asks.

"Maybe they got more questions. And if they see him, they have him put down."

It is not like Eric to have a brain wave, but he has one now.

"They've never seen him before," he says. "We just tell them Edith got a new dog."

"Yeh, but Edith give them a description of the dog."

"Ah ..." Edith begins, and immediately trails off. Everyone looks at her. She shifts uneasily and prepares herself for a confession. It is not in her nature or upbringing to be dishonest, but she has been less than honest with the police. It wasn't only Reg's part in it all that she fabricated, nor the excuse that Tyson attacked him because he took him for an intruder. When the police had asked for a description of Tyson, sensing what might happen if they found him, Edith simply recalled what had once been her idea of the perfect dog; "Sleek, dark, graceful, long legs," she said. Nothing like Tyson at all.

At the end of her confession, Edith looks sheepish, not knowing that all assembled are staring down at her with a mixture of wonder and admiration.

"... So all this time," Unity says, "the police have been looking for the wrong dog."

"Well," says Edith, "I suppose they've had other things to do."

"You wily old bird," says Bridie under her breath, then, as she silently raises her glass to the old lady, she becomes aware of her proximity to Tyson, and even though Eric is still holding him on the leash, her mouth twitches.

"Right," she quickly goes on, "time to get the party underway."

"I thought it was underway," says Edith.

"No," Bridie says, stepping towards the house and putting some distance between herself and the dog, "we need some music."

She places the needle on the record she selected earlier, and within a moment the celebratory but poignant tones of Richard Strauss's "Four Last Songs" burst into the garden. Although Eric doesn't know the music as well as Edith, he knows it well enough to be aware that it is a song about old age staring death in the face, and he isn't sure that he would have chosen it for Edith's ninety-eighth birthday celebration.

"Oh, very cheerful, Bridie," says the old lady.

"No, listen, everyone," Bridie announces from the step. "This is Edith actually singing. Er ... where did you say you performed it?"

"The Wigmore Hall," Edith replies.

"That's it," Bridie continues. "She sang it at the Wigmore Hall."

"Yes, alright Bridie," Edith mutters. "I think everyone's got the message."

By now, Bridie's judgement has almost entirely deserted her, but she is still remarkably steady on her feet, and her speech is not slurred. Indeed there aren't many who could match her drink for drink and still remain standing. She steps into the garden and smartly up to Unity, who is swaying slightly to the music.

"Nurse Geest?"

"Yeh?"

"Would you care to dance?"

"What — to this!?" but before she can protest further, she finds herself gripped firmly in a ballroom stance,

Bridie adopting the gentleman's position. Unity giggles and daintily rests her hand on Bridie's shoulder.

Edith sits quietly, stroking Tyson's broad neck, sturdy and steady beneath her hand. She closes her eyes and looks up once more to the sun, which she has not seen for more than fifty years. 'I'm not far off my centenary,' she thinks. 'I've gone through two world wars, been blown up and blinded, and then, in the twilight of my life, almost murdered.'

"What a life!" she says, as the music draws her back to the Wigmore Hall all those years before. She pictures herself, standing proud and nervous on the stage, in a sumptuous, new evening gown bought especially for the occasion, facing out over the upturned, expectant faces of the audience, which she could no longer see. She hears a hush descend, so knows that the lights have dimmed, and feels that old, familiar thrill as the conductor taps his baton.

Eric watches her quietly, then, after a glance over at the nurse and housekeeper, who are dancing dreamily together, he rises from his chair and steps over to the old lady.

"Edith – would you care to dance?"

She fixes him with her inimitable gaze.

"I'm not sure that I could."

"Yes you can. I'll be holding you."

A smile lights up her face.

"Alright Eric. Yes. I'd love to."

He bends down, lifts her slippered feet and pushes the footrests of the wheelchair aside. Then, wrapping his arms around her, he gently draws her up, until she is straight and poised. Supported more by him than by herself, Edith feels lighter on her feet than she has done for years.

"… It's funny," she murmurs, "I didn't think one could dance to Richard Strauss. Johann, yes, but not Richard."

"We seem to be managing alright."

"We are."

"So are Bridie and Unity," says Eric, glancing over at them again.

At that moment, Bridie is whispering in Unity's ear, "I like your hair like that. Au natural. I think I might have mine cropped. Long hair's such a nuisance."

Unity smiles shyly. She doesn't believe her, but she loves her for saying it.

Eric and Edith dance on. It is more a pas de trois than a pas de deux, for Tyson, being still attached by his lead to Eric, has no choice but accompany them. He looks up curiously at the old lady and the younger man, and even though they are his favourite humans, he thinks again what a strange species they are.

*

March, 2003. Last night.

I am on a dark plain. It is a desolate place. There are flashes of sheet lightning but no sound of thunder. There is no sound at all. It's as if I am watching a newsreel but there is no soundtrack. And it's all in slow motion.

The lightning continues, intermittent, and there is the odd explosion, but I only know it is an explosion because I see the flash. There is still no sound.

Then there is a sound. Almost imperceptible at first. Very distant. A low, rumbling droning – gradually – very gradually – getting louder. Whatever it is, it seems to be coming towards me. And I have that feeling you sometimes get. That feeling that something is about to happen. It's never wrong, that feeling. Whenever I get it, something always does happen.

I look into the sky. The light is strange. The near-darkness has a dull glint to it. It's a warning glint. I try to think of a term to describe it, and the term that comes into my head is "post-apocalyptic." I like that. Nice to get your tongue around.

And then I see it. Minute at first, and I can't make out what it is. But I think I know what it is. And as it gets closer – or less distant – then I know I know what it is.

It's an aeroplane. But there's something strange about it. It doesn't look quite right. It looks like a child's toy. An inflatable, plastic aeroplane. But it's full size. Bomber size.

Now I can see that it *is* coming straight at me. It's chosen me, and this place, out of all the other places it could have gone to. Nobody's flying it. Nobody needs to fly it. It's pre-programmed. Predestined.

Then I hear another sound. It's a voice. And the voice says, "Wrong time. Wrong place," and I think … I know that voice. And I answer it.

"That means this is the right time and the right place."

It certainly feels like the right time. Has done for ages.

I watch it getting closer – listen to it droning louder – and I think to myself, "This time – this is really it," and the voice says, "This time – this is really it," and I say to the voice, "It's not going to be like last time. Last time it didn't quite get me," and the voice says, "It's not going to be like last time."

And now it's really close. I feel I could almost reach up and touch it. If I had a pin with me I could burst it. But I know they wouldn't let me do that. They mean business this time. And the voice says, "They mean business this time," and then the voice says, "This is the hand," and I say, "What hand?" and the voice says, "This is the hand that takes."

At first I don't understand. Then I do. And I feel such relief. It's as if I've been in the wilderness for years and someone has just come along and said, "Here – take my hand."

Then it's almost on top of me – this big, inflatable toy aeroplane that looks so harmless – and I suddenly realise something. It's something so obvious I wonder why I didn't realise it before. … If I'm watching all this – that can only mean one thing.

I've got my sight back!

And that's when everything goes black.

Unity finds Edith dead in her bed one morning in early March, 2003, and it is fortunate for Unity and all concerned that Edith is indeed quite dead, for had she been called upon to attempt resuscitation, the old Bajan nurse would not have known quite what to do.

Edith had died in a state of readiness and disquiet. One morning, just a few weeks before her death, she and Eric were sitting in the garden, Tyson curled up comfortably against her feet. One of the old clocks was chiming twelve.

"We ought to get on," she said, as so many times before. "It's not that long to lunch."

Eric opened the paper and scanned the headlines.

"It's all about Iraq again," he said, knowing what her reaction would be.

"Oh no!"

"D'you think it's going to happen?"

"Yes. I think it probably is."

She thought for a moment.

"Mr. Blair is too much in thrall to Mr. Bush."

Her tone was flippant but Eric could tell she was serious. She had developed a habit of grinding her jaws when she was disturbed, and she did so then.

"Oh dear. It's all so depressing. I've lived through one pointless war. I don't want to go through another."

Eric was perplexed. Edith had told him many stories about the war, and her role in it, and she had always sounded proud of it.

"I've never heard you talk about the war like that before."

She looked at him quizzically, and then realised that she hadn't made herself clear.

"I'm not talking about the Second World War. There was nothing pointless about that. I was talking about the First World War – the so-called Great War. Well let me tell you, Eric, there was nothing Great about it. It was an unmitigated tragedy and disaster. We lost a whole generation of young men. And for what? I tell you – Churchill got it right when he said, "Jaw-jaw better than war-war." And that was our greatest war leader. But even he could see that it had to be a matter of last resort."

Eric watched her quietly, surprised by the vehemence with which she spoke.

"I'm sorry," she went on. "I'm telling you things you already know."

"No-no," he assured her. "I went to public school – I know nothing."

She smiled, and seemed about to say something, but then remained silent. They sat, listening to the birdsong, but Edith was still clearly troubled.

"It's as if we haven't learnt anything from it all," she said.

She took a sip of her whisky. Eric did likewise. He found himself in a curious situation. Over the time that they had known one another, they had tended to keep away from politics, for although neither was particularly political, Edith's leanings were more to the right and Eric's more to the left, and so it had seemed the safer policy, but here they were now, he thought, divided by age, background and experience, and the old lady had just said things more likely to have come from himself. And how distressed she seemed to him in that moment.

The truth was that although over the years she had become inured to the folly of nations and their leaders, curiously, as she got into great old age, she had become touched by it all again, and genuinely feared for the world, even though she sensed she was about to leave it.

"Dear Lord," he heard her murmur. "Don't let me witness another war."

Eric folded the paper and put it down on the grass, for clearly it was not wanted that morning. A moment later, as if she had seen him do it, Edith said, "You know, I think I might cancel my order for the paper. ... Just until the world becomes more sensible."

"I could be out of a job then," Eric said, little realising the prescience of his remark.

"Oh no," she assured him, "we've always got the books."

"Do you want to carry on with the Siegfried Sassoon?"

This was a book that Edith had particularly requested. She had read it, she told him, before the war, and she wanted to hear it one last time.

"Have you got it with you?" she asked.

"Yes."

He opened it at the mark.

"We're nearly at the end."

Twenty minutes later, when Bridie stepped into the garden with top-ups for the reader and the Mistress, she heard Eric reading Sassoon's conclusion.

""It has been a long journey from that moment to this, when I write the last words of my book. And my last words shall be these – that it is only from the inmost silences of the heart that we know the world for what it is, and ourselves for what the world has made us.""

Struck by the beauty of the insight, Eric just stared at the page, while Edith stared up at the sun. Bridie hovered at the threshold, wondering if she had arrived at the wrong moment, and not realising that she had arrived at exactly the right one.

*

Two or three week's later, and unable to prevent the war Himself, God answers Edith's prayer by ensuring that she is not around to see it. Because in recent months she has become extremely feeble and in need of more attention, Unity has started coming in earlier, which is a considerable feat for her. She herself is becoming frail and has difficulty now in climbing the stairs, so she often uses Edith's stair-lift.

One morning, shortly before that fateful day of March 20th, when people watching their TV screens saw the buildings of Baghdad being vaporised, Unity goes up on the Stannah only to find that the stair-lift will never be needed again. Bridie is down in the kitchen, having decided to make an early start on the last and most ambitious recipe in her latest book on French cuisine. When she hears Unity crying out from the top of the stairs, she says, "What's that woman blathering about now?"

Tyson has sensed Edith's death approaching, and knows immediately what has happened. He himself can no longer climb the stairs, so he sits in the garden below his mistress's window and he howls and he howls and he howls. Bridie cannot console him, nor can Eric when he arrives later, so he gathers him up in his arms and carries the old dog upstairs. Tyson is put upon the bed, and he lies with his muzzle on his mistress's hands, which are folded across her chest. Though drained of colour, Eric observes that Edith's noble, broken face bears an expression of peace.

When the undertakers arrive an hour or so later, Tyson growls and will not let them near her. Eric carries him to another room, where he resumes his howling, and he is still howling when the men in dark suits carry her from the house to begin the final part of her earthly journey.

After they have gone, Unity, Bridie and Eric sit huddled together on the stoop that leads onto the garden. Eric has carried Tyson back down the stairs and he sits beside them now, as they all look across towards the oak tree, where Edith had so liked to sit, her reconstructed face shaded from the sun. They sit silently, with their own private thoughts and recollections. Only Bridie knows that Edith has provided for them all in her will. Tyson is included, and even poor old Reg, now referred to by what few friends he has as Reg-without-Lobe. She has also left a substantial sum to the Saint Dunstan's home for the blind in Brighton. Though she was deprecating about the place in her diaries, this was more to do with her frustration at having to be there, for she had a high regard for what they set out to do. Thinking of Edith's will, Bridie turns to Eric.

"You know she left instructions that her diary was to be burnt."

"Did she?"

"Yes."

A moment later Bridie is surprised to hear Eric chuckling. She looks at him.

"What?"

"It's already been seen to."

Bridie has no idea what he is talking about.

"What d'you mean?"

"Reg saw to it a little while ago."

It takes Bridie a few seconds to catch up.

"I didn't know that's what he'd set fire to."

"Nor did he," says Eric.

Bridie becomes thoughtful.

"But she carried on writing it afterwards. She might have gone back over everything. I'd love to take a look at it."

Eric looks at her sharply.

"Do you read Braille?" he says.

"No. But it wouldn't be difficult to find someone who did."

He looks at her steadily, not feeling comfortable with the turn the conversation has taken. It is not like Eric to take the initiative but he does so now. Rising from the stoop he turns and steps back into the house. He reappears just a few seconds later and walks to the centre of the lawn, where he kneels and places the batch of Braille he has just collected. Taking the top sheet, he puts his Zippo lighter to it. When it is well ablaze, he throws on the next sheet. And the next, and the next, until he has a little bonfire going on the grass. He returns to his place on the stoop where he sits and watches the flames die down. It has all been done so quickly and decisively that Bridie has found herself unable to utter a word.

Tyson eases himself up and limps stiffly onto the lawn. The arthritis in his hind quarters makes even this an effort. He sniffs around the papers, which have already burnt themselves out, and then he moves away, deliberately sniffing for the spot where his mistress's wheelchair was so often placed, and there he lies down, his old, grey muzzle nestled between his forepaws, his large, dark eyes clouded now by cataracts.

Bridie, Unity and Eric watch him in silence. All three are thinking much the same thing. How much the old dog seems to have aged in the few hours since Edith's death. They cannot know that Tyson has resolved that he will not carry on without his beloved mistress.

The humans become reflective. They know that in the Great Chess Game, they are merely pawns, or prawns, as Unity would have put it. For all of them, the world is a mysterious place, and they all know that this is the end of an era.

Edith's death has left them all considering their mortality. Bridie is not a particularly spiritual woman.

Her philosophy is a jumble of superstition, and perhaps a suspicion of a life after death, but she tends to live simply for the moment. She thinks that she might, in a sense, live on in her daughters and her grandchildren, but when she consider what a mess they are making of their lives she isn't sure that she wants to. As she sits there, puffing away on her cigarette, her thoughts go back to Edith, and her abiding image of her is from the day they first met, when she was being interviewed for the post of housekeeper, and how regal Edith had seemed to her, and how piercingly blue were her eyes.

The most religious among them is Unity, who, after so many years attending the Unity Church, has more or less convinced herself that there will be a life for her after death, and that God will forgive her for forsaking her son; for hadn't He, she reasons, forsaken his own son, on the cross? She thinks of her boy again, and wonders once more if she is by now a grandmother, or even a great grandmother. And then she too thinks of Edith, and sees her hunched on the other side of the Zimmer frame, as she drags her back and forth across the bare boards in the hallway, and she wishes in that moment that she had not been so ill-tempered with her. Had Unity still been under the care of Dr. Patrick Smith, back in Barbados, he would have judged her less harshly, and been gratified that she had managed to make some sort of a life for herself outside the institution. "Burnt out schizophrenic" would have been his shorthand in her file.

Of the four of them there, Tyson has the most straightforward philosophy. He certainly has a concept of death, and has inflicted it on several occasions, particularly during those lonely nights that he roamed Battersea Park, and as he feels death approaching him now, it doesn't alarm him. It is, as he sees it, simply inevitable, for he is unencumbered by any notions of an afterlife, and like Bridie, his abiding memory of Edith is from the day that he first met her, and how those flashing, blue eyes both saw and didn't see him. But the greatest gift that she gave him was her loyalty. He knows that he could be difficult and mischievous, but she was always there for him, and provided him, for the first time in his life, with a stable and secure home. After those early traumas with his first two masters, when his faith in humanity had been shattered, she came along and restored it.

As for Eric, he has no philosophy at all. He hasn't even a plan. He just potters along, allowing things to happen to him, sometimes mildly surprised at this or that turn of events, like his father before him – Monsieur Hulot. Reg got it about right when he called him "Eric the Unready."

So, he sits there on the stoop, pulling ruminatively on one of Bridie's cigarettes, and thinking of Edith. He will miss her, he knows, but he can't regret her passing, for he knows that she was ready to die, and that her life had been full. He remembers her saying to him once that she had "lived through interesting times. And that should be enough for anyone." Considering how varied were their backgrounds and characters, they had a remarkable affinity, and as he thinks of her now, and whether or not there might be some essence of her that lives on, he recalls the story that she told him about her dead sister, who returned to her one night to give her support when she was troubled, and how she helped her to the bathroom, and sat on the bath chatting to her, while Edith sat on the WC. It occurs to him in that moment that this was the closest that she ever came to acknowledging some sort of afterlife, and so this becomes *his* abiding image of her ...

Of an Edith rejuvenated, sight restored, lucid blue eyes flashing, exchanging animated gossip with her sister, while sitting on a Grand Celestial Lavatory.

This is Nigel Bowden's first novel, though he has, before, written several plays. "Dark Star," about the First World War poet, Wilfred Owen, has been performed in many English theatres and was broadcast on the BBC World Service, while "Falling," about the Lockerbie bombing, was presented at London's Finborough Theatre. "Meg & Vee," about a woman suffering from schizophrenia, was shortlisted for the Verity Bargate Award and commended in the Croydon Warehouse International Play Competition. His last play, "Who's Saki?," about the short story writer, H.H. Munro, has been presented in a score or more theatres in England and Scotland. He has recently completed a collection of short stories entitled "Le Chat, and other Tales," and is currently writing his second novel. He works also for "InterAct," a charitable organisation that provides a reading service for stroke and cancer patients. (Information on this organisation can be found at www.interactreading.org).